LITTLE ANGEL STREET

BOOKS BY JEROME CHARYN

EDITED BY JEROME CHARYN

LITTLE ANGEL STREET
STREET

JEROME CHARYN

THE MYSTERIOUS PRESS

Published by Warner Books

A Time Warner Company

MYSTERIOUS PRESS EDITION

Copyright © 1994 by Jerome Charyn
All rights reserved.

Cover design and illustration by Bascove

The Mysterious Press name and logo are registered trademarks of Warner Books, Inc.

 Mysterious Press Books are published by
Warner Books, Inc.
    1271 Avenue of the Americas
    New York, NY 10020

W A Time Warner Company

Printed in the United States of America

Originally published in hardcover by The Mysterious Press.
First Printed in Paperback: November, 1995

10 9 8 7 6 5 4 3 2 1

For Georges Moustaki

PART ONE

1

"Sweets."

He was in a field full of ice. But the ice couldn't hold him. His shoes sank under the freezing skin. He didn't drown. He'd created a splinter in the ice, a crack that widened with the bulk of him. He was too big. He'd always been that way.

"Sweets."

He was coming out of a dream. He was in the Hollows, a resort near Morristown, New Jersey, where his daddy had owned a summer and winter palace. It was the most exclusive resort in America. It catered only to black millionaires. And the field of ice had been Sweets' territory when he was a child. It was also heroic grounds. George Washington hid his army in the Hollows during the winter of 1779-80 and outfoxed the British from the same field of ice.

"Sweets."

He opened one eye. Somebody was sitting on his desk, wearing a widebrimmed hat. It was his own point man, Albert Wiggens, who loved to sneak up on him, arrive unannounced. Wig was his most trusted aide, a brutal policeman and member of the Purple Gang, a mythical bunch of Harlem desperadoes. Wig was like some outrider who could cross invisible boundaries and create his own sense of inner space, where no police commissioner, black or white, could ever travel. Carlton Montgomery III, called Sweets, had been a star of the Columbia College baseball and basketball teams. But a knee injury had kept him out of professional sports. He didn't agonize over any missed career. He sat behind his desk, with a begonia he'd inherited from Isaac Sidel, the previous Commish, and dreamt about the Hollows until Albert Wiggens woke him up.

"Wig, you're sitting on an heirloom. This was Teddy Roosevelt's desk."

"A lot of white trash," Wig said.

"But it's my desk now. And remove your butt."

"Oh, I will, Mr. Sweets. I have news for you. I found the Pink Commish."

Sidel would move into Gracie Mansion in another month. He was the reluctant king of New York. And the king had obliged the current mayor, Ms. Rebecca Karp, to have Sweets sworn in as the first black PC. Sweets didn't care about racial gambits, but everybody else did. He had to speak at churches and synagogues and college departments of criminology. He wouldn't accept a personal fee. He donated whatever he got to Cardinal O'Bannon's AIDS hospice on Attorney Street. The cardinal's parishioners didn't want that hospice. But Cardinal Jim was courageous. Sweets admired the man, even though Jim had lobbied against him, had tried to get Isaac to appoint an Irish PC.

"And where is our king?" Sweets had to ask.

"That boy's no king. He craps in his pants morning, noon, and night."

"Where is he, Wig?"

"At the Seventh Avenue Armory."

"What the hell is he doing at a goddamn shelter in Harlem?"

"Sniffing around, like he always does."

"Sniffing for what?"

"Dirty old socks. The white boy's been living at the armory for a week."

"He disappears on us and moves in with a bunch of homeless men? That's weird. He'll miss his own inauguration."

"I'd love that, Sweets. The town runs better without a mayor."

There was malice in what Wig had said. He'd been chief of the mayor's detail, had guarded Rebecca Karp, who sat like a spinster at Gracie Mansion and would see no one. Wig had been her enforcer. And Isaac had sacked him, thrown Wig off the mayor's detail.

"We're going up to the armory, Wig."

"Not me, bro'. I'm not wiping the Pink Commish's ass."

"You'll wipe when I tell you to wipe, or I'll send you to Staten Island to guard all the cow pastures."

"You been around that white trash too long. You beginnin' to look like Al Jolson, a white boy with tar on his face."

"I'll flop you, Wig, I swear."

"Take my gold shield. I'll sell fried catfish on a Hundred and Twenty-fifth Street. I'll make a better living than any police commissioner."

"I'm glad. But you're still going to the Seventh Avenue Armory."

He'd inherited Isaac's black Dodge and Isaac's sick chauffeur, Sergeant Malone, who swallowed pink milk to calm his ulcer. But Sweets preferred to drive himself. He sat up front with his point man. Wig didn't have a daddy who was a millionaire dentist, like Sweets. He'd been brought up by a parade of uncles and aunts on Lenox Avenue. He'd gone to high school in East Harlem and belonged to no honor societies. But he did graduate. Sidel, the wandering police scholar, had talked at the high school, had come with Sweets, one of his rookie adjutants, and Wig hadn't listened to a word, but he'd fallen in love with Sweets' size, six feet six. If the Police Department accepted black giants, then why not Wig? He worked as an auto mechanic, took a crash course in criminology, and passed the police exam. He entered the Academy when he was twenty-two and never even served at a precinct. He was picked up by the First Deputy's office, went undercover, and was like a black Hawkeye in Harlem, sniffing out drug dealers and ambitious bandits. He was shot in the head and was shoved off roofs and fire escapes. He was the most decorated cop in the City, after Vietnam Joe Barbarossa, who was even crazier than Wig until he married Isaac's daughter, Marilyn the Wild. Joe and Wig had sworn to kill each other. Part of the venom came from the fact that they were so much alike. They had no fear out on the street. They'd both dealt drugs and were supposed to be assassins for hire. But Joe didn't have the aura of the Purple Gang around him. He had a suicidal sister and a suicidal wife.

Wig arrived at the Seventh Avenue Armory with Sweets. It was a dusty castle with dark brick walls. He'd never seen a soldier inside the armory, but he'd heard that it had housed a black regiment during World War I. Wig couldn't believe it. His uncle had told him about black cooks and black orderlies who'd attached themselves to white generals and had "grown" into sergeants in the white man's Army, but not one black battler. But his PC was a strange case. Sweets' ancestors had fought alongside George Washington as free men in the middle of the Revolution. That was some powerful shit. Brave niggers kicking some British ass.

Sweets seemed uncomfortable. Harlem had never been his terrain. It was broken country. He couldn't get used to all the abandoned buildings, the yellow grass that grew out of the cracks in the sidewalk, the half-empty beer bottles that lined the curb, waiting for some ghostly drinker.

Wig recognized the men loitering on the steps of the armory. They were whiskey preachers who had lost their congregations, convicted felons who were hiding from the law, brain-damaged psychopaths, Harlem rats who'd gone to school with Wig and couldn't pass the policeman's test. He knew their names, their rap sheets, their sexual preferences.

"Hello, Brother John, hello, Joshua. How's my man?"

"Aw, Wig, you aint gonna bother us?" one of the loiterers said.

"No. We looking for the white king."

The loiterers started to laugh.

"You mean the sucker that's got them delusions? Thinks a mattress in our barracks is better than Gracie Mansion."

"Yeah, that's the king. But don't you belittle him."

"Hell, we wouldn't dis the next mayor of New York. Who's your friend?"

"The police commissioner," Wig said. "Mr. Carlton Montgomery the Third."

"Aint our little fraternity brother still the Commish?"

"No," Wig said.

And the loiterers saluted Sweets. "Hello, Brother Carlton."

Wig shoved them out of the way and entered the armory with Sweets. A guard tried to stop them until he recognized Wig. The guard was carrying a nightstick. He wore a uniform of sorts, with shirt and trousers that didn't match. There was another man behind a glass cage. He was the "night manager," who worked in one continuous eighteen-hour shift, until time and weather merged into some endless midnight fog.

"You can't go in there, Wig, without a warrant."

"You're looking at the police commissioner, Brother William."

"That don't mean much. This is *our* armory, Wig. Them poor mothers have their rights."

"You wouldn't be hiding something, would you, William? Because if you get Brother Carlton angry, he'll come back with a pair of special prosecutors and shut down this stinky hole."

And Wig led Sweets into the heart of the shelter, a bleak barracks with row after row of beds, like some ultimate unwashed world. The smell was unbearable. It seemed to slide off the walls, circle that enormous room, and descend upon Sweets. He began to cough. He could barely breathe. Nothing in his own privileged life had prepared him for this. He'd come out of a place that still carried George Washington's ghost. He'd had his own nanny, who taught him magic tricks. He could have played for the Harlem Globetrotters, bad knee and all, or become a vice president of the Ford Foundation. But he'd discouraged all search committees. He was a police commissioner standing inside a shelter for homeless men, some of whom had covered themselves completely with white sheets, like figures in a morgue.

He recognized Isaac, who sat on a particular bed in his winter underwear, scribbling words in a long pad. He had no neighbors to bother him. The beds around Isaac were emptied of lost souls.

"Hello, Mr. Mayor."

"Not so loud," Isaac muttered. "I'm using an alias. Geronimo Jones. And don't call me 'Mr. Mayor.' I'm only the mayor-elect."

"But you're our king," Wig said.

"Did you have to bring him?" Isaac asked the police commissioner. "He's a hired gun. I suspend Wig, and you put him back on the payroll."

"That's right, motherfucker," Wig said. "You're a stinky old man. And I'd off you without a contract. I'd do it for free . . . how's your son-in-law, Barbarossa? He still sell drugs to college kids?"

"Enough," Sweets said. "Isaac, you can't occupy this bed."

"Why not? I needed a holiday. I can meditate in this room."

"Isaac, you have an apartment on Rivington Street. The City doesn't have to shelter you."

"Sweets," Isaac said, staring at Wig. "Will you send him away? I can't bear him. He gives me the creeps. How the hell did he find me?"

"Harlem's his crib."

"Baby," Wig said to Isaac. "I could have done you while you were asleep, put my piece under your pillow and shot your brains out. I was tempted, Brother Isaac, listening to you snore like a walrus. I could have strangled you, nice and clean."

"Why didn't you?" Isaac asked, with a child's look in his eye.

"I wouldn't make Sweets a widow." Wig started to laugh and walked right out of the shelter.

"He gives me the creeps."

"Isaac, I can arrest you for malfeasance. You're not allowed to impersonate a homeless man."

"Sweets, I'm scared."

"Scared of what? You had eighty-six percent of the vote. It was a landslide."

"Ah," Isaac said, "the Republicans put up a dog."

"The town's crazy about you. It's the hottest romance we've ever had. You can do what you want. The town will go with you, Isaac. You have an open ticket."

"Do me a favor, Sweets. Move into the shelter with me, and we'll talk about tickets. I've read the budget. What happens in nineteen eighty-six? Do we build more shelters?"

"Ask your budget people. I'm not the mayor. I can't tell you what the City can afford."

"That's the problem, Sweets. No one can predict the City's fucking revenues. A two hundred million dollar surplus, they said. And we had a fucking shortfall. I can't find out how many teachers are in the school system. Teachers come and go. That's the answer I get. We're living inside a Leviathan. I can't change things. I'm doing a little research. That's why I'm here. I see guards stealing from people, I see them asking for sex."

"They're like jailors, Isaac, that's all."

"But this isn't a jail."

Isaac put on his shirt, pants, and shoes, knotted his tie, and got into one of his famous winter coats from Orchard Street. He liked to dress "downtown." He needed a shave, but he was still the mayor-elect.

"The cardinal's been asking for you, Isaac."

"I don't talk to cardinals these days."

"I thought Jim was your friend."

"I have no friends. I have supplicants and seekers."

"And what the hell am I, Mr. Sidel?"

"My former First Dep. You'll start asking me favors in five weeks, after my coronation as king. But there might not be a coronation, Sweets. I could skip town, you know."

"Wig would find you," Sweets said.

2

Isaac began to miss that armory the moment he arrived on Rivington Street. He was fifty-five years old, almost fifty-six, and the woman he loved was off somewhere with the FBI. Margaret Tolstoy, a refugee from Roumania. She'd split with the Justice Department, but Frederic LeComte, Justice's cultural commissar, had lured her out of Isaac's bed and back into the fold. She'd been Isaac's roommate for a little while, some kind of guest. The newspapers had discovered her during the campaign, had called her "the mystery woman, Anastasia." But all the papers loved Isaac, and they wouldn't reveal her past.

She'd gone to Odessa during World War II, as the infant bride of Ferdinand Antonescu, the Butcher of Bucharest, who'd slaughtered gypsies and Jews near the Black Sea. He was finance minister of Russian Roumania, and advertised her as his niece. They'd lived in a mansion on Little Angel Street. But when Ferdinand began to starve along with the rest of Odessa, he stole children from the insane asylum and devoured their flesh. He was a fucking cannibal without a future. Ferdinand sneaked Anastasia onto a Red Cross boat and she arrived in America, a lady of thirteen. She joined Isaac's junior high school class. It was love at first sight for Sidel. But it didn't last. Anastasia was whisked away, returned to Roumania, and was only a little item in the war between the FBI and the KGB. She attended a KGB kindergarten, lived with a general, seduced scientists, changed identities until she had one constant in her skull: a dark-eyed boy who reminded her of a gypsy. Sidel.

He'd married, had a child, Marilyn, and now a son-in-law, Joe Barbarossa, but nothing could jolt him as much as that junior high school princess, Anastasia with her torn socks.

The king was all alone. Isaac couldn't inhabit Rivington Street without Anastasia and all her wigs. He believed in astral bodies, but he never seemed to bump into Margaret's emanations in his own little rabbit's hutch of rooms. And so he'd lived at the Seventh Avenue Armory for a week as Geronimo Jones, a fictitious man who didn't have to respond to telephone calls and entreaties from politicians and businessmen and all those other seekers of Sidel. He'd have to form his own administration, find commissioners and secretaries, hire and fire, but he was stalled. He'd be mayor in a month and he'd interviewed no one.

He slept for sixteen hours, like a grizzly bear. Then he looked at the calendar he kept on his shirt cuff. He was due at the Waldorf for a power breakfast with three of the City's biggest real-estate barons. They'd all contributed to his campaign. Papa Cassidy, who was a Mafia go-between, Jason Figgs, the lord of residential real estate, and Judah Bellow, the architect-builder who'd once been an apprentice of Emeric Gray, the baron of an earlier time. Isaac loved Emeric, who'd built apartment-house palaces between the wars, with ornamental balconies and terra-cotta tiles, who'd had a kingdom of artisans at his command, who'd covered water towers with brick turrets, who'd never skimped on materials. Emeric didn't die a rich man. He lost whatever he had during the Depression and was run over by a trolley car when he was eighty-six.

Isaac's deepest pleasure was to turn a corner and stumble upon an Emeric Gray, with its terra-cotta pieces that were like musical scales on a brick and stone wall. Ah, he might have been an architect in another life.

He arrived at the Waldorf. The three barons had rented a private room. They had their own butler. Isaac ordered shirred eggs, like a country squire. Jason Figgs was forty-nine. He'd inherited his father's fortune and quadrupled it. He was old society gelt, a Protestant in a Catholic and Jewish town. Papa Cassidy had married a pornographer's model, Delia St. John. He laundered Mafia money. He'd tried to have Isaac killed, and had become the treasurer of Isaac's campaign. That's how alliances were made in New York. Judah Bellow was the wealthiest of the barons. He'd started with towers of black glass and then returned to the brick and stone of his master, Emeric Gray. But Judah's buildings were dull masterpieces, without Emeric's desire to delight. Their elegance weighed upon you, their ornamentation was much too announced. Isaac despised every single Judah Bellow, but he liked the man.

Judah drank his grapefruit juice. "I made a bet that you wouldn't show. You've been scarce, Mr. Mayor."

"Ah," Isaac said, "you're my favorite pharaohs."

They were looking for tax abatements, to build their towers with Isaac's help. But they didn't mention any towers.

"Isaac, we're worried," Jason said. "About Schyler Knott." Schyler was president of the Christy Mathewsons, a bunch of baseball antiquarians. He was also an investment banker, but how could he harm the three barons? And then Isaac realized what the hell the breakfast was about. Schyler Knott had a passion for old buildings. He was chairman of the Landmarks Preservation Commission, and Isaac's barons were the only three realtors on that commission.

"He's incompetent," Jason said.

"A turkey," Papa said.

"He's a dangerous man," said Judah. "He wants to landmark everything."

"That's his privilege," Isaac said. "That's his point of view."

"Then how are we supposed to build?" asked Papa Cassidy.

"I don't know."

"The tax structure will fall to shit."

"Come on," Isaac said. "You have meetings. You fight a little. Schyler's no fucking dictator."

"He's worse than that," said Judah Bellow. "He'll destroy us all."

"How?"

"We have a parcel of land."

"The three of you?"

"Yes," Papa said. "On Fifty-sixth and Third. And there's a matchbox sitting on it, a sixty-year-old monster with rats in the cellar."

"Who designed your matchbox?"

"Emeric Gray."

"Judah," Isaac said, "you ought to be ashamed of yourself. Emeric was your master."

"It's still a matchbox. I wouldn't touch one of his classics. It's an undistinguished building."

"A tenement, Mr. Mayor, with cockroaches," said Jason Figgs. "We could put up a beauty. Coca-Cola will take a couple of floors. We could show you Judah's designs. It would mean a lot to the City, Mr. Mayor. Millions."

"You're all geniuses," Isaac said. "Couldn't you find another parcel?"

"We'd lose six months. Coca-Cola will walk."

"Boys," Isaac said to the three barons. "Build on top of Emeric's castle, secure the air rights."

"Schyler's against it. He says it will hurt the contours of the building, invalidate the roof. He's out of his mind, Mr. Mayor."

"No. He's Schyler Knott. I can't help you, boys."

Jason tried to bully Isaac. "We could go to the governor."

"Be my guest."

"He controls the purse."

"I agree," Isaac said. "We're paupers. But if he interferes with my Landmarks Commission, I'll break his leg."

Isaac abandoned the three barons. He started singing to himself until he had a vision of Margaret Tolstoy in one of her red wigs. Ah, if only he were eighty-six. He might not think of Margaret so much if his sexual powers ever waned. But he wouldn't want to get crushed under the wheels of a trolley, like Emeric Gray. And then Isaac recalled that there were no more trolley cars in Manhattan.

He visited with Rebecca Karp, who sat on the porch at Gracie Mansion, in her rocking chair. She'd grown paranoid about the City of New York, wouldn't venture into the streets, but she was Isaac's main advisor, his secret secretary of state.

"Appearances, Isaac. You have to look like a maven."

"Me a maven? I can hardly put on my pants."

"That's because your gun is too heavy."

Mayors weren't supposed to carry guns, but the new Commish had let him keep his permit. Isaac and Sweets both had Glocks, guns with plastic noses.

"Becky," Isaac said with a grin, "I'm not wearing my Glock today. I just came out of retreat at the Seventh Avenue Armory."

"Cocksucker," she said, "you haven't even been sworn in and you start taking advantage of the homeless. Do you want to sink us? I'll lose my rocking chair if you're impeached."

"Come on. I had to feel what it was like to live inside a shelter."

"The homeless can't save you, Isaac. They never vote. And you have more important projects. You'll need a first deputy mayor. I have a candidate. Malik."

Isaac started to groan. Martin Malik was the trials commissioner at One Police Plaza. Isaac had picked him. Malik was a Moslem and a Turk whose ancestors had been mathematicians in Istanbul. He was a hanging judge who stripped cops of their pensions. The Republicans were grooming him as the next governor. He'd been dating Delia St. John until Papa Cassidy wooed her into his marriage bed.

"Malik's my enemy," Isaac said. "He thinks I was Papa Cassidy's pimp, that I took Delia away from him. He'll never join my administration. He's too ambitious."

"He'll join a man who got ninety percent of the vote."

"Eighty-six," Isaac had to declare. "Don't exaggerate."

"Malik will keep the minorities off your back. And he won't let the barons bite your ass."

"I had breakfast with them," Isaac said. "Papa, Judah, and Jason Figgs. They want me to muzzle Schyler Knott, kick him off the Landmarks Commission."

"They're right," Rebecca said.

"You appointed him."

"He's been intransigent, Isaac. We have to side with the builders. They're our bread and butter."

"But they want to tear down an Emeric Gray."

"The matchbox on Fifty-sixth? It's cockroach country. We can afford to lose one Emeric Gray. And if we frustrate the barons, they might run to another town. It's always a delicate dance, Isaac. Schyler will have to go."

"Then you fire him."

"Isaac, you asked me to appoint Sweets as police commissioner, I appointed him. I can't fire Schyler Knott. All the conservationists will come down on us. And they'll know your hand was behind it. I'm Ms. Rebecca, the lame duck. You'll ease Schyler out, appoint him to another commission."

Rebecca's cordless telephone rang. She picked it out of her lap, muttered a few words, and handed the phone to Isaac. "It's for you."

"Sidel here," he growled.

It was his son-in-law, Barbarossa.

"Boss, there's a dead man in your bed."

"Joey, speak a little slower, will you? What dead man?"

"Geronimo Jones."

"I'm Geronimo Jones," Isaac said.

"Not anymore. He's lying in your bed at the Seventh Avenue Armory with a knife in his neck."

"Joey," Isaac said, "I'll be uptown in five minutes," and he leapt over the porch rail like a useless gazelle.

3

Lieutenant Quinn, chief of the mayor's detail, drove him up to the shelter. Isaac darted around the glass cage and entered the big dormitory. There wasn't much of a commotion. The medical examiner had arrived. He stood with a patrolman, a homicide detective, two lads from forensic, and Joe Barbarossa around Isaac's former bed. A naked man was lying in it. The knife had been removed from his neck. A very narrow mark remained, clotted with blood. Otherwise, he was as pink as Isaac Sidel.

"Who found him?"

"I did," Barbarossa said. "I was looking for you and . . ."

"Weren't there any witnesses?"

"Boss, it's a shelter, for Christ's sake. Nobody hears, nobody sees. This Geronimo died all alone."

"Why are you sure he's Geronimo?"

"That's the name he had when he was logged in. Geronimo Jones."

"It's a scam," Isaac said. "Some mother is sending me a kite. 'Watch your ass, Sidel. You won't live long enough to have a coronation.' I want every single man in this barrack questioned. We'll bring in twenty detectives from Manhattan North."

"Boss, you're not the police commissioner."

"Yeah, Joey. The commissioner works for me."

"That's the problem. He doesn't work for you. You're not mayor yet."

"But I will be." And Isaac started to interrogate the medical examiner. "Boris, was there a struggle, some kind of fight?"

"I'd have to say no. The cut is too clean. That poor bastard died in his sleep."

And Isaac drove downtown with the escort Sweets had assigned to him, his own son-in-law. Isaac wasn't very talkative. He didn't ask about Marilyn the Wild or the new apartment they had in Tudor city, which was like its own small town on a cliff above Forty-Second Street. Isaac couldn't afford to buy them the apartment. The money had come from his estranged wife, Kathleen, the Florida real-estate goddess.

He stopped off at Rivington Street, collected his Glock, stuck it under his belt, because he wasn't fond of holsters, and shoved his way into Police Plaza with Joe. He was still the Pink Commish, even if he had no real status at One PP. A future king didn't have much of a portfolio. He rode up to the fourteenth floor, barked at Sweets' aides, and entered the commissioner's office. Sweets and Wig were watering Isaac's plants.

"Wonderful," Isaac said. "A devoted couple . . . I want that man arrested, Sweets."

"What the hell are you talking about?"

"He killed Geronimo Jones." Isaac turned to Barbarossa, who was at his heels. "Joey, will you cuff Wig and read him his rights?"

"Boss," Barbarossa said.

"Nobody's cuffing me," Wig said. "Not your little asswipe, Barbarossa."

The three of them, Isaac, Wig, and Joe, pulled out their Glocks.

"I'm calling in my sergeant," Sweets said. "I'm putting you all in the clink."

"I'll fire you first," Isaac said.

Barbarossa had to whisper in his ear. "Boss, you can't fire anybody. It's floating time. You're one more civilian until the new year."

"Tell him," Wig said. "He's a white ghost."

Sweets started to rock. "I won't have drawn guns in my office. Holster them or get out."

The Glocks disappeared.

"Now, will you enlighten me a little?" he said.

"Joey found a corpse at the Seventh Avenue Armory . . . a white homeless male with a knife in his neck. He was registered as Geronimo Jones and living in my bed."

"And where does Wig enter the fucking picture?"

"Didn't he promise to kill Geronimo Jones? Didn't he say he would off me if he had the chance? He was amusing himself. He offed another Geronimo Jones to give me a fit."

"He's not that fancy, Isaac. Wig's not a poet."

"But he's a member of the Purple Gang."

"Do I have to listen to that old song?" Sweets said. "The Purples are a myth. You know it, I know it, Wig knows it. Ask Joe."

"I never saw a Purple," Barbarossa said.

"That's settled . . . Isaac didn't dream up that dead man, Wig. How did he get there?"

"Shit, Sweets. I'm not a witch doctor."

"But Seventh Avenue is your department store. A man named Geronimo Jones dies in Isaac's bed . . ."

"It's not Isaac's bed. He happened to sleep there. Should I tell you how many George Washingtons and Abraham Lincolns there are at the shelter?"

"But there was only one Geronimo Jones," Isaac said. "Me."

"And how did I spot you, bro'? Every moron in the neighborhood knew that King Isaac was registered at the armory as Geronimo Jones. I didn't have to do diddly. I followed my nose to the big stink."

Sweets stared at Wig. "I still don't like the percentages. Two Geronimo Joneses landing in the same bed."

"Aw, Sweets, that mother could have been offed anywhere and dropped in *Isaac's* bed. I'll bet you a hundred dollars there's no rap sheet on Geronimo. Call Crime Scene."

"It's too early," Isaac said.

"Crime Scene can tell you about the hairs in a dead man's nose."

"It's too early," Isaac muttered. "We were with the M.E. and two lab technicians an hour ago."

"Sweets," Wig said, "call the wizards."

Sweets made two quick phone calls. Then he shook his head. "There's nothing on Geronimo Jones. He was a floater, Isaac. He has no history. He was never processed downtown at the main shelter. No one sent him up to the armory."

"But his name was in the logbook. Joey saw it."

"Logbooks can lie," Sweets said. "I'll have Wig look into it."

"Not Wig," Isaac said. "Not Wig."

"Are you telling me how to run my shop, Mr. Mayor?"

"No," Isaac said. "Wig will be our explorer . . . come on, Joe. We're a couple of outcasts. We aren't welcome on the fourteenth floor."

"The cardinal's been asking for you again," Sweets told him.

"I keep my own fucking calendar," Isaac said, but he had Barbarossa dial the cardinal's office after they'd returned to the car, which was a battered blue Plymouth Joe had swiped from the police garage. His boss was no aristocrat. Isaac was the people's king.

They found the cardinal at a recreation center near the Williamsburg Bridge. The locals were against the AIDS hospice Jim had opened on Attorney Street. They wanted to shut it down. They talked about the plague Jim had brought to their streets.

"Jesus," Jim said, with a cigarette in his mouth. He'd been a bantamweight boxer in Chicago before he was a priest. He wasn't wearing his cardinal's robes. He looked like an ordinary parishioner. His pants were wrinkled. His tie was askew. He loved to move about his parishes in mufti. But his flock was shouting at Jim.

"Your Eminence, we don't want our young children involved in the plague. Move your hospice into another parish."

"There is no other parish," Jim said.

"AIDS is the Devil's disease."

"Then we'll fight the Devil," Jim said. "But with kindness and compassion."

There was a constant chant. "Move the hospice, move the hospice."

"I will not abandon dying children and women and men."

But the criers drowned his voice and defeated Jim. His cheek began to twitch. He chewed his cigarette. And then there was a bit of silence. The king had entered the recreation hall without Barbarossa. Isaac had put him on the case of Geronimo Jones. It wasn't legal. But Isaac couldn't survive without his own minuscule police force, and that force now consisted of his son-in-law, Joe.

The king approached Cardinal Jim.

"You deserted me, boyo," Jim said. "I'm a forlorn prince of the church. I'll have to go on retreat."

"Stop moaning," Isaac said. "I'll handle this."

And he faced the parishioners like some Mussolini, with the Glock sticking out of his pants.

"With all due respect, Mr. Mayor," said an Irish accountant from one of the middle-income projects on Essex Street. "Would Cardinal Jim, bless his heart, have invaded Park Avenue with his hospice?"

"No," Isaac said. "Some millionaires' club would have crippled him. The millionaires and their wives could have gotten an injunction from a friendly judge and no hospice would have ever been built."

"Then why do we have to suffer?"

"Because this is the Lower East Side. It's where politics began. We protect the weak."

"Our schools are bad enough without sick children. We don't want a plague."

"I'll tutor the children myself. Do you feel better? I'll devote ten hours a week."

"Sonny," the cardinal whispered, "don't promise what you can't deliver."

"Keep out of it, Jim. I have my own parish."

And the local citizens had their king. He was much less remote than an uptown cardinal from the powerhouse of St. Patrick's Cathedral. Isaac was one of their own. He wouldn't betray them. They drank schnapps with him out of paper cups and went home.

Isaac stood in the deserted hall with Cardinal Jim and a mountain of cups.

"Sonny," Jim said, "I was wrong about you. You'll be a formidable mayor. But we have to arrange a meeting, your lads and mine."

"Ah, those wonderful monsignors. They're sharks, Jim. I couldn't survive in the same room with them. They'd steal my pants and the City's revenues."

"I'm a cardinal," Jim said. "I have to steal. I run half the City, boyo. And don't you forget. I campaigned for you. I delivered the Catholic vote."

"Pish," Isaac said. "You wanted a Republican mayor so you could rule this town. You had your monsignors contribute to the Republican treasure chest, and don't you deny it."

"Jesus, I had to hedge a little. And you had a real liability, son. That Tolstoy woman. She grew up around the Nazis. I hear she ate orphan boys in Odessa."

"she was a child, Jim."

"Old enough to marry the Butcher of Bucharest. Antonescu, wasn't it? Drank gypsy blood. He was a genuine ghoul."

"He was her ballet teacher."

"Ah, that's a laugh. The lord of Transnistria, his own fake little country by the sea. A Nazi prince."

"You must have kept your monsignors busy doing research."

"Not at all. I had a chat with Frederic LeComte. He couldn't lie to a cardinal, could he? You'd better drop the Tolstoy woman as soon as you can. The town won't take to a Nazi princess."

"Don't talk about Anastasia."

"Ah, the little bride of many names."

Isaac walked out on the cardinal, left him standing there with his tobacco fingers and a cigarette butt. He returned to Rivington Street. He took off his clothes. The king didn't have to drop off into some dark sleep. He dreamt of Margaret Tolstoy while he sat inside his kitchen tub. He'd forgotten to fill the tub with water. Isaac would have to endure one of his dry baths. His head fell onto his shoulder. He was off on one of his astral trips. He'd gone to Odessa from his magic tub. It was the middle of World War II. Isaac saw a mansion. It didn't have wooden shutters or a wooden porch, like Rebecca's house. It was made of stone. It sat on a hill. Isaac was near a harbor. He could smell the sea.

Ah, it was Little Angel Street, where his own beloved, Anastasia, had lived with Odessa's Roumanian prince, Antonescu. There were rats riding under the stones, a whole population of starving rats that formed herds around Isaac. He couldn't avoid bumping into them with his shoes. They had long, bony bodies that were like some horrible gray armor. But Isaac got through the door, into Antonescu's house. It was cluttered with rats.

"Anastasia," he moaned.

"I'm right here."

Isaac the Brave had to blink. He wasn't in wartime Odessa. He was back in his tub, like a naked beast. And his darling wasn't Little Orphan Annie in the clutches of a false Roumanian prince. She was Margaret Tolstoy, wearing a blond wig.

"I was dreaming," he said. "About Little Angel Street . . . how did you get in?"

"Mr. Mayor, I still have your key. And I'm a resourceful girl. I could have picked your lock in my sleep. Do you like to bathe in the cold? . . . I remember. You're a polar bear. What were you doing on Little Angel Street?"

"Looking for you."

"Do you have to invade my privacy, Isaac? Odessa is the only past I had. And there was no Little Angel Street. It was called the Deribaskova. Uncle Ferdinand decided to rename the whole town."

"He had the right. He was a prince."

Anastasia laughed under the folds of blond hair. "You only say that because you're another grand seignior. A king, in fact."

"You shouldn't have abandoned my bed."

"Had to, dear." She undressed, got into that dry tub with Isaac, and they kissed with a passion that seemed to pull at the roots of Isaac's eyes. He was Little Orphan Annie. And she was LeComte's little soldier . . .

He found himself in his own bed. He must have made love with Anastasia. He couldn't recall a bloody thing. He was an amnesiac, always an amnesiac. But *this* Anastasia didn't have a wig. She was bald and beautiful, like a wondrous mannequin with cropped gray hair.

"You left without a word. Packed your bags and boom! You're Frederic's toy again."

"I'm not a toy," she said. "I'm chasing a child trafficker, a mutt who sells blond, blue-eyed boys and girls from Roumania."

"Ah, one of Ceausescu's ministers."

"Don't laugh," she said. "I was born in Roumania."

"I thought you were a citizen of the world."

"I am," she said. "The KGB took away my country, and the FBI won't give it back. But I still have Odessa, Isaac . . . and the Lower East Side. Let's say I'm a sucker for blue-eyed orphans."

"Who is this mutt?"

"He calls himself Quentin. He has massage parlors all over

23

the place. He deals a little coke. And he has connections with the rich and the super rich. That's where he finds his customers."

"And LeComte sent you over to sleep with him, huh?"

Anastasia searched for her wig. She was that blond creature again, Margaret Tolstoy.

"LeComte's your pimp."

"He's everybody's pimp, darling. Didn't you know that?"

"Not mine," Isaac said.

"You went on the road for him, dear. You were his Hamilton Fellow, the Justice Department's traveling man."

"But I don't travel anymore."

"Well, I still do . . . I hear your namesake was killed. Geronimo Jones."

"Ah, LeComte told you that. Justice already has a file on Geronimo."

"You shouldn't sleep in shelters, dear. It's dangerous."

"It wasn't dangerous. The apartment has too many ghosts. I had to get away. And the Purple Gang offed the other Geronimo Jones."

"There is no Purple Gang. You mean Wig."

"Yeah, Sweets' little deputy. He was running dope right out of Gracie Mansion. I suspend the mother, and Sweets brings him back."

"He's the best cop in New York City. He can walk Harlem, Isaac, and you can't."

"I'm a downtown man."

"Then what were you doing in a Harlem shelter?"

"I told you. I was taking a rest."

She kissed Isaac on the mouth. He began to moan. "Where can I find you? Give me a telephone number, Margaret."

"No numbers. I'll find you."

And she was out of the king's arms and out the door, and Isaac had to live with Margaret's ghost and the memory of Little Angel Street.

4

He was the Purple Gang, alias Albert Wiggens. He'd been shot in the head, and he'd never really recovered. He could have had a disability pension, retired at thirty-three, but he wouldn't retire. He'd hidden a few medical reports, faked a couple of others. He had tiny fragments of lead in his skull, and he had crippling headaches that not even his doctor knew about. He'd fainted several times in the middle of the street. No one molested him. His Seventh Avenue "cousins" would sit beside him until he woke. He was Wig. Seventh Avenue might have become Adam Clayton Powell Jr. Boulevard to the mapmakers and tourists who wanted a glimpse of "darktown," but Adam's boulevard belonged to Wig.

He was at the Seventh Avenue Armory with Brother William, the night manager, in William's glass cage. His head had begun to throb. A steel ribbon snaked above his eyes like some terrible screw. He had to keep one hand on William's desk. "Geronimo Jones."

"Aw, Wiggy, it was nothin' but a joke on the big Jew. Parks his ass in our dormitory. I had to take revenge."

"But how did that stiff get into Isaac's bed?"

"I put him there, Wiggy. Carried him in my arms."

Wig slapped the night manager across the face with his free hand and almost fell. William blew his nose and started to cry.

"Have I ever threatened you, Brother William?"

"No," William said, sulking like a penitent.

"Have I ever hurt you or your sister?"

"No, Wiggy. Not once."

"But I'll kill you, William. And it won't be with a knife in the neck. Didn't you realize that when you fucked with Isaac, you were fucking me?"

"How's that, Wig?"

"I'm responsible for that little king. I'm his black angel."

"But you hate him, Wiggy, and he hates you."

"That don't matter none. I'm his angel."

"Nobody took the time to tell me that."

"You're my beacon, William. You're my early-warning system. And you play a fool trick. Where did the corpse come from?"

"Midtown," William said.

"It was your sister's doing."

"Rita Mae wasn't involved, Wiggy."

Wig took out his Glock and held it between William's eyes. "What happens when people lie to me, William?"

"They don't ever get no second chance." The night manager was blubbering now. "He was just a john who died on Rita."

"She robbed him, right?"

"Wig, he wanted pussy and he couldn't pay. He tried to strangle Rita and take her money. She had to defend herself."

"With a pigsticker she put in his neck."

"That's Rita's way. She has her habits, Wig. She's too old to change. But there's nothin' to worry about. The john didn't have any address."

"A homeless man from out of town visits your slut of a sister with the intent to rip her off?"

"Aw, don't call her a slut, Wiggy. Rita's wild about you."

"Quentin has him brought uptown in one of his wagons and you accept the delivery, right?"

"I had to, Wig. She's my sister."

"I warned you, William. No more deliveries. The shelter's

no dumping ground for other people's corpses. The fat days are over. I'm not living at Gracie Mansion anymore. I can't supply morgue space. The tit is gettin' tight."

"I'll behave, Wiggy. I swear."

Wig had to put his Glock away. He wasn't going to off Brother William.

He rode down to Times Square in the commissioner's black Dodge. He hated these streets. It had become a camping ground for young bloods who had nowhere else to breathe. The poorest of them had metal chains around their necks. Homeboys without a home. He was a cop, and it didn't matter how many bloods were in the Department. All cops—brown, red, yellow, and blue—were white. They had to protect white power. And that's why he hadn't severed himself from the myth of the Purple Gang. Black assassins rising from the ruins of Harlem . . .

He entered the Ali Baba, a porno mill on Eighth Avenue, near the *New York Times*. It was a multimillion-dollar show, the biggest sex supermarket in Manhattan, its own indoor red-light district. The Ali Baba had no rivals. It was run by the Maf and Quentin Kahn, a slumlord, a psychopath, and a master pimp. Quentin's trademark was a yellow condom that his hostesses supplied to all the johns. He wouldn't allow buggering at his dream palace. He was some kind of crazy Puritan. Girls could be beaten or whipped, but not sodomized. And the johns had to have their peters inspected by a nurse.

But the Ali Baba was mostly a boulevard where out-of-town johns mingled and watched the different attractions. The entrance fee was five dollars. And once they passed through the Ali Baba's golden gate, they could watch as long as they liked. Quentin's girls stood behind glass booths, wearing negligees or nothing at all. A john could enter a booth, but there was always a window between him and the girl. He could talk dirty, undress himself, or make a date with the girl, meet her at some bedroom closet or tiny sauna in Quentin's labyrinthian upstairs rooms. He had to be careful. The Ali Baba wasn't a house of prostitution. It was a lonely hearts club, according to Quentin Kahn. And his "researchers," who stood behind one-way mirrors, could almost smell an undercover cop.

But Wig was always welcome at the Ali Baba. He had his own "touch," a tiny percentage of the profits that he shared with Mario Klein, the mayor's secretary. That "touch" might end after Isaac became the one and only king. But Wig had other "touches" here and there. He wasn't rich, but he could also find a bed at the Seventh Avenue Armory, become the new Geronimo Jones.

Quentin's boulevard had glaring blue lights, and Wig had to create a little visor with his hand or he wouldn't have discovered Rita Mae's booth. She sat behind her window, looking bored. She was wearing a white negligee. Wig entered the booth.

Rita Mae yawned, then cupped her breasts without looking up at him.

"Honey," she said, "I'll show you mine if you show me yours."

He'd lived with Rita once upon a time. She'd been his old lady, but he was a wild man, filled with coke. He fell off a roof. He had other old ladies, and Rita drifted down to the Ali Baba. He could have bombed that lonely hearts club, set it on fire, offed Quentin if he had to. But Rita was already gone.

"Show me yours," she said, and Wig knew she'd been smoking crack. She was a girl with incredible cheekbones and hazel eyes. He peered into her glass wall until she noticed him.

"Wig, honey, I thought you was a john."

"I am a john," he said. "Take off your little housecoat."

"No," she said. "I'm naked enough."

"Where's your pigsticker?"

"What you talking about?"

"Your knife, Rita. Where's your knife?"

"That old thing, I lost it, Wig."

"In some poor sucker's neck."

"Who told you that?"

"William. He buried that sucker in one of his own beds at the armory."

"He's lyin'. The last time I had to stick a john was two years ago. Quentin called the doctor, and they put him on a bus."

"Yeah. He bled to death on the way to Miami."

"It's not my fault, Wig, if Quentin's doctor couldn't stop the blood."

"Take off the housecoat. I want to look at you."

Rita stood up and wiggled out of her negligee. Her breasts had fallen a tiny bit. Her pubic hair was like a brown diamond. Her nipples were larger than he'd remembered. Her knees were slightly bowed. His headache got worse and worse. He wanted Rita. She was his fox even if she slaved for Quentin Kahn.

"I'm gonna buy up your contract, Rita."

"What for? So you can put me in your own glass house? I'll stay where I am, Mr. Albert Wiggens. It's Ali Baba," she said. "The land of yellow condoms."

Wig raised his arm. Was it to break through the window? That metal ribbon in his skull pressed against his eyes. Wig was going blind. A whole world of colors began to bleed around him as he fell to the floor . . .

He woke in Rita's arms. He was in a closet behind the glass booth. Rita was rocking him, singing some Christmas song about a red-nosed reindeer. Fuck Christmas. He'd have banned reindeer from Harlem if he could.

"Honey," she said, "I have to get back to my booth. Quentin will . . ."

"Yeah, he'll kill you, Rita Mae. And I'll off him. But that won't bring you back."

She was thirty-one years old, with a runny nose. She'd had a child when she was seventeen. The boy, Harwood, lived with her on Lenox Avenue. He'd dropped out of school, spent his time in several crack houses. He was taller than Wig, with his mama's hazel eyes. He couldn't write a sentence. But he'd read like a little devil when Wig had been around. Fucking Harwood! Wig loved the boy, but he hated to admit it.

"Rita, I'm all right."

"Those blackouts are getting real bad."

"I'm all right."

He climbed up onto his own feet. He was dizzy. "Girl," he said, "you go back to your booth. You have a line of customers big as a block."

But there was no one on line outside Rita Mae's booth. There was only that boulevard of stragglers. Wig joined those stragglers under the blue light. It was almost paradise.

He walked into Quentin Kahn's corporate headquarters, passing a pair of bodyguards. Quentin Kahn sat behind a desk that had been part of Cornelius Vanderbilt's railroad car. He was older than Wig. He'd made his fortune as a slumlord and then took over a failing pornography shop and turned it into the Ali Baba. He'd been buying and selling buildings since he was seventeen. He had a kind of bold handsomeness, with light brown hair. He was a pingpong player, like Barbarossa and Sidel's dead angel, Manfred Coen. He had a table in his office and he would fly in champions from Roumania and Portugal to hit the ball with him for half an hour. These foreign champions were always coming into or out of his office. Quentin had his own magazine, *Pingpong Power*. He was wearing a red jersey from some forgotten pingpong club.

He wasn't alone. Sidel's Roumanian murderess was with him, Margaret Tolstoy.

"Hello, Wig," she said. She had purple lipstick that looked like a magical wound over her mouth.

"Ah, you kids know each other," Quentin said. He liked to talk with the gruffness of a landlord.

"Yeah, we met," Wig said.

"Before or after the king's campaign?"

"A little before," Wig said. "I'll come back later, Quent."

"No, no. Margaret was about to leave."

She kissed Quentin on the cheek, traveled across the room, and disappeared.

"You are a dumb motherfucker, Quent. That is Dracula's daughter. She only has one kind of kiss. She poisons you and sucks out your blood."

"Relax," Quentin said. "I'm alive, aint I?"

"Not for long. If she's around, Quent, it means the Feds have you under surveillance and are moving to indict."

"I'm always under surveillance. So what? I'm a registered Republican. I can't be touched."

"LeComte must have microphones in every little corner."

"I'll laugh him out of court."

"Quent, what the hell was she doing here?"

"She's close to Isaac, aint she? And I'll need some favors from the king. I own too many buildings. I have to get on his good side."

"With Margaret Tolstoy?"

"Who else? It's like having your own lobbyist in the Sidel administration."

"A lobbyist who's a vampire."

"Don't worry, I'll pay you to off her when the time's ripe."

Wig rolled his eyes and Quentin started to laugh. "Come on. We'll go to my living room. The FBI can't disturb us."

They went out a door behind Cornelius Vanderbilt's old desk and landed on a fire escape with a ladder that looked like metal vines. Wig had a view of the battered fields between Eighth and Ninth Avenues. It was a dead garden. Wig saw abandoned refrigerators, rotting motors, collapsed tents. Then he realized that people were living in the garden. It was a haven for the homeless, much more appealing than the Seventh Avenue Armory, even if you risked freezing your ass.

"Quent, you've been reviving your ambulance. I can't afford to have another stiff at the Seventh Avenue Armory. Try Brooklyn or the Bronx."

"Wig, I was doing you a favor. Your little mama knifed a john. I had to get rid of him."

"Rita swears she didn't use her pigsticker."

"Would you like to have some witnesses? Her knife was in his neck."

"Who was the john?"

"Nameless. No ID. There's nothing to link him to us or Rita Mae. I wiped the handle of her pigsticker."

"That's considerate of you, Quent. I work for the police commissioner. I can't feed him a fucking fairy tale."

"There's no ID."

"He'll send in a team of homicide boys."

"They can't find shit. We'll pin it on the competition. I'll pay a couple of kids to swear the john was knifed at the Stardust Palace."

"Quent, you're a businessman. Don't play cop. The Stardust Palace will lead those homicide boys back to Ali Baba."

"I could offer Rita a little vacation."

"No. She's more anonymous in a glass booth. I'll invent a story. But it's the last time."

Wig started to prance down the fire escape. His headache was gone.

"Hey," Quentin shouted, "don't you want your envelope?"

"Not today."

He'd have to distance himself from Quentin's weekly "touch." He watched the homeless men and women living under blankets and tiny tents. Their hands were black. They had no running water in this ruined garden.

He didn't want to go back and interrogate Rita again. She was lying or Quent was lying or both of them were covering up. It had something to do with Margaret Tolstoy. That was Wig's guess.

He walked out of the garden.

PART TWO

5

There was a second corpse. Also Geronimo Jones. At the Atlantic Avenue Armory in Brooklyn. Then a third. Under a blanket at Grand Central Station. There was no ID. Just a xeroxed note stuffed in his mouth. Crime Scene had to test the saliva before they would return the note to Sweets. It was some weird manifesto.

> We are sick of hoboes and mongrels and niggers and kikes.
> We believe in the virtues of Old New York.
> —The Knickerbocker Boys

> Monte Ward
> Will White
> Jay Penny
> Long John Silver
> Sam Wise
> Jesse Nichols
> Morris deMorris
> Alexander Hamilton
> Herman Long
> Tobias Little

Isaac kept perusing that row of fictional madmen. "Long John Silver" had come out of *Treasure Island*, of course. And "Alexander Hamilton" was a slap at Isaac, who'd been the first Hamilton Fellow. But the other names haunted him. Will White, Will White. It was like a poetic laundry list. Isaac brooded about the names and the homeless men who were being killed.

He met with Sweets and Wig.

"I'll need my own team. Twenty cops and a command post."

Sweets covered his eyes with his huge basketballer's hands. Then he peered out at Isaac.

"Keep away from my cops."

"Your cops?" Isaac said. "Who's the mayor?"

"Rebecca Karp."

"She's sentenced herself to a rocking chair."

"Becky's still my boss."

"Not for long," Isaac said. "I had to twist her arm to take you on as the Commish . . . I'll be your boss come January."

"This is December, baby."

"Sweets," Isaac said, "I'm a cop."

"Yeah, the Pink Commish," said Wig.

"Sweets, will you shut him up? He offed the original Geronimo Jones."

"I'll massacre both of you," Sweets said, lunging with his basketballer's hands. "I want some peace. We have a band of crazies out there. The Knickerbocker Boys."

"Honkey motherfuckers," Wig said.

"Sweets, give me something. I can't go it all alone. I'm stranded."

"He flopped my whole detail at the mansion," Wig said. "Let him borrow some of Rebecca's new boys."

"I don't want Rebecca's boys."

"You have Barbarossa," Sweets said.

"He's my son-in-law. No one will take me seriously if I run around with Barbarossa all the time."

"Then you'll have to tough it out until January," Wig said.

"I could embarrass you, Sweets. I could ask the D.A. to deputize me. He knows his politics. He'll let the mayor-elect form his own squad."

"You'll still have nothing," Sweets said. "I'll change that fucking squad every day of the week."

"All right," Isaac said. "What have you come up with?"

"On the Knickerbocker Boys? Precious little. The names don't add up to much on our computers."

"Not even Long John Silver?"

"I'm not talking literature, Isaac. I'm talking facts."

"But isn't there a make on the three homeless men?"

"Nothing," Sweets said. "They're like characters out of a missing book. No positive ID. They could have fallen off another planet."

"There has to be a reason that they're so anonymous," Isaac said. "Who's dumping dead bodies in our lap?"

"Crazies . . . freaks."

"No. There's a pattern. I haven't found it yet."

And Isaac slipped out of the PC's office, muttering to himself.

"Resign," Wig said, "or you'll have that honkey on your hands."

"I can live with Isaac," Sweets said. "Wig, what the hell is going down?"

"Honkeys are dying in different parts of town."

"Stop stroking me," Sweets said. "And cut this 'honkey' shit. I'm not a black man once I get out of bed."

Isaac got into his usual bum's clothes and was about to go undercover when he received a telephone call from Rebecca's rocking chair.

"He quit," she said. "He left Landmarks."

"What?"

"Schyler Knott, you dope. He's given up his chairmanship. You ought to be glad. Now all the barons will be on your side."

"Wait a minute. Why would Schyler suddenly quit? He's the toughest preservationist in town."

"Ah, he's gone back to baseball," Rebecca said. "That's his first love."

"I won't accept his resignation."

"Schmuck," Rebecca said. "I already did. You can't afford Schyler. He's a nuisance. Isaac, builders have to build. You can't shackle them with a maniac like Schyler. Let him devote his life to the memory of Joe DiMaggio and Willie Mays."

"Schyler's an antiquarian. He doesn't want to remember Willie Mays."

"Didn't I tell you? He's a racist. And we got rid of him."

"Madam Mayor," Isaac said, "did you pressure him to resign?"

"I haven't talked to Schyler in six months."

She hung up on the mayor-elect, who hiked to Greenwich Village in his bum's clothes. Schyler lived in an Emeric Gray on Horatio Street. The building had been put up before the big Crash. It was a 1927 classic, with colored stones above every window, a revolving door furnished in cherrywood, a canopy with gorgeous brass poles. The building was owned by one of the barons, Judah Bellow.

The doorman was very superior with Isaac. "Sir, I'm sorry, but I can't allow beggars in the building."

"Why not?" Isaac growled, revealing his Glock. "Do you have some kind of fucking dress code? It's illegal. I didn't come in without my shoes and socks. That's all I need."

"I'll have to call the super."

"Call him, but get me Schyler Knott on the intercom. Tell him it's the Pink Commish, Isaac Sidel."

The doorman started to blush. "I'm sorry, Mr. Mayor. I didn't catch your disguise."

"These are my winter casuals," Isaac said. And he rode upstairs to Schyler Knott, who had five rooms on the seventeenth floor, with windows that seemed to wrap around New York. Isaac could see the Hudson and the Empire State and the heartless country of glass towers that had been put up by the barons.

Schyler wore a red polo shirt. He was an investment banker who'd retired at thirty-eight to devote himself to landmarks and the Christy Mathewson Club. There was an incongruity about all this. He looked like some Robert Redford who'd missed his chance on the screen.

Schyler was a health nut. He prepared a pitcher of carrot juice for Isaac and himself. Isaac hated carrots, but he had to drink. His lips turned orange.

"Schyler, I want you back on Landmarks."

"What's the point? I'm tired of sitting with those real-estate sharks."

"I'll chop off their heads. We'll have a whole new commission."

"It will come to the same thing. Isaac, they're ready to tear down Emeric Grays."

"Yeah, I heard about that fiasco on Fifty-sixth. The pharaohs can fuck themselves. They're not getting that parcel."

"Did you ever read the first New York City Master Plan? It's a remarkable document, written in 'twenty-nine. It wouldn't tolerate pharaohs without a vision. No builder could interfere with the integrity of a neighborhood or destroy a sense of the past. Isaac, that's how we breathe. Every stone is our second skin. And when we kill one or two Emerics, it's an act of self-mutilation."

"I love Emeric," Isaac said, between sips of carrot juice. "He's my hero. I know the exact spot where that trolley car ran him down."

"Your City, Isaac, is a landmark that's about to die. We had our pyramids, and we lost them."

"Like the old Penn Station," Isaac said.

"I could tell you about reservoirs and banks and music halls and the first Madison Square Garden . . . Antonio Gaudí was supposed to build a skyscraper in New York. Can you imagine what it would have been like? Ever been to Barcelona, Isaac? Ever see Gaudí's Church of the Sagrada Familia? It was never finished."

The king was ashamed to admit that he'd never been to Barcelona. But he remembered that Gaudí, like Emeric, had been hit by a trolley car.

"Isaac, Gaudí's skyscraper would have been a tall fun house, a Coney Island cathedral. But he couldn't get it financed. So it sits like a ghost in our dreams, one more phantom building."

"We'll find a new Gaudí," Isaac said.

"It's too late," Schyler said.

"But we'll fight the pharaohs, and we'll win."

"And live with a shrinking tax base, Mr. Mayor?"

"I don't care," Isaac said.

"I'm your white elephant. I had to go, or the realtors would all scream. 'Schyler wants to landmark every stone.' And I would . . ." He shut his eyes, as if he were practicing some incantation. Isaac could feel Schyler's face begin to close. The king would get nothing more from Schyler Knott.

"Would you consider some other chairmanship?" he said.

"In your administration? Isaac, I wouldn't fit. I'm a purist. I can't make compromises. I'm better off with the Christys."

"But you can't contemplate Ty Cobb and Shoeless Joe Jackson for the rest of your life . . . come in as one of my deputies."

Schyler clutched his forehead. "Please . . . no more chairmanships, no more commissions. I belong with Shoeless Joe."

6

Isaac was out in Indian country again, off the charts.
Sweets had a special task force out looking for the mayor-
elect. But Isaac wouldn't seem to surface. He loved to live in
some no-man's-land of his own making. He was like a medieval character inventing every kind of quest. Sweets had all
the armories and shelters combed and checked. He stationed
a man outside Isaac's apartment, Isaac's cafeteria on Delancey Street, Isaac's other haunts. He went up to the self-en-
closed castle land called Tudor City and visited Isaac's
daughter, Marilyn the Wild, and Isaac's son-in-law and offi-
cial police escort, Joe Barbarossa. Tudor City reminded
Sweets a little of the Hollows. It wasn't a community of black
millionaires, and it hadn't been a camping ground for the
Continental Army. But it had its own restaurant and market
and bicycle shop, and anyone with enough money could camp
in Tudor City for the rest of his life and never climb off that
hill of apartment houses . . .

Marilyn offered him a cup of dark coffee and some peach
cobbler she'd learned how to make during one of her many
marriages. Barbarossa was her tenth husband. She'd been in
love with Isaac's original angel, Manfred Coen, aka Blue
Eyes. She wanted to run off with Coen. Isaac wouldn't allow
it. He'd hurled Coen into his war with the Guzmanns, a gang

of Peruvian pimps, and Coen got killed. Marilyn never forgave him . . . until she met Joe, another blue-eyed orphan, crazy in the head. Barbarossa played pingpong with a white glove on his hand. The hand had been burnt while Barbarossa was in Saigon.

"Isaac's MIA again," Sweets said.

Marilyn wrinkled her nose. "I don't get it."

"He's missing in action."

"What action? My father's not in the middle of a war."

"But he's the mayor-elect. He can't keep disappearing inside the elephant's ass."

"He wouldn't be Isaac if he didn't disappear."

"But it's less than four weeks to his coronation."

"And two weeks to Christmas," Marilyn said. "So what?"

"I'm responsible for him, Mrs. Barbarossa."

"You drank my coffee. You can call me Marilyn."

"Joey," Sweets said. "You're his escort. You weren't supposed to let him out of your sight."

"He's no minor," Barbarossa said.

"Yeah, he's the mayor-king and the Pink Commish."

"That's the problem," Marilyn said. "My father has too many titles. A king's business is hard enough to define. But he's fallen into the crack between City Hall and Police Plaza. He isn't mayor yet, and he still dreams like a police commissioner. It's a bitter month for dad."

"I have to protect your father, Ms. Marilyn. That's my job."

"But he has the right of any civilian to remain anonymous."

Sweets winked at Joe. "I'd like to bring her into the legal department at One PP."

"Three of my husbands were lawyers," Marilyn said.

"I give up," Sweets said. "Joey, will you help me find the king?"

Sweets had his third coffee and left. Barbarossa put on a lumber jacket.

"Joe," Marilyn said. "Isaac needs this time. He's like a wounded bear."

"Ah, I won't push him," Barbarossa said. "I'll check his hideouts and see . . ."

"Darling," she told him, "please don't turn up dead."

"I'm not Blue Eyes."

"I didn't mean Blue Eyes . . . I meant this mad business about the Knickerbocker Boys and those poor homeless men."

"I'm not homeless, but I'll have to take a risk. Crazies are crazies."

He kissed Marilyn, and the two of them swayed in their living room, which opened upon the East River and Roosevelt Island and the U.N. And Marilyn had to admit that this tenth husband of hers did remind her of Blue Eyes. He was quiet and dangerous and gentle, but never dangerous with her. He was like all pingpong players, demented and in love with a little white ball.

Barbarossa stood under the Williamsburg Bridge. It was the king's favorite haunt, a tiny patch of Sheriff Street where he'd been glocked a year ago by a crazy police captain. Isaac had lain in a coma more than a month, dreaming of some lost baseball team, the New York Giants of 1944, and its star outfielder, Harry "Bomber" Lieberman, who disappeared into the Mexican leagues in 1946. The king came out of his coma and couldn't seem to recover from Harry's fall. But it was the bridge, the bridge, that concerned Joe. He'd hoped that Isaac would be loitering about in his bum's clothes. The king had played here as a boy, had bartered ration stamps so he could buy gifts for his sweetheart, Anastasia, now Margaret Tolstoy. It was Isaac's magic place. But there was no Isaac under the bridge, just a raw December wind and a pair of homeless men who hadn't even heard of the king.

Barbarossa trudged to Isaac's favorite Newyorican restaurant. The bum wasn't at his table, gobbling white rice and black beans. Joe went up and down Manhattan in his blue Plymouth. He crossed into Brooklyn, tried coffeehouses on Arthur Avenue in the Bronx. The big bear had to drink his cappuccinos. But Joe couldn't uncover a sign of Isaac. He gave up. And to relax his nerves, he drove down to Columbus Avenue and stopped at Schiller's, the last pingpong club in Manhattan. Joe had lived at the club until he got married. It had been his headquarters. He'd inherited Coen's table. A Cuban-Chinese bandit had killed Coen here, in the middle of a pingpong match. Joe had fallen in love with Marilyn at the same table. She'd come on a pilgrimage to where Coen had been shot . . . and met Barbarossa.

Joe hadn't seen Schiller in months. He couldn't even remember where his pingpong paddle was, he'd been so occupied with Marilyn and with Isaac's election campaign. He felt like a fucking stranger. The club was booming. All five tables were occupied, even Coen's table. The kibbitzers recognized him right away. "Joey, Joe . . ."

Schiller wasn't with them. He was at the fifth table, an old man with a rope around his middle, the Columbus Avenue philosopher. There was a scraggly man in gym shorts at the far end of Coen's table, playing with a Butterfly bat. The guy had irregular strokes. He hopped around like a bear. It was the king, Isaac Sidel. And Barbarossa was baffled.

Schiller despised Isaac, blamed him for Coen's death.

"Schiller," Joe said, "I can see you have a new friend."

The old man shrugged his shoulders. "What can I do? I have to take in the homeless."

"He's the fucking mayor-elect."

"That's what I mean. A mayor who has to move into a mansion is a mayor without a home."

"That's wonderful," Joe said, "but what about the memory of Blue Eyes?"

The old man started to sniffle. "There's a time to mourn and a time to forget. Ask the kibbitzers. Isaac came here, got down on his knees, and begged my forgiveness. So I forgive."

"Dad," Barbarossa shouted to Isaac, "is that true?"

"Scram," Isaac said. "I'm practicing my strokes."

"And I am going crazy," Barbarossa said.

"Joey, you shouldn't have abandoned us," Schiller said.

"I didn't abandon . . . I got married. I'm a cop. I had to guard my fucking father-in-law . . . dad, will you introduce me to your pingpong partner?"

"That's King Carol," Isaac said. "The champion of Roumania. Carol's my coach."

King Carol was a thug in his fifties who had formidable strokes. He could have been a champion. How could Joe really tell? Carol had a mustache with scars down the middle, white spots where no hairs would grow. It lent him the look of an athletic Satan; the champ of Roumania had knotty, muscular legs. He shook Barbarossa's hand. He also was playing with a Butterfly. Joe preferred the Stiga, which had a heavier handle. But he'd been the unofficial champion of Saigon, nothing more. He couldn't have matched the Roumanian's strokes.

"King Carol," Joe said, but he couldn't even finish his sentence. Sweets and Wig arrived, right upon Barbarossa's back.

"Hello, Mr. Mayor," Sweets said. "That's pretty smart. Hiding behind a pingpong ball."

Isaac wouldn't answer him. He kept hitting the ball with King Carol.

"You've been following me," Barbarossa said to Sweets. "And you brought your triggerman."

"I'm no trigger, Joey," Wig said. "I'm just one more colored scout in the white man's war."

"Cut it," Sweets said. And he reached out with his huge paw and grabbed the ball out of the air. "All right, Mr. Mayor. You can have your command post. This pingpong club. And two men. Wig and Barbarossa."

Isaac groaned. "They'll kill each other. I'll never catch the Knickerbocker Boys."

"That's all you're getting, Mr. Mayor. Good-bye."

And Sweets abandoned Isaac to the pingpong club and his little gang of cops.

7

Isaac couldn't understand this new language of rubber and sponge. The players around him kept ripping off the rubber skin of their bats and gluing on other skins. Nothing seemed stable in the world of pingpong. He had his coach, King Carol, and his Butterfly. Now he wore short pants all the time, like a little kid. He hadn't meant to make this voyage to Schiller's club. It was utterly unconscious. He'd arrived in his bum's clothes, Schiller glaring at him. Isaac saw Coen's table and started to cry. He missed that blue-eyed angel. He'd messed up Coen's marriage, and he'd have to bear the truth of his own machinations. Manfred's wife divorced him, and the kid floated into his own alpha state with a pingpong ball. Marilyn fell in love with him. Isaac was jealous. He himself had gone into deep cover, lived in a candy store with the Guzmanns as a disgraced cop. Manfred Coen got caught in the middle and died at the pingpong club.

"Schiller," he'd said, "it's my fault . . . shouldn't have left Blue Eyes out there all alone . . . ah, he was a good kid. I have conversations with him in my head . . . forgive me, please."

He was shivering. The old man put a blanket around him, adopted this bum who was also the mayor-elect. And Isaac had his sanctuary, Coen's table and Coen's closet. The kibbitzers couldn't make up their minds about Isaac, whom they

46

considered both a killer and a king. It was Schiller who laid down the law. Isaac had become the club's personal pilgrim. And anyone who showed him disrespect would be cast out of the club.

The weight of his own solitude fell off Isaac. He had a mentor, Emmanuel Schiller, and a coach, Carol, who wasn't a real king but had a similar name to Isaac's former adjutant, Caroll Brent. Caroll was Papa Cassidy's son-in-law. He'd quit the Department and had become a private detective in New Hampshire. But he wasn't a pingpong player like King Carol. Isaac knew that Carol was a lout, but he developed a camaraderie with the Roumanian. They talked pingpong. He listened to his coach.

"You have to love the ball," Carol said.

"But what if I can't?"

"Then you won't find any peace at the table."

"You'll be caught in a dark closet," said Schiller, the club's Rousseau. And Isaac learned to love the ball. Pingpong was a meditative game in motion. He was like a monk who had to find his own particular light. But he had too many ghosts behind the bite of his Butterfly. He'd never reach satori. But he tried.

"Schiller," he said, "I'm going to abdicate."

"Keep quiet."

"I'll devote my life to pingpong."

"We don't accept shirkers at this club. If you won't walk to your coronation, then we'll carry you."

"Can we move the club into Gracie Mansion?"

"Not a chance."

"They'll isolate me, those budget directors and their builder friends. Will you become my first deputy mayor?"

"Shut up, Sidel. I never finished high school . . . you'll convene at the club once or twice a week. You'll play and we'll have a dialogue. But don't shove me into your administration."

Isaac didn't have Margaret Tolstoy, but he was as happy as a mayor-king could get under the circumstances. He was still haunted by his alias, Geronimo Jones. A fourth Geronimo was found dead with a note stuffed into his mouth.

Must we pay taxes for all this vermin?
—The Knickerbocker Boys

There was the same poetic list of madmen:

Monte Ward
Will White
Jay Penny
Long John Silver
Sam Wise
Jesse Nichols
Morris deMorris
Alexander Hamilton
Herman Long
Tobias Little

Isaac could have sworn that he knew Jay Penny and Tobias Little somewhere in his life. He sent out his own unlikely team, Barbarossa and Wig, to find some fucking handle. There was a Tobias Little in the Manhattan phone book. But he was eighty-seven years old and had lost the power of speech. There were two Will Whites, but neither of them seemed close to any lunatic fringe.

Isaac concentrated on his game. If he loved the ball enough, it might bring him some answers. Monte Ward, Sam Wise . . .

A woman with a blond mop walked into the club. Margaret Tolstoy. And a companion she didn't have to introduce. It was Quentin Kahn, publisher of Pingpong Power, the bible of all the kibbitzers at the club. Quentin traveled throughout the world, reporting on every major tournament. It was Quent who got Carol out of Roumania and installed him at Schiller's, it was Quent who kept the real-estate barons off Schiller's back. The barons wanted to buy out Schiller's lease, destroy the building, and put up one more glass and stone apartment house on Columbus Avenue. Quent ran a massage parlor, but the kibbitzers weren't moralists about other people's money.

Isaac was wickedly jealous. He knew Margaret was sleeping with Quentin Kahn. Quent must have been the trafficker she'd talked about, the mutt who was grabbing blue-eyed children out of Roumania. Isaac had to take another look at King Carol. His coach was one of Quentin's pirates. And Isaac had to use all his power to separate this pirate from the art of pingpong and continue to love the ball.

"Isaac," Margaret said, "this is Quentin Kahn, one of your admirers."

"Mr. Mayor," Quentin said, "it's a treat to know that you're a fan of table tennis."

"I'm not a fan," Isaac said, attempting to hide his truculence. "I'm a beginner . . . King Carol is my coach."

"His name is Michael Cuza. He was the number five player in the world. I'm the one who began calling him Carol. Carol was the first king of Roumania, and his grandnephew, Carol the Second, was also a king."

"I know all about Roumania, Mr. Kahn. And Carol's a terrific coach."

"Would you write an article for us, giving your impressions of table tennis? I run a little magazine. Schiller must have told you about it."

"Pingpong Power," Isaac said.

"That's it. Nothing formal, Mr. Mayor. Just your impressions. Our readers would love it. The magazine is published all over the world."

I'm sure it is, you fucking child buyer, Isaac muttered to himself. He was growing paranoid in Margaret's presence. He wondered if Schiller had something to do with the scam. No, he decided. Not Schiller. Not his gallery of kibbitzers. Just Quentin Kahn and King Carol. Margaret smiled at Carol, and that other king didn't like it.

"I'd love to take you to lunch, Mr. Mayor."

"That could be considered a form of bribery," Isaac said, with a barbaric smile.

"You haven't been installed yet. You're not a sitting mayor."

"But I will be."

"Then we'll have to have our lunch as soon as we can."

"I'll consult my calendar and get back to you, Mr. Kahn."

"Please. I'm a friend. I contributed to your campaign. Didn't Papa Cassidy tell you that?"

"I never discuss finances with the treasurer of my campaign."

"That's a novel idea. Mistreating your own contributors."

"I mistreat no one," Isaac said. "I'll have lunch with you. Next week."

Quentin Kahn shook Isaac's hand and left with Margaret, who smiled at Carol for a second time but wouldn't even wink at Isaac. He wasn't heartbroken. He was morose. But he had a sudden flash of pingpong satori. Quentin's magazine was the perfect vehicle for selling blue-eyed kids. A want ad, a personal column with a very discreet message.

He had murder in his blood. He'd come to pingpong with his own odd innocence, the vagabond king. And he'd uncovered one more nest of rattlesnakes. It wasn't Schiller's nest. Isaac had grown to love the old man in less than a week. Schiller wouldn't buy or sell children. But the Roumanian would. Isaac had to smile at his coach, treat him like some Zen master. But he'd destroy Quentin Kahn and make Carol choke on a pingpong ball.

Ah, he forgot. He had to love the ball. He couldn't use it as a weapon.

8

The king showered at Schiller's, shampooed his hair. He had to look presentable. He changed his clothes, sang a little song to himself. *Will White, where are you?* But the Knickerbocker Boys would have to wait. Isaac walked down to the Ali Baba, paid his admission fee. He was in an enormous cave lit with blue lamps. He passed the different booths. None of the girls appealed to him, black, white, or brown. They had a hard, lascivious look, like demons in a blue haze. But he did see one girl whose eyes didn't swallow up Isaac with some pretended lust. She was black, around thirty. She yawned and Isaac entered her booth.

"Honey," she said, "I'll show you mine if you show me yours."

"What's your name?" he asked.

"Are you a cop?"

"Yes . . . no. I'm not a cop. I'm about to start a new job. What's your name?"

"Yolanda," she said.

Isaac insisted. "Your real name."

"Josepha Church."

"Please," Isaac muttered. She must have felt the persuasion of a king in Isaac's eyes. She didn't yawn now.

"I'm Rita Mae. And who are you, hon?"

"Geronimo Jones."

"Mistuh," she said, "that's not a healthy name to have. You are a cop."

"No. I'm also Isaac Sidel."

"The white boy who's gonna be mayor?"

He wagged his head.

"Shame on you. Trying to trick a girl. Why the hell are you in a snatch house? Doin' some research, Mr. Mayor?"

"I saw your face, and . . ."

"My face, huh? And my ass and my tits. Show me yours, Mr. Mayor."

Isaac was caught in his own fucking trap. He started to stutter.

"Show me yours," she said.

He unbuttoned his fly, held his own prick in his hand. He was amazed at its magnificence. Rita was the only other woman who'd given him a hard-on since Margaret Tolstoy reentered his life. Isaac already felt unfaithful. It was madness. Margaret seduced gangsters for the FBI, and Isaac was inside the Ali Baba with a black prostitute.

"Hon, do you want a date?"

"I'd like to talk to you, Rita."

"Still doin' research, huh? There's a little chapel upstairs. We could pray together, hon . . , but I can't talk about the price. Meet you in ten minutes."

A dark curtain dropped over her window and Rita Mae disappeared. Isaac went back into the long corridor of blue light. He continued to carry that elephant stick inside his pants. He whistled to himself, *Will White, Will White*. He seemed to float. He wasn't floating. Several pairs of arms were carrying him along. He was whisked away from the blue light, deposited into some secret closet inside another closet. This closet was equipped with radios and recording machines. Isaac could smell the FBI. Fucking Frederic LeComte had established his own little station inside the Ali Baba. He didn't have his usual Mormon accomplices. Frederic's agents were all black. They had contempt for Isaac Sidel, the vagabond king.

"Where's LeComte?" Isaac asked.

"Shut your mouth."

LeComte arrived like some sword-swallower through a trick door. He wagged his finger at Isaac. He wasn't dressed in his ordinary blue on blue. The Ali Baba was a different country. He looked like a hayseed, an out-of-town hick in red socks and a mail-order suit. It was a clever disguise, Isaac had to admit. The cultural commissar of Justice was playing himself, without the color blue.

"This place is off limits. Isaac, do you read me?"

"I'm the mayor-elect. I walk wherever I want."

The black agents laughed at Isaac. They had brilliant white teeth.

"You're nothing . . . shit on a stick," the agents said.

"You'll blow our cover," LeComte said. "You're the most recognizable man in New York. That's a fact. Not even Paul Newman gets as much eyeball as Isaac Sidel."

"Yeah, I'm a superstar," said the king.

"It's honeymoon time. Enjoy it."

"Fuck you, Frederic."

The black agents formed a close circle around Sidel. But LeComte wouldn't let them have their circle. He shooed them away from the king.

"Where's Margaret?" Isaac had to ask.

"You know where she is. With Quentin Kahn. You're not going to spoil my case against Quent. That mother is going down. And don't you meddle."

"I wouldn't dream of it, LeComte. But grab him before January. Because my first act as mayor will be to shut the Ali Baba."

LeComte started to groan. "Get out of here. Go on. Chase the Knickerbocker Boys. That's your meat."

"I guess the FBI doesn't give a fuck about homeless men."

"We don't have jurisdiction over the shelters. That's a local affair."

"Local affair," Isaac muttered. "And Quentin Kahn is more important, huh?"

"He's marketing children, Isaac. He's stealing them out of Eastern Europe and making a fortune. Can you imagine? Mothers and fathers selling their own kids?"

"You'll sell anything if you're hungry enough."

"Or greedy enough. It's like running a chicken farm. You take a blue-eyed kid, fatten him up, sell him to the highest bidder."

"It's just another kind of madness."

"Madness? It's a multimillion-dollar industry. And Quentin Kahn is behind it all . . . you'll blow it for us if you come here again."

"Quentin contributed to my campaign. I'm having lunch with him next week."

"You'll never make it to that lunch. I'll tie you to your pingpong table."

"Grand," Isaac said. "I'll have long discussions with King Carol about the children's market in Roumania. Good-bye, LeComte."

The black agents walked him out of LeComte's closet. He'd lost his erection while he was with the FBIs. He thought of Rita Mae behind her window. One more damsel in distress. He loved Margaret, but he was Rita's knight. He left the blue haze of the Ali Baba and blinked his way back into the sunlight.

9

Reporters began showing up at Schiller's club. LeComte must have given them the king's new address. Isaac had to hold a press conference near the kibbitzers' gallery.

"Mr. Mayor, can you tell us something about your administration?"

The king had to lie a little. "It's firming up."

"Will Martin Malik be your main deputy?"

"I'm considering Malik, but that hasn't been decided yet."

"But you haven't named one commissioner."

"I'll have my team in place by Christmas."

"What about the budget, Mr. Mayor? Will fiscal 'eighty-six be a bounty year? Or will we have less in the pot than 'eighty-five."

"I won't anticipate revenues," the king said, sounding like a mayor. "That's premature."

"Can you tell us anything about the Knickerbocker Boys? Are they white supremacists, part of the Ku Klux Klan?"

"Maybe. I'll destroy them, whoever they are."

"Has this club become your control room until Ms. Rebecca vacates the mansion?"

"I don't have a control room. You don't do politics at a pingpong club. You play pingpong. And Ms. Rebecca isn't leaving the mansion. She'll stay on as my guest."

55

"How are we to interpret that?"

"There's nothing to interpret. I'm allowed to have guests."

"Will Ms. Rebecca be part of your administration?"

"Officially? No. But she will advise me."

"Aren't you getting a little too close to one of New York's least popular mayors?"

"She's been a good soldier. I value Rebecca Karp."

"But soldiers belong on a battlefield, Mr. Mayor."

"This is a battlefield, believe it or not."

Isaac closed the press conference, but other reporters camped out in the kibbitzers' gallery, watched his every move. Isaac couldn't concentrate on his game. And suddenly the biggest real-estate barons in New York turned into ping-pong players. Jason Figgs and Judah Bellow showed up in short pants, clutching Butterflys. Schiller wouldn't lock them out. He was a philosophe. He couldn't discriminate against any man who happened to be a pharaoh.

Isaac had to warm up with Jason and Judah. He was furious.

"You got rid of Schyler Knott, didn't you?"

"He resigned," said Judah Bellow.

"With a little push from his real-estate friends."

Isaac was only a beginner. He couldn't love the ball and Jason Figgs or Judah Bellow. He withdrew into Coen's closet. He tried to meditate, but his mind was like a river of dark sludge.

He ran downtown to his apartment, changed his clothes. The king did have one appointment. The Modern Language Association had come to town, and Isaac was scheduled to speak to a gang of college professors about the ritual of baseball, its own private language and literary life. But the profs didn't really want a speech. They were baseball fanatics. They wanted to learn about the Bomber, Harry Lieberman, and that vintage year of 1944, when the majors were composed of "garbage teams," rejects, retirees, and bush-league kids.

"Are you asking what baseball was like without Joe DiMaggio? It was glorious," Isaac said. "We all missed

DiMaggio. And his wonderful isolation in center field, his sense of grace. But it was a little crippling to me. I preferred the Bomber. He wasn't DiMaggio, but he was the first Zen player in the history of baseball. Harry's movements were like a koan. He never tried to get beyond his own awkwardness. His awkwardness was Harry. And each home run he hit floated into the stands like a stunned bird."

Isaac traced the arc of that bird in his own head. *Will White, Will White.* And he fell upon the saddest revelation in his life. He knew Will and Sam Wise and Herman Long and Tobias Little. They were all players out of the nineteenth century. That's why the names had been so fucking familiar.

Isaac's little auditorium at the Sheraton Centre was packed. His was the most popular seminar in the whole MLA. He drank coffee with the profs. But he was dying to look at his baseball almanac, confirm his suspicions about Will White.

His hands were shaking when he returned to Rivington Street. He could barely hold the almanac. Tobias Little played for Louisville in 1887. Jay Penny was a third baseman in the Players League, which only lasted one year: he arrived and vanished in 1890. Sam Wise won thirty-seven games for the Toledo Americans in 1884. Jesse Nichols was a journeyman catcher with Brooklyn, Pittsburgh, and Philadelphia in the 1890s. Will White pitched six hundred and eighty innings for the Cincinnati Nationals in 1879. Monte Ward was an in- fielder-outfielder-pitcher for Providence and New York. Her- man Long was a hard-hitting shortstop. Morris deMorris was a player-manager with Buffalo for half a season. And there was also a Long John Silver in the National League. He played for the Chicago Cubs. Even an Alexander Hamilton, who played with Columbus and Cleveland.

The list was complete. Isaac had mapped all the Knicker- bocker Boys. He had bitter feelings in his blood. The Knicker- bocker Boys were an antiquarian's code and a personal kite to the king. Only one man could have sent that kite. A fellow an- tiquarian. It had to be Schyler Knott. Schyler was descended from the early Dutch farmers of New Amsterdam. His forebears had once owned a piece of the Bowery. And Schyler owned buildings all over the place. He was the landlord *and* president of the Christy Mathewson Club. His vision of baseball ended around 1940. Harry Lieberman was a Christy, but he couldn't be included in the Christys' own annals. He'd joined the Giants in 1943. He was a couple of years too late.

Isaac had never heard Schyler talk of hoboes and mongrels and niggers and kikes. And he couldn't conceive of Schyler murdering homeless men. That wasn't the mark of a preservationist, but it was Schyler who'd invented that dream team of nineteenth-century players. Nine men and one manager, Morris deMorris.

The king went to Schyler's house on Horatio Street. But Schyler wasn't there. "He's gone, Mr. Mayor," the doorman said. "Packed his bags . . . told me to collect his mail."

"When will he be back?"

"Mr. Knott didn't say."

The king walked uptown to the Christy Mathewson Club. But its doors were closed. The club was being renovated and wouldn't open again until Isaac was crowned as mayor-king. Isaac had to ride the "A" train to Washington Heights, where the Bomber lived alone in a very long retirement. Harry had had a mujer in Mexico and a baby girl. The girl died of the measles and Harry came back to New York without the mujer, did odd jobs, and banished himself to a couple of rooms on Fort Washington Avenue. He was the Christys' watchman and bailiff, and he helped coach the Delancey Giants, Isaac's baseball team in the Police Athletic League. But Isaac wasn't close to the Bomber, and Schyler was. The patrician had befriended Harry, had made a home for him at the club. It wasn't only the bond of baseball. Perhaps Schyler could appreciate a man who hid from his own past.

The king didn't have such a talent. Harry was his hero. And he couldn't stop dreaming of Harry's home runs.

The Bomber lived in a walk-up near a tiny park with a stone pingpong table. Isaac listened to the clack of the ball and then climbed upstairs to Harry and knocked on the door.

Harry let him in, and Isaac had to keep from crying. The Bomber was a gray-necked boy. He'd grown old around Isaac, but he had that agile innocence of someone who belonged in center field.

"Bomber," Isaac said, and he did start to cry, because Isaac's own innocence was linked to Harry's. They were like a pair of icemen frozen to 1944, when Harry was the reluctant star of the National League and Isaac had Anastasia and the New York Giants.

"You can't come in here," Harry said, "if you won't wipe your eyes."

The king didn't have a handkerchief, and Harry had to lend him one. His apartment was as gray as the hair on his neck. There wasn't a single memento on the walls, not one picture of Harry as a Giant.

"Harry," Isaac said, "do you remember that game with the Cubbies when you hit three home runs?"

"I never hit three home runs in a game."

"Harry, I was there. It was July 'forty-four."

"I was in a slump most of July," Harry said. "Now shut up about baseball."

"I didn't mean anything, Harry. I was reminiscing a little."

"Reminisce on your own time, Mr. Mayor. What do you want?"

Isaac sat in Harry's living room on a chair that had lost its springs, so that he felt he was falling, falling into some eternity of a lost baseball league.

"Schyler's missing."

"Who says?"

"Harry, he gives up his chairmanship on the Landmarks Commission, shuts down the Christys, and disappears from Horatio Street."

"That's not a crime," the Bomber said.

"It is if he created the Knickerbocker Boys . . . Harry, do I have to spell it out? What is Schyler doing with a band of maniacs who kill homeless men?"

There were flecks of blood in the Bomber's eyes. "This

town is falling to shit. I caught a bum in our cellar at the Christys. He turned our sink into a toilet."

"Harry, answer me."

"You could be wrong about Schyler."

"No. Ten Knickerbocker Boys. And they're all antiquarians. Will White. Long John Silver. Monte Ward. Morris de-Morris . . . that's Schyler's own fucking team."

"Schyler doesn't have a team, Mr. Mayor. What if the Knickerbocker Boys belong to me?"

"I don't believe it. You're the Bomber."

"Sure. Harry the hero. I hate Jews and colored people."

"Stop it," the king said.

"Arrest me, Mr. Mayor."

"I can't. I'm a civilian, like Schyler and you."

"I hit on the homeless, I bombed them into hell."

"Ah, Harry you should have stayed in center field."

"Arrest me," the Bomber said.

Isaac started to leave. Harry twisted him around with his gigantic paws.

"Arrest me . . . I'm confessing to a crime."

"You're shielding Schyler."

"You think I couldn't have dreamt up Monte Ward and all them guys?"

Isaac wouldn't answer. He thrust Harry's hands away from him and walked out of that grim apartment that was like a quiet grave.

10

He didn't tell Sweets about his talk with the Bomber. Sweets wasn't a cabalist or an antiquarian and wouldn't have understood the enigma of nineteenth-century names. He could have had Wig and Barbarossa watch Harry around the clock, but he would have had to spend all his resources on the Bomber. He'd get to Schyler on his own. He still had informants and spies at One PP. He was the Pink Commish. He called a lady captain in the chief inspector's office.

"Marge," he said, "two things. There's a black pros at the Ali Baba. Calls herself Rita Mae. I'd like her pedigree. And I need a few personals on Schyler Knott, K-N-O-double T. He kicked himself off the Landmarks Preservation Commission. He never married, but I remember something about a broken engagement. Who was the girl? . . . thanks, Marge."

The king had picked Marge right out of the Academy, and Marge had remained his cadet, no matter who was PC. She was like his own intelligence unit within the walls of Police Plaza. Marge phoned him at the pingpong club. Isaac took the call in Coen's closet.

"Rita Mae Robinson," Marge said. "Lives on Lenox. Has a fourteen-year-old boy, Harwood. He's a crackhead."

"Does she have a steady beau?"

"It's hard to research her love life, boss. She's a pros."

61

"What about Schyler Knott?"

"All I could come up with was Schyler's shrink. A certain Dr. Lillian Campbell, a psychiatrist with degrees from Columbia and Cornell. And guess what? Schyler's been sleeping with the good doctor."

"He's having an affair with his own fucking psychiatrist? How did you discover that, Marge?"

"Shame on you, boss. You told us to keep a file on all of Rebecca's people."

"Come on, Marge. I have to protect the commissioners from themselves. Some monkey could blackmail them. And the whole City would be compromised. How old is Dr. Campbell?"

"Thirty-eight or -nine."

"Is she a looker?" Isaac asked. Marge was silent, and Isaac had to confess his sins. "Okay, I'm a chauvinist pig, but . . ."

"Boss, she's a knockout, a redhead with lots of freckles . . . should I undress her for you, Isaac?"

"Stop that," he said. "I'm your commander in chief."

"You are not. You're a king without a crown, and a very bad boy. I have to run. Sweets will kill me if he finds out I've been talking to you."

Isaac made an appointment with Dr. Lillian Campbell, insisted on seeing her that same afternoon. He had to use all his weight as the mayor-elect. Dr. Campbell fit him in at five o'clock. The king had to smile. Dr. Campbell's office was on Horatio Street. She had a penthouse in Schyler's building. It sounded like incest to the king.

His knees dipped when he saw the redhead. Marge hadn't been wrong. Dr. Campbell was a knockout. She had intelligent cheekbones, an animal's brooding eyes. She reminded him of Maureen O'Hara, an actress out of his childhood. It was like looking at a beauty with her whole face on fire. The king had to be careful. He couldn't win any contest with Dr. Campbell. But he'd have to use his little trump card. Her love affair with her own patient.

He sat on the patient's couch in Dr. Campbell's office,

which looked out onto the terrace and a view of Wall Street and the Woolworth Building in the early winter dusk. Darkness seemed to fall like a folding bomb. Ali Baba, Isaac thought. The sky could have been the roof of some magical cave. The king would never recover from New York.

"You're here about Schyler, aren't you?"

"He's vanished, Dr. Campbell. And I believe Schyler's involved with the Knickerbocker Boys. He's their ringleader . . . help me, Dr. Campbell. Bring him in."

"And conspire against my own patient, Mr. Sidel? Do you really think he would murder poor harmless men?"

"I'm not sure. But the Knickerbocker Boys are his invention. They're all professional baseball players from the nineteenth century. No one but Schyler could have composed that list."

"That makes him a minor-league poet, not a murderer."

"But if he's cohabiting with murderers, then he's their accomplice . . . or their stooge. Please. I don't want to argue. Help me."

"I can't give Schyler's secrets away."

"I'm not asking for secrets. But you could tell me about his mental state. Was he depressed, Doctor? I mean, he quits the Landmarks Commission. He closes the Christys."

"There's nothing mysterious about that. The club had to be overhauled. And he couldn't sit on the same commission with a gang of realtors. He was bound to clash. You know Schyler's sentiments. He'd landmark the living and the dead if he could."

"Doctor, you're fencing with me. Schyler's in trouble. I don't want to pounce on him, but the cops will."

"Unless I talk to you. But I'm not talking."

Isaac was already defeated by her red hair. He grew mean. "Doctor-patient privilege, huh? Like some voodoo priest. But do you sleep with your other patients, Dr. Campbell?"

She'd been leaning on her desk, poised like a magnificent statue, when she reached over to slap the king with all her might. His jaw rippled, and his body fell deep into the couch.

"We were engaged once, Mr. Sidel, long before he was my patient. I haven't slept with Schyler Knott in seven years. Does that satisfy you?"

"Sorry," the king said, holding his face.

"You're pitiful, like any bloodhound. But I did vote for you, Mr. Sidel. Schyler's like a damaged Christ. Manhattan is his own particular cross. For him New York has no future, only a past. And Schyler lives in that past. But he wouldn't kill for it. You'll have to take my word."

"But people are dying around that stupid, racist banner of the Knickerbocker Boys. I don't want to hurt him, Dr. Campbell. Ask him to meet with me."

Isaac scribbled his phone number at the pingpong club. Suddenly he began to shake. He'd have to move into the mansion in a couple of weeks. He couldn't survive without the bargain counters of Orchard Street and the whiteness of a pingpong ball.

He took the Seventh Avenue Express up to Harlem. He had to kiss two babies and shake hands with a little band of blind students. The king was recognized wherever he went. Crowds formed in his wake. He couldn't promise anything. No one could predict whether there would be a windfall next week. The king might inherit a pauper's mantle the moment he was sworn in as the City's one hundred and seventh mayor.

He passed a playground on Lenox Avenue, watched a young black man in enormous white sneakers shepherding four blue-eyed brats. The brats were holding hands and laughing in a language the king couldn't understand. They had very blond hair and could have been "perfect" children out of some crazy genetics program. They looked about six or seven in their winter coats. They wore mittens. Isaac had a rage in him. The young man had to be Harwood, and his own mom, Rita Mae Robinson, was the den mother for Quentin Kahn's Roumanian connection.

The king could have been wrong. Suppose this wasn't Harwood. And the brats were simple refugees. Isaac went up to the shepherd boy, who barely noticed him.

"Harwood," he said.

The boy's eyes were half closed. "Who wants him?"

"Ali Baba . . . I'm a friend of Quentin Kahn's," said the king.

"Quent owes me and my mama two hundred dollar. You got the money, mistah?"

"Tomorrow," Isaac said. "Tomorrow."

He didn't try to steal the brats from Harwood. He didn't run to Rita Mae. He didn't go down to the Ali Baba and crack Quentin's skull. He went to Jerry DiAngelis, lord of the Rubino crime family. The Rubinos ran New York. And Jerry was as much a king as Isaac or Cardinal Jim. Isaac had once been part of the Family, had been Jerry's war counselor, while he was the Commish. Isaac had sat in jail for being a little too close to the Rubinos. But he'd won his case in court. And now Jerry and his father-in-law, Izzy Wasser, the melamed, were almost Isaac's enemies.

The king stood outside the Baron di Napoli Club on Mulberry Street. He didn't knock on the window. He waited. It was a long silent siege. Jerry DiAngelis came out in his fabulous white coat. Isaac looked like a pauper compared to that coat.

"Don Isacco, what the fuck do you want?"

"We have to talk."

"Then talk," Jerry told him.

"Not in front of LeComte and his sound trucks."

"Leave me alone. I'm retired."

"You're five years younger than I am. And you're worth about a hundred mil. You can't afford to retire. Your own captains would chop you to pieces."

"Don't discuss my Family," the don said. They went to Ferrara's, an enormous pastry shop on Grand Street that had become a tourist trap. Not even LeComte's wizards could have wiretapped every table. But it was difficult to talk. people kept coming up to Isaac and Jerry and kneeling in front of the table. Jerry had to shout at them. "Jesus, can't we have a coffee break?"

The king had a cappuccino. And Jerry had a caffè tinto, black coffee with a single drop of milk.

"Jerry, I can hurt you when I'm mayor, hurt you real bad."

"Fuckface, you come to me with threats? I'll strangle you in Ferrara's, in front of two hundred people."

"You own the Ali Baba," Isaac said.

"I own shit. I get a percentage of the gross. That's my deal with Quentin Kahn. I don't ask questions. He gives, and I take. And he's smart enough not to make me suspicious."

"Did you know that he's a scumbag, that he traffics in stolen children?"

"Isaac, I told you, I get a piece of the cake, a big piece. I don't disturb any of his rackets."

"You'd better think again, because LeComte has his own little shop right inside the Ali Baba. He'll sink Quentin Kahn, and you'll drown with him."

"Maybe, maybe not. Quentin has a rabbi, Don Isacco, and that rabbi isn't me."

"Rabbis won't be able to help him once LeComte starts to pounce. The man is warehousing blue-eyed children. I saw them, Jerry, with my own eyes. Lean on him a little."

"You lean," Jerry said. "Quentin's rabbi can take on LeComte."

And he walked out of Ferrara's, leaving Isaac to pay the bill.

11

The king was losing time. Days passed. Another homeless man was killed, with another note in his mouth. "Trash," the note said. "All the men's shelters are filled with homos." There was the same list of Knickerbocker Boys, starting with Monte Ward. And the Crime Scene tecs couldn't gather any clues. "One more Geronimo Jones," they said.

Isaac began to curse his own alias. Who the hell was dogging him? He had to go back into the Ali Baba, but LeComte's black commandos would toss him out on his ass. So the king had to play Sherlock Holmes. He didn't disguise himself as a bum. LeComte would have made him in half a minute.

He stood in front of his mirror and penciled in a mustache. He looked like some Latino prince. He discovered an orange suit in one of the barrels on Orchard Street, and soon he looked like a pimp. He was anxious about what to call himself. People seemed to die around Isaac's aliases. He didn't want to create another corpse.

He arrived at the Ali Baba, dove into the dark without a name. It soothed him to be ripped of all identity. He could float across that blue haze, free as a fucking bird. He didn't have to bear the brunt of his own coronation. He wasn't Sidel.

He got past the first black commando. He was so conspicuous in his orange pants that nobody bothered to notice him.

He was one more masquerader, one more undercover man. He presented himself at Rita Mae's booth like a lovesick caballero. Rita's nipples stood like merciless darts under a web of white silk. But those darts weren't for him. She already had a customer in her booth. This caballero wasn't wearing orange pants. He was dressed in corduroy. It was Judah Bellow. Judah whispered through the glass wall that separated him and Rita. There wasn't any boredom in Rita's eyes. She didn't cup her breasts or try to excite Judah.

Isaac was paralyzed. There was something so intimate about that crazy talk between the glass that he just couldn't spy on Judah. He stepped back into Ali Baba midnight, waited for the whispering to end. The real-estate baron came out of Rita's booth, walked within a hair of Isaac. Judah was crying. He patted his face with a silk handkerchief and disappeared. Like a fucking ghost.

Isaac took Judah's place. He scrunched inside the booth. The boredom had crept back into Rita's eyes. She flicked her tongue at Isaac.

"Honey, I'll show you mine if you show me yours."

"You've already seen mine," Isaac groaned.

Her eyes seemed to startle inside her head. Then she laughed.

"Shame on you, Mr. Mayor, trying to take advantage of a working girl."

"How did I take advantage?"

"Sneaking up on me in a mustache."

"It's nothing," Isaac sad. "The FBIs are all over Ali Baba. I couldn't get past them without a fancy costume."

"You mean Mr. Frederic and his niggers? They been propositioning me."

Isaac groaned again. "It's entrapment, Rita. You shouldn't be talking to them."

"Yeah, baby, I get the message. You my protector now."

"Rita, why the hell was Judah Bellow here?"

Rita Mae pressed up against the glass. "I aint no tattletale."

"You've been warehousing children for Quentin Kahn. I

know that. I saw them with Harwood. Little blue-eyed monsters from Roumania."

"Did Harwood talk to you? That boy has a big mouth."

"Is Judah part of the scam? Is he Quentin's boss?"

"Hush," Rita said. "Meet me in the chapel upstairs. And don't you disappoint me, like you did the last time."

"LeComte kidnapped me, Rita, tossed me right out of the Ali Baba. I couldn't . . ."

"Hush."

The same dark curtain dropped over the glass, and Isaac felt horribly alone without Rita Mae Robinson. He fumbled in the dark, climbed upstairs, and found the chapel, which was really a closet with a single prayer desk and a treasureful of crack vials and yellow condoms on the floor. He waited for Rita, but Rita never showed. Isaac went back down to her booth. A different girl sat behind the window, with watery eyes and a wounded smile. He ran from that look and bumped into a black commando.

"Hey, watch your fuckin' feet."

Isaac fled the Ali Baba in his orange pants. He didn't bother to change clothes. He'd become a subway jockey. He rode up to Lenox, entered the brownstone where Rita Mae lived, a little rotting mansion with a rat's nest of apartments, rapped on Rita's door until he realized that the door wasn't locked. He walked in. The apartment was tranquil enough. Rita sat on the sofa with a plastic bag twisted around her head. There were no signs of struggle. Her fingers didn't claw at any material. Her back was straight. Her eyes stared out at Isaac from under that plastic veil.

He didn't rock in front of Rita like some guy in a prayer shawl. But he blamed himself. He should have grabbed a police car and shot uptown with the siren screaming. Then he might have saved her.

But he was saddled with the ambiguity of a mayor-king. The election had hobbled Isaac, left him to drift in some void. Like everything he did right now, he was a little too late . . .

There was something very, very neat about Rita's veil. She

was a lost bride on a death date. Isaac didn't have to stare at the tiny coloration in the plastic, marks of Rita's breath.

He pulled off the veil. "Rita, do all the girls at the Ali Baba like to play dead . . . or only the ones who are minding Quentin's store?"

Rita's eyes began to roam. She reached around and lunged at Isaac with her pigsticker, a knife that was like a featherless dart. Isaac caught her at the wrist.

"I'm not a homeless man anymore," he said. "I stopped playing Geronimo Jones."

But he shouldn't have been concentrating so hard on Rita. A pair of burly characters wrestled Isaac to the ground. He recognized Brother William, the night manager at the Seventh Avenue Armory, and Harwood, Rita's moon-eyed boy. They held him with his neck fastened to the floor.

"Rita Mae, stick the honkey," William said. "Stick him before he gets us killed . . . he aint no king. He's working with the FBI and *the* Mafia *and* that motherfucking Judah Bellow."

Isaac was scared, but not because of the pigsticker. He'd never been surrounded by such a wild and willful gang.

"I could kill you . . . I really could," Rita said, nicking Isaac's ear with the knife. Even with all the pain, he couldn't stop admiring her hazel eyes.

"I'll show you mine if you show me yours."

"We already done that game, Mr. Mayor. I don't like it when you follow me home. It's dangerous. People are starting to talk."

"Then you shouldn't wear a plastic veil in front of strangers."

"You're not a stranger," Rita told him, and she found some witch hazel and a cotton ball and started to swab Isaac's injured ear and wipe the mustache from his mouth.

PART THREE

PART THREE

12

He wasn't a complete flop. He did learn that the night manager was Rita Mae's big brother. But Brother William couldn't have led this gang. He didn't have the brains or the courage. He was like an extra rib. And Harwood had already graduated to some other world. It was Rita who kept them from falling into chaos and supplied the glue that any gang had to have. She was part of Quentin Kahn's kindergarten class. But she wouldn't talk about Quent or the children or Judah Bellow.

"Rita, it's rough out there ... and how can I help if you leave me in the dark?"

"You can't help us," William said. "You just Dr. Death ... people die wherever you sleep."

"But I'll have to arrest all of you if I catch you warehousing any more of Quentin's kids."

William's whole face started to quiver. "Stick him, Rita, while we still got the chance."

"I can't," Rita said. "He's one of my best clients. I've seen the Commissioner's pickle."

Even Harwood came out of his moon country long enough to laugh.

Isaac returned to Rivington Street, took a bath, changed his clothes, and went to see Judah Bellow. Judah occupied three floors on Madison: Emeric & Company, in honor of his mentor, Emeric Gray. Isaac didn't have to schedule a meeting with this pharaoh. He was summoned into Judah's office in the middle of a conference. The conference broke. All the junior partners scattered to the ends of the hall. And Isaac was left alone with Judah in an office that could have contained King Tut's royal tomb. Judah even had his own tomblike table.

"Isaac, what happened to your ear?"

"Rita bit it," he said. "She's getting kinky."

"Maybe you ought to introduce me to this Rita."

"Come on, Judah. I saw you with her at the Ali Baba. Rita Mae Robinson. She's like a gypsy. Has her own booth."

Judah Bellow didn't bother to blink. He had that raw power of a pharaoh in his own glass box.

"Have you been spying on me, Mr. Mayor?"

"Nah. I've given that habit up. I'm between and betwixt. Neither the mayor nor a cop. It feels like an empty house."

"And so you visit the sex shops on Times Square."

"Judah, you sat at Emeric's feet. You studied with the great man. You ought to be more precise. Sex shop? The Ali Baba is an empire . . . I'm planning to close it down. Soon as I inherit Gracie Mansion."

"Close it down," Judah said.

He was a little younger than Isaac, and he didn't like to show off his wealth. He dressed in the shabby genteel way of his dead master. He wore ancient corduroys and a blue workman's shirt. Emeric Gray stopped building apartment houses after the Depression. He'd fallen out of favor with those modernists who didn't believe in ornament. It had become too costly to construct an Emeric Gray. All the artisans he'd collected around him began to die. Emeric sat in his workshop for twenty-five years like a madman with his models and plans. Judah had come to him as a boy in his teens, kept him company, ate sandwiches, drank champagne in the hook of an afternoon while the master's hearing began to fail. They'd sit in silence until Judah could breathe the master's thoughts. He studied the design of a building, and its soul. One day, while Judah was still at high school, in a tournament with the fencing team, Emeric marched into the street without his hearing aid ... and a trolley ran him down. There was hardly a remembrance of him in the newspapers. One more builder who'd grown out of touch with contemporary design. Then half the city seemed to wake to the constellation of brick palaces Emeric had constructed for the middle class. There were no Emeric Grays on Park Avenue or Madison or Beekman Place. He was never the architect of the rich. His palaces had no river views or indoor swimming pools. They sat on some narrow plot, with their terra-cotta motifs, lyrical and all alone. And Isaac was jealous of Judah, who was Emeric's last confidant.

"Did he wear bow ties?" Isaac had to ask like a beggar.

"Emeric? He did have a fondness for the bow tie. They had to be very soft. His skin was quite sensitive."

"How come he never married?"

"He was always too busy ... and then he wasn't busy enough. He had mistresses, Isaac, up to the very end."

"But no daughters, no sons? An architect ought to have children."

"Ah, that's a potent thought."

"I mean, to continue his line ... as a builder. But you could have been his adopted son."

"Emeric didn't adopt me. I studied with him. That's true. But he wasn't a man who liked to talk. He didn't dwell on the past, Isaac. He didn't feel sorry for himself. He'd outlived his own building materials. What he had loved lost their validity in the marketplace. He'd priced himself out of existence. And he wouldn't adapt."

"But he must have told you *something*. He couldn't have been in mourning year after year."

"Isaac, the man had no hobbies or outside interests. He was in exile, a builder who couldn't build ... he went to his office every day. He did have a few commissions. But nothing came of them. He was too unyielding, too ambitious. He anticipated all our problems with the homeless. He wanted to put up a handsome barrack near the Great Hill in Central Park."

"A visionary," Isaac said. "There's no such thing as a handsome barrack."

"You're wrong," Judah said. "But it wasn't practical. Speculators would have forced the homeless out of Emeric's barrack. He never really understood Manhattan real estate. Quality drives up the price. And Emeric would only consider the very best."

"Like his disciple."

"I'm not his disciple. I ate lunch with Emeric out of a paper bag . . . I was just a kid."

"Tell me, Judah. Is Rita Mae also 'quality'?"

"I could have my lawyer answer that. But it isn't a crime to come and go in the Ali Baba. Frankly, Isaac, Rita Mae Robinson is none of your fucking business."

"Come on. You could have any hooker on the planet. So it isn't about love or a little S-M. I'd say Rita is acting as your broker. You're paying her and Quentin Kahn to get you a blue-eyed Roumanian boy or girl."

"Prove it," said the pharaoh.

"I can't. But if you're caught with a stolen child, I'll name you as an accomplice, Judah, and no lawyer will help."

"Then I'll have to take my chances, won't I?"

"Judah . . ."

"Your Honor, do you realize how difficult it is to adopt a child, *any* child?"

"Particularly a white one, huh, Judah?"

"It's dead out there. The supply has completely diminished. The local lawyers, the judges, the agencies all have their cuts, and so there's a terrific boom in black-market babies."

"But these aren't babies, Judah. The kids I saw were at least seven or eight."

"Yes, that's the market of last resort. You don't have to deal with a pregnant girl who can decide on a set of parents and then change her mind, ask for the baby back after she gives birth. Her lawyer can hold you up for hundreds of thousands of dollars . . . it's much safer with the Roumanian connection.

Most of the children are orphans, Isaac. They'll have a much better home here in America."

"Judah," Isaac said, "it sounds like slavery . . . is Quentin Kahn running a goddamn club for pedophiles? Is it bondage time at the Ali Baba?"

"Isaac, you have my guarantee."

"What's your part in all this? You come out of the Ali Baba with tears in your eyes. Tell me, Judah. *Why?*"

The pharaoh patted his mouth with a red silk handkerchief. "There was one particular child . . . a little girl, Natalia. I'd been corresponding with her, sending her money. I'd grown fond of the child. And don't call me a pedophile. You know what those State orphanages are all about. I could protect her, bribe a few of the doctors and the guards."

"Rita was the conduit, your personal letterbox."

"That's it."

"You handed her the money, and she gave you letters from the little girl. Natalia. Are you sure the letters weren't a fake?"

"I talked to Natalia once . . . on the phone. They have English classes at the orphanage. Her voice was marvelous, magical . . . more than I could ever have imagined."

"More than you could imagine. And Quentin Kahn was going to smuggle her out of the orphanage, send her across the ocean in a secret canoe."

"Nothing like that. I didn't want to adopt. I . . ."

The pharaoh chewed on the red silk. Isaac tore the handkerchief from Judah's mouth. "What happened?"

"I put a hold on the girl. I didn't want anyone else to adopt her . . . Isaac, you have a daughter?"

"What does she have to do with this?"

"My daughter killed herself."

"I'm sorry, Judah. I didn't . . ."

"There was no chronic depression. She was a painter. Rather successful, I think. Had a couple of shows. Sat down in the bathtub one night and slit her wrists."

"Judah, what was *her* name?"

"Why do you ask?"

"It was Natalie, wasn't it?"

"Yes. Her name was Natalie."

"And Quentin Kahn got in touch with you *after* Natalie slit her wrists."

"Yes," the pharaoh said.

"He found your Natalia in the orphanage, like some perfect package."

"Package? What are you driving at?"

"Judah, did Rita Mae tell you that little Natalia was dead?"

"How did . . . ? She caught a chill. Died of pneumonia. Just like that. I might have saved her, Isaac. I should have brought her out of Bucharest. To hell with all the legal stuff."

"Judah, can I have a look at her letters, please?"

"No."

"I won't confiscate them. I promise."

"A policeman isn't supposed to promise."

"Judah, I'm not a policeman anymore. I'm a month from being mayor."

"It won't matter to you. You'll dig up all the dirty garbage, you'll poke around in other people's affairs. That's your nature, Isaac."

"Help me, Judah. I'm getting awful pissed at Quentin Kahn. I don't like the services he provides . . . did you know that Schyler Knott is missing?"

"He resigned from Landmarks. That's all I care about. Good riddance."

"But he's tied up with the Knickerbocker Boys."

"Been murdering homeless men. I'm not surprised."

"But they're not really homeless men. They're fictitious people. Without the least identity. They . . ."

"Isaac, I don't have the time to become a sleuth. And if you mention Natalia's letters, I'll swear they're something a mayor-elect cooked up to keep himself busy."

The pharaoh began summoning all his junior partners, and Isaac became a superfluous man at Emeric & Company. He stared at images of Emeric on the way out: Judah had surrounded himself with portraits of Emeric Gray. The master had had a very weak chin. He was fond of cigars. Emeric Gray looked like an impoverished accountant, and not a character who had marked Manhattan with palaces for the middle class.

13

Isaac returned to Schiller's club. He hit the ball with his coach, who was one of Quentin's traffickers. Isaac was convinced that Michael Cuza, alias King Carol, ran Quentin's pipeline from Bucharest to Manhattan. He could have been a member of the Securitate. King Carol loved to tell stories about Nicu and Zoia, the great dictator's children, who lived like royal brats, their pockets stuffed with cash.

"Did you ever dance with Zoia?" Isaac asked his coach.

"Me dance with a princess? Little father, I was nothing but a pingpong player."

"But you won medals, didn't you, Michael?"

"I was a finalist in six international tournaments. But that was long before the Ceausescus."

"And you met Quentin Kahn at one of those tournaments?"

"Quent? I met him much later. He sponsored me, brought me out of Bucharest."

"And you've been loyal to him ever since."

"Yes, little father. I'm loyal to Quent."

Isaac started to dream. Should he kill his guru before or after the coronation? No. Michael was more valuable alive. A proper pingpong coach was hard to find.

"Take me to Quent."

"He'd love it, little father. He's been dying to have lunch. You know that."

"Then arrange the lunch, Michael. I can't court some guy who owns the Ali Baba. I'm the mayor-elect."

It was Michael who called the Ali Baba, who whispered with Quentin Kahn and drove Isaac out to the River Café, under the Brooklyn Bridge. Quentin Kahn was already in the restaurant, at a table that looked out upon the harbor and the Statue of Liberty. A speedboat shot past the restaurant's glass wall. It was like sitting with a river in your lap. The bottom of the Brooklyn Bridge reminded Isaac of the flattened belly of a monster snail.

King Carol excused himself.

Quentin Kahn ordered a bottle of two-hundred-dollar wine. Isaac growled at the price, but the wine was delicious.

"Pomerol," said Quentin Kahn. "My favorite red." Quent had salmon, and Isaac had a swordfish steak in a bed of spinach.

"Quentin," Isaac said like a debutante. "I thought you're supposed to drink white wine with fish."

"An old wives' tale. You can drink Pomerol with shoe leather if you like. I have a weakness for good red wine."

"How's the child market, Quent?"

Quentin's eyes began to glow from the Pomerol. "Somebody's been slandering me. I do favors now and then for people in high places."

"You fuck," Isaac said, across the bottle of Pomerol. "Judah's daughter kills herself, so you and King Carol invent a phantom girl for him. Little Natalia of Bucharest."

"She's no invention, I promise. And what did we do that was illegal? There was an exchange of letters . . . Judah contributed toward Natalia's upkeep at the orphanage, gave her an allowance. And then she died."

"And then she died," Isaac said.

"It was an accident, Your Honor."

"Save the titles. I might never get to Gracie Mansion. I could also have an accident."

"She caught pneumonia. We couldn't interfere. The doctors . . ."

"Can I see the little girl's death certificate?"

"I could requisition it for you. We'd have to write the orphanage."

"Never mind. You'll shut your factory, Quent. You'll get out of the child-buying business. And you'll release Rita Mae Robinson from her bondage."

The glow in Quentin's eyes was gone. There was a meanness to his mouth. "Rita's not a slave," he said.

"Yeah. She's a whore who happens to babysit for you."

"You're working with LeComte . . . bugging the Ali Baba."

"Me? I got lucky. I caught Harwood chaperoning a small country of blue-eyed kids."

"Harwood's a crackhead. I can't predict his moves."

"But I can predict mine. Come to my inauguration, Quent. The minute I'm sworn in, I'll sign an executive order closing the Ali Baba."

"I have a license . . . and a lawyer. You can't sign me out of existence. You can't rule by decree."

"Don't count on it. I'm a dragon. I eat up lawyers and constitutions . . ."

Isaac heard a buzz behind his neck, as if he were being attacked by a magnificent bee.

"You're so charming, dear."

It was Anastasia in a white jumpsuit and orange wig. She looked like a model from Mars. Isaac was instantly jealous.

"Quentin, did you tell Margaret about our lunch date?"

"I swear, I—"

"He didn't have to tell me, Isaac. I've been following you like a hawk. Quentin, it's time to go."

"We didn't order dessert," Isaac said. "They have sherbet on the menu, with marzipan flowers and chunks of white chocolate. It's arranged like a little garden. This is the River Café."

"I know," Margaret said.

"We haven't even finished our Pomerol. It's two hundred dollars a pop."

"He can take the bottle with him, dear."

"It's not the same thing as having a picnic in a restaurant, with the Statue of Liberty floating in back of your head."

"Then he'll have to suffer," Margaret said.

Quentin Kahn patted his lips with a napkin and disappeared.

"Spider Lady," Isaac hissed. "Do you discard all your lovers like that?"

"I don't have lovers, Isaac. I'm devoted to you."

"But you sleep with Quentin Kahn."

He wanted to grab her wrists, fly out the window with Anastasia, and crash around in the water like a couple of mermaids. He didn't have the heart to be mayor without her.

"Isaac," she told him. "You're stepping on Frederic's toes."

"I'm glad."

"He can toss me out of the country."

"Margaret, you can always marry me."

"I'm not fond of arrangements," she said. She'd married Ferdinand Antonescu when she was twelve, the bride of Little Angel Street, had eaten human flesh, or she would have starved in Odessa.

"Arrangements?"

"Shhh," Margaret said, one of her fingers slicing across his mouth. "We can't afford to close the Ali Baba . . . not right away."

"Ah, that's a new twist. I thought you were tracking Quent because of the Roumanian kids. I thought you were going to pounce."

"We were, but there's a glitch. Quent has a champion now."

"Judah Bellow."

Anastasia laughed under her wig. Isaac felt like a schoolboy. He couldn't forget the orphan who'd first come into his class. Anastasia was a wound he'd have to wear all his life.

"LeComte isn't frightened of pharaohs," she said.

"Who is he frightened of?"

"Isaac Sidel."

"Come on," Isaac said. "He owns the one person on this planet I adore . . . who's Quent's rabbi, who's his hook?"

"I'm not supposed to tell."

"I'll find out, Margaret. I'll tap all of Frederic's lines, I'll bug the Ali Baba. Who's Quentin's hook?"

"Billy the Kid."

She was talking about the governor, who had a whole series of nicknames.

"Billy's a Democrat. Justice ought to love that. Did he invest in the Ali Baba? Or did he give a stolen child to each of his daughters as a Hanukkah present?"

"The governor's Episcopalian. And he doesn't have any daughters."

"What's the difference? Write your own script. Frederic always does."

Isaac growled at the head waiter. "Where's the check?"

"Mr. Kahn took care of it, sir."

"Nobody asked him to," Isaac said, reaching for his wallet. But he couldn't even have paid for the Pomerol. He had fifty dollars in his pants and a canceled credit card. The pension he collected from the City of New York went to the Delancey Giants. It was expensive to equip a baseball team. And Isaac had to save some cash for his brother Leo, who was in and out of alimony jail. Leo was a notorious shoplifter. And it was Isaac who had to fight with the detectives of different department stores to preserve his brother's skin. Leo would probably shame him once Isaac sat in City Hall.

He couldn't slink out of the River Café. The bartender demanded his autograph. Customers saluted him. He'd become a celebrity in spite of himself. He signed his name on a napkin, dreaming of Margaret Tolstoy.

"Come home with me."

"Can't," she said. "Frederic is waiting."

"I'll close down Quentin Kahn. You'll see."

"Darling, don't play with fire. You can't win."

His sweetheart from junior high kissed him on the lips. It

was enchantment, nothing less. He couldn't spin free of Anastasia.

The parking attendant produced Anastasia's car, a red Jaguar that must have been a gift from Justice, the spoils of some drug war the DEA had won.

"Darling, can I offer you a lift?"

"I'll walk."

"Isaac, it's the Brooklyn waterfront. You might get lost."

But he loped away from Anastasia.

"I'll manage," he said, and Anastasia sped out of the little parking lot.

He crossed the Brooklyn Bridge on foot, like a fucking pilgrim. Bikers and pedestrians stared at him. But Isaac looked beyond them, through the wires of the bridge, and onto the ruined silhouette of lower Manhattan, glass pyramids that killed the grace of an older skyline. These were the pyramids of Judah Bellow and Jason Figgs. Isaac already missed the clarity of Schyler Knott, his devotion to a softer past.

He'd stood on this bridge forty years ago with Anastasia, had watched the glory of Manhattan stone and glass through the morning fog, towers that seemed to invent themselves in Isaac's mind. He wanted to catch the moment by the tail. Schyler was right to resign from Landmarks. Those real-estate barons had pissed upon the town. Isaac would have to find another crazy warrior to run the Landmarks Commission.

There was another pilgrim waiting for him on the Manhattan side of the bridge. This pilgrim was dressed in blue. Frederic LeComte, without his black commandos, at the mercy of the wind. His tie had traveled around his neck; the wings of his collar had risen. He looked comical on the bridge.

"Wouldn't go to the governor if I were you."

"Jesus, Frederic. He's only a Democrat."

"But he's *our* Democrat," said the cultural commissar of the Justice Department, a wind-ripped boy.

"You bought the Gov?"

"Isaac, think like a politician, for God's sake. You'll have your own mansion in a month. You're the king."

"Stop that. I'm Isaac, remember me? I was your Alexander Hamilton Fellow. I traveled around the country like a worthy son, making speeches about all the fucking complexities of crime."

"But you abandoned the tour, Isaac, you didn't keep your promise."

"I wouldn't talk about promises, Frederic. You got yourself a toehold on this town while I was gone. You're the one who profited from my fellowship."

The wind slapped at Isaac. He had to bite his own words. He was standing on the Brooklyn Bridge with a commissar who could wreck anyone's career.

"You've tarnished the spirit of Alexander Hamilton," said LeComte. "You've killed people."

"So have you . . . LeComte, you bought the Gov. Admit it."

"He'll be running against the president in 'eighty-eight. He's a known commodity. We'd rather have him on the ticket than some wild man who might hurt us at the polls."

"So you're protecting the son of a bitch from any scandal, huh? You can't afford to let the governor fall. Is he boss of the Ali Baba? Does Quentin Kahn work for him?"

"The governor was a little foolish, that's all. He has a favorite niece."

"Ah, let me guess. She had fertility problems. Couldn't conceive. So Quentin Kahn found the governor's niece a magical child."

"That's the thrust of it."

"Blue-eyed? A boy? Fresh from an orphanage in Bucharest. What's the boy's name?"

"Oskar, I think . . . listen to me. The niece had adopted a baby boy before Oskar arrived. But the courts returned the boy to his mother. The niece went into mourning, Isaac. She wouldn't leave the house. It got so bad they had to administer electric shock. Nothing could cure her . . . until Quentin brought Oskar to the house. She crawled out of her depression the moment she laid eyes on him."

"Oskar's an orphan, right?"

"Almost. He did have a mother. But she sold him to Quentin Kahn."

Isaac couldn't control himself. He grabbed LeComte by the lapels, shook him against the wind. "That's monstrous. No mother would sell her child. She was coerced, wasn't she, LeComte? Ceausescu's people blackmailed her, threatened to—"

"Not at all. It was a simple transaction. Five hundred dollars and a bill of sale . . . let go of me, Isaac."

"Bill of sale? A boy's not a horse, not even in Roumania."

"Let go of me."

Isaac released the commissar. He didn't want to cry in front of LeComte, but his shoulders started to heave.

"Isaac, it was dollars and cents."

"Don't say that," Isaac said. "Don't ever say that, or I'll throw you off the bridge."

"Listen. Five hundred dollars could feed her for a year . . . and she gave the boy a future he could never have had."

"I suppose it's patriotic to give your child away to a governor's niece. But I come from a different school. Losing a mother is like losing a limb. Worse than that. If my mother had sold me to some pasha, I would have screamed and screamed."

"Oskar didn't scream. He has a tricycle. He goes to a terrific school."

"I'd like to meet the boy."

"Isaac, I'm not the governor's social secretary."

"I'd like to meet the boy."

"Isaac, if you bother the Gov, I'll make your life at City Hall one long, uninterrupted hell."

"You'd disappoint me, Frederic, if you did anything less."

Isaac swerved around LeComte and walked off the Brooklyn Bridge, into the belly of Manhattan.

14

The governor was a ghost in the City of New York. He had his own executive offices at the World Trade Center, but he seemed in constant exile whenever he was away from his Albany mansion. He didn't have Isaac's mark. He was a creature of the suburbs, an upstate man. "He'll play in Kansas and Mississippi," his advisors like to boast. They were grooming him for the White House. A Democrat with a conservative trim. He wouldn't piss money away on undesirables. He had no plan for the homeless. He was mute on most topics. His ship of state was a prairie schooner composed of platitudes. Billy the Kid had all the blue-eyed handsomeness of a narcoleptic gunslinger.

Isaac didn't have to shove his way past secretaries. LeComte must have phoned the governor, who was waiting for Isaac with a homburg on his head. Billy the Kid, his shoes shining like dark and bitter glass.

"How are you, Billy?"

"Don't spar with me, Sidel. You're no better than a common criminal . . . come on, you wanted to meet my grandnephew."

"Grandnephew?"

"Oskar Leviathan, my niece's little boy."

"I didn't—"

"Shut up, Sidel."

They rode down the elevator with the governor's bodyguards, who looked for suspicious characters in the basement garage. Isaac sat with the governor and the bodyguards in a sleek limousine and found himself sandwiched between several sedans in Billy the Kid's wagon train.

The Gov was brutal in front of his bodyguards, talked around them as if they were deaf and dumb. "Sidel, I could have you whacked. No one would know. I'd use professionals."

"Ask LeComte. He'll help."

"Fuck LeComte. You're the most visible man in America, mayor of New York. The whole Party will be judged by you, Sidel."

"Ah, I'm an amateur," Isaac said.

"And I'm Billy the Kid, but you're the king."

They arrived at a modest little ranch house in Yonkers. Billy the Kid and Isaac got out of the car, crossed a stone path, and entered the ranch, where Billy's niece and the boy were waiting for them. The niece's name was Rose Leviathan-Smith. She was in her thirties, with iron-colored hair and a slight tic in her cheek. The king liked her instantly. And he liked the boy, who was nine or ten, and stood with his body against hers, as if he could protect her from some profound malady.

"Rose," the governor said, "this is Sidel. I told you about his inquisition. Wants to take Oskar back to Bucharest."

"I didn't say that, Billy."

"Oh, he's brilliant. He'll smear me before I can mount a proper campaign. But I've considered putting a price on his head. I'll rub him out, Rose. I will."

"Uncle Billy," the niece said. "Go back to the car."

"I wouldn't leave you alone with him. He could be wired. He's a stinking policeman."

Billy the Kid looked into Rose's eyes and trudged out of the ranch. Isaac followed Oskar and Rose into an enormous kitchen, where he settled in with black coffee and Mississippi mud pie. He was starving after his lunch at the River Café. Ever since he woke up from his coma he couldn't control his appetite.

"Ma'am, I'm not here to judge. I . . ."

"You can talk to Oskar. Ask him whatever you like."

And she walked out of the kitchen with that shivering wound in her face.

"Scrumptious," Isaac said, his mouth filled with mud pie.

"I take care of Rose," the boy said.

"Don't you miss your mother?"

"I'm Oskar Leviathan. Rose is my mother now."

"But you must have had friends in Bucharest."

"Only one. Tudor. We played chess. But baseball is better for American boys. Willie Mays visited my school. He is also a refugee."

"He was born in Alabama," Isaac said.

"But he caught a terrible cold when the Giants moved out of Manhattan. That's what Uncle Billy says."

"Billy's right." How could Isaac explain the betrayal he'd felt when the Giants fled to San Francisco? Mays was an outcast and an orphan inside the windy walls of Candlestick Park. Or perhaps it was Isaac himself who was orphaned without Willie Mays.

"I have my own team, Oskar. Would you like to play for it? I could arrange a tryout."

"I am a disaster. I am dreaming of chess on the baseball diamond. I am getting confused. The outfielders are like horses. And the catcher is my king."

"Happens to me all the time."

Isaac had another piece of mud pie and returned to the governor's limousine.

"I maligned you, Billy. The boy is great. I would have adopted him myself."

"Always talking, aren't you, Sidel?" the governor said, with his hat in his hand. "Let me give you a little hint. Long John Silver is closer than you think."

Isaac stared at Billy. "Governor, what the hell do you know about the Knickerbocker Boys?"

"Nothing much, except that Schyler is missing, and he's a member of that unfortunate club."

"Who told you that?"

"Schyler Knott. Don't look surprised. Landmarks isn't my province, but I've been monitoring Schyler. I am the governor, Sidel. And Schyler kept sending me manifestos. *To Billy the Kid from Long John Silver.* Stuff about the City's decline and the purity of its Dutch past, the good old Knickerbocker days."

"Knickerbocker days? Billy, the Dutch were mongrels, like me and you. Did you encourage Schyler, did you excite his fantasies?"

"Of course not."

"Why didn't you talk to the police?"

"I'm talking to you, Sidel. And I have no hard evidence that Schyler himself was involved in the murder of homeless men."

"What if the victims weren't homeless? What if they had been taxpayers, pillars of the community?"

"Then I would have gone on prime time and howled my head off. But there's nothing here to milk. I'm doing you a favor, Sidel. I'm giving you an edge."

"Billy," Isaac whispered in the governor's ear. "You never did a favor in your life."

They dropped him off in the middle of Harlem. Billy the Kid wanted to lend him a bodyguard. Isaac said no. He was safe among the ruins. He felt like visiting the Seventh Avenue Armory, crawling into his old bed, playing Geronimo Jones. He'd been much happier as a homeless man, living in some foggy present tense, without a future or a past. He'd brought a bag of books on his first trip to the shelter. He'd read Pascal, a short life of Spinoza, some Patricia Highsmith and Dashiell Hammett. Isaac had been a voracious reader ever since his one semester at college. He didn't have any degrees, like his First Dep. But he loved dark lines on a page, the feel of a sentence, the ordered forest of words.

His pager began to vibrate like an electric worm. He unclipped the pager from his belt, looked at the telephone number inside the plastic window. He couldn't recognize the number. It wasn't Gracie Mansion or Police Headquarters. He stepped into a telephone booth and dialed. Someone answered gruffly at the other end. "Who's this?"

"Sidel."

"What do ya want?"

"Dunno. I was paged."

"Yeah, yeah. You're the Commish. I paged ya. We had a little accident."

"Who are you?"

"It's confidential. I'm calling from Brooklyn."

"Is this the River Café?"

"It's a warehouse. Plymouth Street, number nineteen and a half. The Maggione Paper Company. You can't miss it."

Isaac hailed a gypsy cab. He and the driver both got lost. They kept circling under the Manhattan Bridge. It was a scary neighborhood, beside the old Brooklyn Navy Yard and the Farragut housing project, where rats and wild boys roamed the streets. The driver began to shake. "Lots of murders around here."

"I know. It's a Mafia dumping ground."

"Who's afraid of the Mafia?"

They still couldn't find Plymouth Street. Isaac paid the driver and got out of the car.

He walked up Prince Street, turned onto Gold, where he discovered a rat that amazed him. It was all furry and moved with the assurance of an alligator. Isaac got out of the rat's way and stumbled upon Plymouth Street and the Maggione Paper Company. He recognized one of Jerry DiAngelis' soldiers. The soldier saluted him. Isaac went inside. It was like a cave with huge bundles of compressed paper. Isaac couldn't bear to imagine the heart ripped out of so many magazines and books. He was a Talmudist. Words on any scrap of paper had a totemic charm to the Pink Commish.

A woman lay beside one particular bundle. She had a bodkin behind her ear, the same sort of needle-knife that had dispatched all the homeless men. But Isaac didn't find a note from the Knickerbocker Boys. He couldn't seem to forget how lovely the woman was in her strange repose. Rita Mae Robinson with her arms curled on the ground.

A rat crossed Isaac's path. He looked up. Jerry DiAngelis was near him in his white coat.

"Can't you cover her, Jerry? Before the rats eat her eyes."

"Don't worry about the rats."

"Who taught you how to page me? The number's supposed to be a big secret."

"Don Isacco, you don't have any secrets."

"Yeah. You caught me in Rita's booth with my cock out."

"She was your friend. A lot of people know that."

"How did she get here? She wouldn't have come to a rat-infested factory on Plymouth Street. It's the end of the world."

"What are you saying?"

"She was killed uptown somewhere and dumped in your lap."

"And you think it was my piece of work? I ordered her execution, huh? And then I paged you to cover my ass. I'm a clever man . . . I found her, Don Isacco. I could have dropped her in a sink, but I saved her for you."

Isaac had one of Jerry's henchmen call Joe Barbarossa. He kept staring at that girl on the factory floor. Rita's eyes were like dark candles. Her body could have been a displaced flower. She'd died with a sweetness on her face. Whoever attacked her wasn't a stranger. A word, a kiss, and a bodkin in the neck.

Barbarossa arrived with Albert Wiggens. Isaac didn't even say hello to Wig.

"Joey, you'll dust for prints. I don't want Crime Scene mixing in our affairs."

"Boss, we're cops. Sweets will hang us on a tree."

"Ah, there's lots of time for lab reports. Joey, some fat fuck carried her here. He would have had to cradle her in his arms, dance with her almost. A fat man, I'm telling you."

"Boss, what's her name?"

"Rita," Isaac said, and then he noticed Wig, who was shivering in this cave like some casualty of war.

"Wig, can I get you a chair?"

Wig never answered. He walked right out of the paper company.

PART FOUR

PART FOUR

15

He didn't have vengeance on his mind. Wig had to find Harwood before he began punishing people. Harwood was floating around in crack heaven with his unlaced Adidas. The kid was in danger. Harwood couldn't read, but he kept his mama's books inside his head. Wig drove across the Manhattan Bridge in Sidel's own car and raced up to the Ali Baba. He found Harwood in one of the back rooms that served as a drug canteen. Harwood was smoking some dreadful shit out of a dirty glass pipe. His hazel eyes had gone yellow. Wig had to slap Harwood awake. He shoved his coat over the boy's shoulders, walked him out of the Ali Baba, brought him up to the crib he had in Harlem Heights, and tied him to a chair.

"It aint right, Wiggy," the boy said, with his constant sniffle.

"You'll run downstairs and beat up on some old man for a dime bag."

"Not me. I swear on my mama's life."

And Wig, who'd fallen off roofs without a blink, started to cry. "Your mama's dead."

Harwood's lower lip hung out like a hyena. That was how a crackhead laughed. "Stop shittin' me, Wig. Mama made me sandwiches this morning."

"This morning don't mean diddley. She's dead."

"Aw, Wig, mama wouldn't leave me alone."

"King Isaac found her in a factory. On Plymouth Street. With a pigsticker in her neck."

"Did that white king off my mama, Wig? He been nosing around, askin' questions. Me and William had to jump on him."

"He wouldn't have hurt Rita Mae. He has dumb ideas about women. It's called chivalry."

"Chivalry is a whole lot of shit. It's for white women. And what was she doin' in a factory?"

"Getting ready to be eaten by rats. Somebody brought her to that graveyard. Made it look like the Mafia. But it has all of Quentin's marks. Did he have a fight with your mama?"

"No, Wig. He pays us and we watch the foreigner kids for him. But he's stingy. He was blackmailin' mama a little."

"On account of the john she knifed? That was two years ago."

"Makes no difference to Quent. He has it written up in his books."

"I had to ride that corpse down to Florida."

"See? You workin' for the man too. You get your touch, like everybody else."

"Quentin doesn't own me like he owns your mama."

"She dead. And the white king killed her."

"I told you, boy. Isaac doesn't kill women, white or black."

"Then who stuck her if it aint him? Mama was valuable to Quent."

"Yeah, like cattle. Did she quarrel with that other king?"

"Carol? Mama never had no dealings with him. Only Quent."

"Harwood, you've been around crackheads too long. Your brain's ready to rot. That Carol is the man behind the man. He does the dirty work. How do you think Quent imports those children? Through King Carol . . . I have to leave you in my crib."

"Don't, Wiggy. I'll die in this chair."

"It's the only safe house I have. And I can't untie your

hands. You'll bolt on me. You'll do your crack. And you'll be dead in a couple of hours. Because whoever got your mama will go after you."

It sickened him to sentence Harwood to a chair, but he couldn't take the boy with him. Harwood would give all his moves away. Harwood had cocaine eyes and a runny nose. Wig got into the king's car and drove back down to Ali Baba country. He was just like Isaac, who was always crying. He should have known that Rita wouldn't survive her booth at the Ali Baba. But he'd lent her a cloak—his reputation out on the street. Quentin knew that Rita had once been his old lady. And Quentin would have to pay for that.

But death was always doing funny tricks. Rita was inside him, like a lost wife. If he hadn't been such a bandit, he might have settled with her, had his own child. All he had was a fable. The Purple Gang. But he couldn't kiss a fable, hug it in the dark, hold its hand. He'd pushed Rita toward the Ali Baba, made her into a pros. Sweets wouldn't have done it. But Sweets had the Revolution behind him, black aristocrats who could sit for family portraits and consider law school for their sons. Wig had never even said hello to his papa. And his mama had scrubbed floors in honkey houses.

Aint no excuse, Mr. Albert Wiggens. Your fox is dead, and don't you blame it on your breeding.

He walked into the Ali Baba with his ankle holster and his Glock. Wig was the house sheriff who collected his toll every month, that "touch" he shared with the mayor's secretary. Mario Klein had introduced him to Quentin Kahn when Wig was chief of the mayor's detail. He was Mario's bodyguard and bagman. The little secretary was loyal to Rebecca Karp, but it was Mario who managed New York and maneuvered behind the mayor's back. And Wig carried so much cash around in his pockets, he felt like a freight train. He'd stroll into clubs that had never seen a black man come through the front door. He'd sit in the poshest chair, smoke a Cuban cigar with all the potentates, and tell stories about the Purple Gang. He loved all those lies. But Sidel got to Mario Klein and tossed Wig off the mayor's detail. And the only "touch" he had left was the Ali Baba, with all its memories of Rita Mae's booth.

He got past Quentin's bodyguards, but that pingpong priest had gone off on a holy mission, so his bookkeeper said. Quent was traveling in behalf of *Pingpong Power.* The bookkeeper's name was Eddie Royal. He was a former jockey who'd studied accounting on his own. He was also a thug who controlled all the girls at the Ali Baba and kept the johns supplied with yellow condoms. He wore a Glock in his pants. He was five feet two and vicious as a poisoned, aging doll. He sat behind Quentin's desk and handed Wig two fat envelopes stuffed with hundred dollar bills.

Wig returned one of the envelopes. "I don't bag money for Mario anymore.'

"Ah, do us a favor, Wig. Mario's got a bad cold. Make the delivery."

"When can I meet with Quent?"

"I told ya. He's covering a tournament in Yugoslavia. He's nuts about table tennis. You know that. It's like a religion to Quent . . . I'm sorry about Rita, Wig. Where should I send the flowers?"

Flowers. Wig forgot. He'd have to arrange the funeral with Brother William. Rita had no other kin. Harwood. William. And Albert Wiggens. It was Wig who'd have to get Rita into the ground after all the labmen and other ghouls poked around with her body.

"No flowers, Ed. Just contribute something to Rita's favorite charity."

"Sure, Wig. What is that?"

"The Roumanian Orphans' Association."

"You shouldn't joke like that," the jockey said. "It could cost you."

"Yeah, Ed. Like it cost Rita . . . was the FBI closing in?"

"Not so loud," the jockey said. "I wouldn't trust these walls."

"What happened? Did LeComte grab a kid and the trail led back to Rita?"

Eddie Royal pulled the Glock out of his pants. Wig reached across the desk in one swoop and knocked the gun out of Eddie's hand. The jockey was mortified. He didn't even shout for Quentin's bodyguards.

"Quent's the real executioner. He ordered the hit. Why?"

"Don't get crazy on me, Wig. I got nothing to do with children. That's a separate account."

"Yeah, Eddie. It always is. A separate account. But you tell Quent for me that I'm also an executioner. All the pingpong tournaments in the world can't save him."

Wig took Mario's envelope and drove up to the mayor's mansion. He had trouble at the gate. Larry Quinn, the new chief of Rebecca's detail, wouldn't let him inside.

"You're not welcome here, Mr. Wiggens."

"I came to see Mario," Wig said.

"Ah, that lad isn't receiving visitors today."

"I suppose King Isaac has him under house arrest."

"You're misinformed, Mr. Wiggens. We have no kings at Gracie Mansion. Only a convalescing mayor."

"I heard that," growled Rebecca Karp, who'd come down off her porch to greet Wig. "Larry, let him in. I've been lonely without Wig. That cocksucker Isaac took him away from me and sent a bunch of spies."

"I'm not a spy, Your Honor," said Larry Quinn.

"Of course." She took Wig by the hand. They climbed up the tiny hill to her porch. Each of them sat in a rocking chair. It was the best gig he'd ever had, Rebecca's personal bodyguard. He lived on coke and scrambled eggs. He had a chauffeured limousine, a bedroom at the mansion, a maid, a cook. He sold drugs. He collected cash from the Ali Baba, he offed one or two of Mario's enemies. Police captains saluted him. Mafia princes offered him money. The Secret Service consulted him whenever Ronald Reagan was in town.

He had mint juleps with Rebecca on the porch.

"Be careful of that cocksucker."

"I'm always careful around Isaac, Miz Rebecca."

"I'm a prisoner in my own mansion. I never leave the porch."

"That's the shame of politics, ma'am. It makes exiles of us all."

"Were you looking for Mario? The little bastard's in his room."

Wig excused himself, went into the mansion, and located Mario in his tiny bedroom behind the stairs. Mario was sucking steam out of a vaporizer. His eyes were bloodshot. He'd been the brains behind Rebecca until Isaac banished him to the back rooms, one more kingmaker who could no longer make a king.

Wig tossed Eddie Royal's envelope onto the bed. Mario counted all the cash like a greedy child.

"That's the last tit you'll ever see from the Ali Baba. I'm gonna whack Quent soon as I can find him. He offed Rita Mae."

"What if he didn't off her?" Mario sniffled with a towel over his head to preserve the last dying puffs of steam coming out of the vaporizer.

"Talk sense."

"It could have been one of the Knickerbocker Boys."

"Quentin Kahn *is* the Knickerbocker Boys. He was always good at moving corpses. And you can't deny it. We own a piece of his ambulance. I've been checking around. And them poor mothers he's been moving aint hoboes. They're Hungarians or something. Mules he's had to get rid of."

"Of course. He promises them hard cash and then King Carol kills them."

"And Carol killed my Rita."

"You want Quent. You want Carol. You're a one-man shooting gallery, but Quentin Kahn has Billy the Kid on his side."

"Fuck Billy."

"And Carol is probably a colonel in the Securitate."

"I eat up colonels every day of the week."

"Not this colonel, Wig." And Mario coughed into the vaporizer.

"What should I do, Mr. Mario? Lie down for Quent, tell him it's okay to get rid of Rita? Why the hell did he finish her, huh? Rita aint with the Securitate. She's never been to Hungary."

"Roumania," Mario said. "There's a difference. And she was caught in the middle, I imagine."

"The middle of what?"

"I don't know. Between Billy the Kid and the FBI. Between Quent and his money people. She was holding his children. Quent was probably trying to cover up his tracks."

"Then you ought to be his next victim."

"I'm impregnable," Mario said with a meager smile. "I have my own palace guard."

"If you mean Lieutenant Quinn, you'd better start worrying."

And Wig was out the door.

"Where the hell are you going?" Mario groaned from under his towel. "Keep away from Carol."

That metal ribbon in his skull started to expand. Only a fool, he muttered, gets shot in the head. He couldn't afford to have a blackout, not right now. He was driving Isaac's blue Plymouth, and he could only see out of one eye. Fucking Cyclops, he said. Quent kept his ambulance at a deserted firehouse on Eleventh Avenue. The firehouse had a caretaker called Archibald Harris, a nigger who was down on his luck. He was one of those unfortunate troubadours who'd played baseball in the nigger leagues and never got to bat for the New York Giants. He was just a little too late. He was a thirty-three-year-old second baseman with the Brown Bombers when Jackie Robinson broke the "color barrier" and joined the Brooklyn Dodgers in 1947. Archibald already had a game leg. He began knocking off liquor stores in Harlem. He was sent to Sing Sing for nine or ten years. Wig never liked to talk baseball with Archie Harris. He didn't have Isaac's fever for the game. But he'd met homeless men inside the Seventh Avenue Armory who'd seen Archibald play forty years ago at some nigger all-star game. That fool loved to field ground balls without a glove. He could throw with either hand. He'd clutch the bat way above the handle and slap home runs without even bending his wrists. He had cataracts in both eyes now. He polished Quentin's ambulance, changed the oil, and drove it from time to time, half blind as he was. He carried a pigsticker on him. He learned how to use it when he was with the Bombers, barnstorming from town to town, living like black gypsies. He'd befriended Rita, taught her most of his tricks. But a blind refugee from the nigger leagues couldn't save her life.

He was polishing the ambulance when Wig arrived, caressing the car with his fingertips. It was Brother William who supplied him with most of the drivers, guards from the Seventh Avenue Armory and homeless men with fake IDs.

"That you, Wig?" Archibald asked.

"Lieutenant Wiggens himself, old man."

"Who's an old man? I can still whip your ass."

"And if I closed my eyes and wished for it, I could play second base for the Brown Bombers."

"The Bombers don't exist. I'm a walking scrapbook, the last goddamn Bomber who's still alive, and I'm a young buck. Seventy-three. If diabetes don't kill you, a bum heart will."

"Has Brother William been around?"

"Hardly."

"Was the ambulance used yesterday, Arch?"

"Not that I noticed."

"Arch, Miz Rita is dead. And I'm curious if she was carried into Brooklyn in your ambulance."

"I know she's dead . . . but I didn't drive her, Wig. I loved Miz Rita."

"How'd she get to Brooklyn, Arch?"

"I took a long lunch," Archibald said. "Somebody could have walked in and stole my wagon."

"Somebody like King Carol?"

"I aint seen Carol in a month. I don't much like him. But he has a key. A king can come and go."

"He aint a king," Wig said. "He's a hired killer and a secret cop from Bucharest who pretends he's a pingpong champion."

"You're the one who called him King Carol."

"That's his fucking code name in America. He's a mountain of piss."

Archibald started to laugh. "Water can't make mountains."

"Yeah, old man. What about the monster waves at Coney Island? They're bigger than a mountain."

"Coney's different. Coney aint piss."

Wig couldn't fight Archibald's logic. Arch had come out of the nigger leagues. An infielder who never wore a glove.

Wig drove to the Seventh Avenue Armory. His whole fucking head burnt with blue fire. Can't black out, can't black out, he mumbled like an incantation. Brother William wasn't behind his glass cage. Wig didn't need all the magic lure of the nigger leagues to figure who had brought the ambulance into Brooklyn. Brother William parked his own sister on Plymouth Street. William was the chief of Quent's ambulance corps. He was hiding somewhere, holed up with whiskey and a white woman. He was scared to death of Carol.

Wig walked deep into the shelter. There were no guards around, just miserable fuckers under their tents of dirty white sheets. Wig climbed upstairs to the little gallery where he found one of the guards, a honkey who worked hand in hand with William. Wilson Bright, a forty-year-old scavenger who robbed the homeless whenever he could. He was constantly reprimanded, but he couldn't be fired. His brother was a deputy mayor. Wilson had been studying philosophy at Hunter College for half his life, but he couldn't accomplish a single degree. He'd talk worthless white shit, and when he got bored he'd have sex with the nigger cleaning ladies or dietitians who'd come from human Resources and plan meals that the homeless never got to eat. He carried a billy club for his own protection, and was Quentin's main driver. He should have had a uniform, but the clothes he wore had been ripped off the backs of homeless men.

Wilson was dozing with a book in his lap. Wig examined the cover. He saw the name Wittgenstein and woke Wilson with a brutal kick. The guard fell off his chair, groaned once, recovered the book, and climbed back onto the chair.

"Wilson, what if I tore the book to pieces and made you swallow all that paper?"

"I'd complain to my brother," Wilson said.

"Your brother's with Rebecca Karp. He'll be out on his ass in a couple of weeks. And where will you be?"

"With the Parks Department. I passed the test."

"It won't matter, Wilson. Haven't you heard? I'm Sidel's black angel. I'll cancel your test. Who's Wittgenstein?"

"The greatest philosopher of the twentieth century. You couldn't understand him. You don't have the training."

"Well, summarize him for me. Like they do in Hollywood."

"You can't summarize Wittgenstein."

"I'll kick your head in, Wilson. What did he say?"

"He said words are our only history. They're pictures of life. and if we aren't careful, the pictures will go away."

"Where's Brother William?"

"I haven't seen him, Wig. Not for two days."

"And the ambulance?"

"I've given up driving, Wig. I swear."

"Stop it! You've been carting Quentin's corpses around. You helped William drive Rita into Brooklyn, didn't you?"

Wilson raised his billy, and Wig would have plucked it right out of Wilson's hand if he had been a little less blind. The billy struck his shoulder. He socked Wilson once, and the guard fell off his chair again. Wig stumbled down from the gallery and managed to leave the men's shelter. Wittgenstein, he muttered. Pictures of life.

16

He woke to the image of a man struggling on a wall. This mother had bronze flesh and a hat of thorns. Wig was sharing a room with Jesus. He recognized nurses and nuns. He'd never been inside a Catholic hospital. He'd spent a month at Bellevue after he was shot in the head and two weeks at Harlem Hospital the first time he fell off a fire escape. Sweets kept calling him Icarus. Fucking Icarus. Wig had to look him up in a dictionary devoted to Greek myths. The Greeks didn't have fire escapes. But they did have roofs. And a guy called Daedalus was trying to escape from an island called Crete. He built a pair of wings for himself and his son. Icarus. The wings were made of feathers and wax. Father and son flew down off the roofs and started to cross the sea. But Icarus climbed up near the sun and never even noticed that his wings were beginning to melt. He dropped into the sea and drowned. And Daedalus got all the way to Sicily without his son.

But Wig was an Icarus who fell off roofs and survived. And he didn't have a dad to build wings for him. He didn't have a dad at all, none he could remember. But he did remember falling down a fire escape and landing on his ass in the dry sea of some backyard rubble. He'd relived half his life during that first fall, like a movie camera with images that exploded inside his head—Wig and his mama going to church, Wig making love to Rita Mae, feeling that luscious skin, the perfume of her armpits, Harwood at the door, not peeking, but wanting to be part of whatever his mama had with the wicked policeman. He started to cry. He'd buried *his* mama, but he couldn't seem to mourn Rita Mae.

He could smell a man's shadow near him. He didn't have to look up. It was the king.

"How'd you find me, Brother Isaac?"

There was a fistful of flowers in his face. The king had brought him dandelions from a Korean grocer. Wig could feel the remorse in Isaac's eyes.

"I didn't know about you and Rita, Wig . . . I'm sorry. Joey found you near the shelter. I called Cardinal Jim. We got you a bed right away."

"Where am I?" Wig had to ask. He was wearing a blue gown.

"At Mother Cabrini. The cardinal and all his monsignors have their annual checkups here. It's mostly a hospital for priests . . . you should have told me that you've been having fainting spells."

"Is the Department going to pension me off after my next CAT scan?"

"I'm not with the Department, Wig."

"But you did tell Sweets."

"He doesn't know you're at Mother Cabrini. But if the doctors say it's dangerous for you to be a cop, I will have to tell him."

"Tell him what? Even God wouldn't be a hundred percent if He was shot in the head. I can still walk the street . . . and climb fire escapes."

"Not right away. Who killed Rita? Was it Quentin Kahn?"

Wig clutched the dandelions, took them out of Isaac's hand.

"Quent's out of the country. At a pingpong tournament. In Yugoslavia."

"That's some Yugoslavia," Isaac said. "I just had lunch with him at the River Café."

"He could have left for Yugoslavia after lunch."

"Help me, Wig. Quent buys children from Eastern Europe. Rita becomes his kindergarten mistress, minds the children, and then Rita dies . . . with a needle in her neck. It's the same M.O. as the Knickerbocker Boys, the same style, the same cancellation. But without a note."

"She didn't deserve a note. Rita's black. And she wasn't homeless."

"Wig, did you ever hear of Schyler Knott? He's the poet laureate of the Knickerbocker Boys."

"Sounds like a racist pig."

"No. That's the problem. Schyler isn't a pig. He was with Landmarks. And then he disappeared."

"Maybe he's become an ambulance driver."

"What's that supposed to mean?"

"You are sort of brainless for a king. Quentin supplies the ambulance, which is more like a hearse. And he supplies the corpses. Homeless men. But these homeless men are Hungarians. That's why nobody can ID them. They're mules and babysitters. European honkeys who bring over a bundle of blue-eyed kids, but Quent never bothers about a return ticket. He lets your coach, King Carol, off them, and he creates this trash about the Knickerbocker Boys. It's a scam, a smoke screen for his enterprises."

"But it's not good business to waste the members of your own team. Word might get around. And Quent might find himself without a babysitter."

"What if the mules are damaged merchandise, what if they're tainted somehow? And Quent is collecting money to kill them."

"Collecting from whom?"

"I don't know. Roumania. Bulgaria. The king of Egypt."

"Farouk was Egypt's last king. And Farouk is dead."

"He could still be paying dollars to Quent from the grave. That's how smart Quent is . . . Isaac, the Knickerbocker Boys were your roommates at the Seventh Avenue Armory. Quent stole the idea of Geronimo Jones from you."

"What roommates?"

"Brother William. Wilson Bright . . . they're all ambulance drivers."

"Who are the other Boys?"

"Schyler Knott, maybe. King Carol. Quentin's accountant, Eddie Royal."

"That crooked little jockey?"

"Lemme finish my list. Carol. Eddie Royal. Quentin himself. And the old man who minds his ambulance. Archibald Harris."

Isaac's eyes swelled out. "The ballplayer?"

Wig chuckled behind the yellow flowers, but his head hurt. "You're the cat's ass, Brother Isaac. There isn't the ghost of a ballplayer who could ever escape you."

"But Archie Harris isn't a ghost."

"That's right. Arch was with the nigger leagues. He never played the New York Giants."

"You're wrong. The Brown Bombers played an exhibition game at the Polo Grounds. And they crippled the Giants. It was during the war. Archie Harris didn't wear a glove."

"I know that."

"He'd catch ground balls between his legs. Hit two home runs and hardly swung his bat. Made a monkey out of New York."

"Arch has cataracts," Wig said, feeling left out of all the history this king had in his head. "He can't see for shit."

"I don't get it. Brother William and Arch, two black men, and they're Knickerbocker Boys. How can they believe in all that racist crap?"

"Aw," Wig said, "they're deliverers. They move dead bodies around. They never get to see the notes. And even if they did, Arch is mostly blind and Brother William is illiterate."

"You hate my guts, Wig. Why are you telling me all this?"

"You brought me flowers. And you didn't snitch to Sweets. I sort of owe you a little . . ."

"It's more complicated than that. You knew about the Knickerbockers from the beginning. You could have stopped those murders, but you didn't."

"Why should I give a damn about dead Roumanian mules?"

"You're a cop," Isaac said.

"Don't you lecture me, Brother Isaac. You rob people, and—"

"You were right on the edge, weren't you, Wig? Almost a Knickerbocker Boy."

"Almost don't count in a court of law."

"Where does Arch keep his ambulance?"

"At the old firehouse on Eleventh. But you might not find him there. The Boys had to be desperate, or they wouldn't have delivered Rita to Plymouth Street."

It was his own dead fox that tied him to Sidel. *Rita.* And he started to curse himself. He'd forgotten all about Harwood. He couldn't ask the honkey to go and untie Harwood's hands. Then Isaac would uncover Wig's own little fortress on Convent Avenue.

"Where's Harwood?" Isaac asked like a fucking mind reader.

"Harwood's safe, Brother Isaac. I have him."

Isaac scribbled something on a scrap of paper and handed it to Wig.

"You can reach me day or night at that number," Isaac said, pointing to his pager.

"Brother Isaac, I aint in that much of a hurry."

"Keep it. You can never tell."

And Isaac walked out of Wig's hospital room. His back was hunched like a bear who was carrying half the weight of New York. He'd never last at Gracie Mansion. He'd need his own rocker after a couple of months. Wig didn't have that white man's sense of charity or justice. Loving people could get them killed. He found a telephone near his bed and dialed the firehouse. He'd have to ask a favor from Archie Harris. Wig couldn't crawl out of bed to Convent Avenue. Arch would have to go and untie Harwood and sit him down inside the ambulance. The telephone rang and rang. The old man must have been deaf. Wig would have to tell Arch to move the firehouse or the ambulance before Brother Isaac started riding high on the Knickerbocker Boys.

Someone picked up after the twentieth ring and said hello.

Wig decided to play the fox. "Arch, is that you?"

"Yeah," the voice said. But it wasn't Arch.

"How's the pitching arm?"

"Fine, fine. Who is this?"

"Geronimo Jones," Wig said and hung up on whoever was impersonating Arch.

17

Isaac returned to Schiller's club. Carol was gone. Covering a tournament for *Pingpong Power*. He'd left a note for his pupil. "Never stop loving the ball. And don't concentrate on your strokes. Remember, Isaac. Pingpong is a game of spiritual grace. Warm regards. King Carol."

Isaac crumpled the note and tossed it under his pingpong table. He couldn't control his fury. The Knickerbocker Boys had been invented right inside that armory where he'd slept. He'd have to start punishing people. But a mayor-elect didn't have his own proper war room. He dialed Rebecca's deputy mayor and damage-control artist, Nicholas Bright, and asked him for a meeting up at the club. Bright was a thirty-six-year-old bachelor who behaved like an inspector general. He wasn't a constable or a cop. He had only the power of recommendation. He wrote up reports about each of the city's departments and declared what cuts ought to be made. Nicholas Bright didn't even have his own secretary. He worked alone, without computers or telephones or much of a paper trail. He was a relentless keeper of information, cruel and efficient in his desire to get rid of waste and guard the City's cash flow.

Isaac had never bothered to meet Nicholas until now. He kept putting off the task of shaping his own government and deciding which of Rebecca's deputies to swallow. Nicholas had thick eyeglasses and wore a drab butternut brown suit, like a subterranean creature who only surfaced when he had to.

"Nicholas," Isaac said, sitting the deputy mayor down at a card table in Schiller's back closet that had served as a changing room when Manfred Coen was alive. "I'm afraid we're enemies, you and I."

Nicholas was pale under his eyeglasses. His fingernails weren't as clean as they should have been. His shoes weren't shined. Nicholas was a tactician who couldn't seem to solve the problem of grooming himself.

"Would you prefer that I resign?"

"No, Nicholas. I intend to keep you on. You scare the pants off everybody. That's good. You save us precious dollars. And you don't have much allegiance to the Party."

"Then what makes us enemies?"

"Your brother, Nicholas. I noticed him at the Seventh Avenue Armory. He was a rotten, swindling guard. But all the guards were swindlers, and they were on their best behavior while I was around. I lived at the armory for a week."

"That was clever, sir. Taking inventory."

"I needed a rest. But your brother deceived me. Did you know that he's one of the Knickerbocker Boys?"

"Sir," Nicholas said, "I wasn't altogether ignorant of Wilson's pranks . . . about the ambulance, I mean."

"Jesus," Isaac said, "I was police commissioner. I belonged to a crime family for a little while. And I'm the last guy in Manhattan to learn about the Knickerbocker Boys. It isn't fair."

"Sir, I didn't exactly know . . ."

"I'm not scolding you, Nicholas."

"I realized something was askew when that dead man was found at the shelter, the first Geronimo Jones, but I closed my eyes."

"Nicholas, I was the first Geronimo Jones. But those bastards stole him from me. It was like taking my birthright . . . did Wilson confide in you, did he tell you anything about the ambulance rides?''

"He mentioned a certain black man, mentioned him over and over again. Wilson was in awe of him.''

"Was it Archie Harris?''

"Yes, Archibald. Brother Archibald.''

Isaac had fallen out of love with baseball. It was the land of lawyers and business managers and free agents. Utility infielders becoming multimillionaires. He'd get invited to a game, sit in a box seat, watch the players, and couldn't find pleasure on a single face. He'd never romanticized the Negro leagues. The Brown Bombers and the Homestead Greys were outlaws who lived in poverty, but Isaac would rather have barnstormed with them than with the heroes of modern baseball.

"Nicholas,'' Isaac said, "you're in my camp now. If your brother tells you anything, you report to me.''

"I promise. But will he have to go to jail?''

"Nicholas, I can't say yes or no.''

There was a freckled face standing outside the closet, a red-headed vision—an angel come to haunt Isaac in that grim, gray light. His dead mama, Sophie Sidel. But his mama had never been a freckleface. It was Dr. Lillian Campbell, Schyler Knott's shrink, with her animal eyes. Ah, there were too many women in the king's life. And they all belonged to some elaborate lost and found department. He said good-bye to Nicholas Bright, and Lillian entered the closet.

"You're a hard man to find, Mr. Sidel.''

"Come on, the whole world knows this is my office. Anyone could come in and shoot out my lights. I do nothing. I dance around in the dark. People steal my name. Real-estate barons kiss my boots and plot behind my back.''

"Schyler wants to see you.''

"Grand,'' Isaac said. "But I'm tired of all this intrigue. I ought to have a vacation. Would you like to come along, Dr. Lillian?''

"Are you propositioning me?''

"No. I'm crazy about freckles, that's all."

She took Isaac by the hand, led him out of Schiller's, sat him down in her car, and drove him to the Christy Mathewson Club, with its boarded windows and scaffolding.

"Ah, I should have figured. Schyler has nowhere else to go."

They went in through the cellar door. Schyler sat in his own little bunker. He needed a shave. He'd lost that impeccable lightness, that blond aristocratic mask. He looked more like a homeless man than the president of a baseball society.

"Schyler, Archie Harris of the Brown Bombers and the Baltimore Elites. He's part of your gang."

"I don't have any gang," Schyler said, with Lillian behind him like a freckled panther. "And I never met Archibald Harris."

"And I suppose you didn't write jingles for the Knickerbocker Boys. Schyler, don't waste my time. I'm getting mad. Monte Ward. Will White. Sam Wise. Morris deMorris. Your own Ku Klux Klan. I mean, I could understand baseball antiquarians without Jackie Robinson and Willie Mays. But there isn't one word about the Negro leagues in your annals. No mention of Cool Papa Bell or Josh Gibson—"

"Or Archibald Harris. Don't fence with me, Isaac. Can you name the mental institution where Josh Gibson spent the last part of his life?"

"I know about Josh, how he'd have conversations with Joe DiMaggio in his head. Wouldn't it make you crazy, Schyler, if you were a grown man playing in a children's league?"

"The Negro National League was hardly for children, Isaac."

"Yes it was. Because you could never graduate into the white leagues."

"I didn't invent the color ban. America did."

"And who the fuck is America? Me. You. Lillian."

"Isaac, I never liked your language."

"Then ask Dr. Lillian to wash my mouth. I'd love it . . . you shouldn't have written that crap. About niggers and homeless men."

"I didn't write anything. I only supplied the names."

"And that makes you innocent, huh Schyler, huh?"

"The City I love is dying, Sidel. It's losing the memory of its own past. Do you know why Harlem never had a team in the Negro National League? The major leagues were scared that whites would come and see the blacks play in Harlem and empty the Polo Grounds and Yankee Stadium."

"Aint it a fact?" Isaac said. "Economics is the rudest king of all. You're a cold fish, but I would have wanted you on my Landmarks Commission."

"Even after Monte Ward and Will White?" Schyler clutched Lillian's hand in that damp cellar, sitting in some royal chair that must have belonged to his Dutch ancestors. "In twenty, thirty years you'll have a whole new crop of pharaohs, and they'll fight to bring down every landmark there is. They'll kill, Isaac."

"I won't let it happen."

"Mr. Mayor, this is Manhattan. Land is stronger than merchandise or money . . . and you're a hairy boy who'll inherit Gracie Mansion. The pharaohs will gobble it up."

"Let them gobble. I'll live in a tent. But what's it got to do with a list of forgotten ballplayers? Quentin Kahn isn't in Judah Bellow's league, but he's becoming a pharaoh."

"Quentin Kahn is nothing. I paid him to start the Knickerbocker Boys."

"Shhh," Isaac said. "The man happens to deliver corpses. Schyler, wake up. These aren't homeless men on a merry-go-round. They're Roumanians who swindle children into the country."

"They aren't Roumanians."

"Has Quentin been reading you fairy tales?"

"He swore to me. He was collecting dead people and depositing them at different points . . . as a lesson to the City."

Even in that little heart of darkness Isaac could see the hot pain coming off Schyler's face.

"What lesson, Schyler?"

"That soon we'll all be homeless. The City is a cesspool. The plague is upon us, Isaac. We've inherited other people's dirt, and we're being punished. I had to do something. I couldn't shut my eyes. There's no place for the Christy Mathewsons in this town."

"Schyler, tell me, how did you get involved with Quentin Kahn?"

"He joined the Christys about a year ago."

"Quentin Kahn just marched into your club?"

"No. The governor introduced him to me."

"Ah, he came with a recommendation from Billy the Kid. That's grand. And what did Billy say? That Quent was one more antiquarian who happened to run the Ali Baba?"

"We have similar interests . . . we want to keep the pharaohs from tearing down that Emeric Gray on East Fifty-sixth."

"And you think that a prick like Quentin Kahn cares about Emeric?"

Isaac touched Dr. Campbell's elbow. "Lillian, please, get him into a sanitarium . . ."

"Schyler isn't crazy . . . he cares about your town, Mr. Sidel."

"But it could get slippery for him. Quentin Kahn isn't a radical city planner. He runs a murder factory. He's using Schyler. He could call him a partner one day and kill him the next. And I don't have the resources to watch over him."

Isaac walked out of the Christys' cellar and ducked back into the street. He'd have to find which Yugoslavia Quent was in. And trap him, with or without Carol. But he couldn't stop thinking about that hospital on a hill. Mother Cabrini. Here he was, like a grandpa, worrying about Wig.

18

He found his own Yugoslavia, at a kiosk on Forty-second Street. *Pingpong Power.* Quentin Kahn was publisher and editor in chief. Michael Cuza, aka King Carol, was contributing editor. And that retired jockey, Eddie Royal, was treasurer of Quentin's little mag. Isaac had a bitter smile. *Pingpong Power* was edited and printed at 23 Plymouth Street, a couple of doors away from where the rats tried to feed on Rita.

The king read from cover to cover. *Pingpong Power* was a source book, itinerary, and bible that had nothing to do with the American Table Tennis Association. It didn't list local tournaments or the ratings of top American players. The publisher lamented the sad state of pingpong in New York, the lack of tables, the public disregard. "There are more pingpong tables in Belfast or Carcassonne than in all of Manhattan. The nadir of pingpong is New York."

He talked about pingpong power in Roumania, Poland, Brazil. "It's the fastest growing sport among women in China, Bulgaria, France." The world's youngest woman champion, Nina Anghel, was a nineteen-year-old Roumanian whose face, body, pingpong skirt, and bat were featured throughout the pages of *Pingpong Power.* She looked like a grown-up Orphan Annie with freckles and frizzy hair. Nina Anghel was interviewed in three separate articles. She had a custom-made bat with pimples on one side and sponge on the other. She posed with Quentin Kahn, Carol, and Margaret Tolstoy. Isaac had a ball of bitterness where his worm had once been. *His* Anastasia and some champion with frizzy hair. He was like some jealous husband, only what did he have to be jealous about? There was Margaret with Nina Anghel on a cruise ship. Isaac devoured the bloody caption like a cannibal. "Nina Anghel and her companion-coach, Anastasia Antonescu, aboard the SS *Silver Eagle,* on their successful tour of the Danube countries."

Isaac saw a swollen river behind Nina Anghel's back, the makings of a forest. He was furious. Margaret Tolstoy had disappeared from Isaac's bed, had abandoned the little comforts of Rivington Street, to play nurse to a teenager that Quentin Kahn had trumpeted into some kind of champion. She'd borrowed the name of her Black Sea husband. Ferdinand Antonescu. It wasn't a legal marriage. Anastasia had been twelve. And Antonescu was the dictator of his own mad country.

There were other pictures of Anastasia and Nina Anghel. At the Kempinski Hotel in West Berlin, posing with different women champions. At the Trocadéro in Paris, where Hitler had stood sixty years ago, admiring the curious iron jewel of the Eiffel Tower. The king had a sudden jolt. His father, Joel, had abandoned Isaac and Leo and Sophie Sidel to become a portrait painter in Paris. Joel had a Vietnamese mistress named Mauricette, whom he'd married after Sophie's death. Isaac had visited his disappearing dad once or twice. Joel was in his eighties now, happier than he'd ever been. Isaac sent him money as often as he could. Joel had once been a millionaire, a manufacturer of cloaks and fur collars. But he didn't have much of a pension as a portrait painter. He might have starved without Isaac's dividends . . .

The king couldn't escape his own roots, not even in *Pingpong Power,* which was a fanciful cover for the buying and selling of children. There were nine pages of personals in a twenty-page magazine. It wasn't hard for the king to break the sad little code of longing behind most of the messages.

"Caucasian couple seeks blue-eyed fox terrier. Box 221, Tulsa."

"Hartford newlyweds wish to correspond with Nina Anghel's younger cousin . . ."

"Serious Boston club would like to borrow Nina Anghel for a month to train a class of gifted eight-year-olds."

"Earnest husband and wife searching for blue bicycle with Bulgarian tires . . ."

Isaac didn't believe that Quentin's mag was about sex for sale. Quent wasn't hunting for pedophiles. He didn't have to. He had thousands of childless couples he could prey upon. Isaac followed the photographs. Quent and Nina Anghel in some Balkan village. Anastasia and King Carol holding hands in Bucharest. Isaac didn't like the look in their eyes. Were they lovebirds? Had Quent been the beard, confusing Carol's tracks, while Isaac's childhood sweetheart was involved in some autumn sonata with another man? A king, no less. A false king.

Isaac was horrified.

A patrol car spotted him in the street. "Mr. Mayor," the driver said, "the Commish would like to see ya?"

"I don't have time for Sweets. Not right now."

Isaac commandeered the car, got the driver to take him to Plymouth Street. "Thanks." He sniffed around like a bear. Twenty-three Plymouth Street was a bottled-up building with a blackened storefront. *Pingpong Power* didn't even have its name on the door. But the king was curious. He hadn't crossed into Brooklyn for nothing. He stood flush against the building, picked the storefront's lock, and crept inside. He'd come to a black hole. He took out his pocket flashlight and shone it into the dark. There were piles of *Pingpong Power* in some sort of pilgrim's progress from the first issue to the last. But Isaac couldn't find a printing press. Just a nudie calendar on the wall that was three years old. And pellets of rat shit all over the place. The king could have been in a library. He glanced through back issues of the magazine. There were photographs of Nina Anghel at sixteen, when she was "vice-champion" of Europe. Without her coach, Anastasia Antonescu. Nina posed with Carol. Isaac put all the old issues back. It was only Anastasia who could intrigue him.

He turned off the flashlight and walked out of Quentin Kahn's phony editorial office. Sweets was standing on Plymouth Street.

"I've been paging you, Isaac. Why didn't you call me back?"

"The damn battery's dead."

"Did winning an election teach you how to lie?"

"All right. I was on a case."

"You're a civilian, Isaac. All your cases belong to me . . . where's Wig?"

Isaac shrugged. Sweets grabbed the future mayor and shook his shoulders. "Where's Wig?"

"Dunno," Isaac said. "I could slap an assault charge on you."

"It wouldn't stick. I'm worried. Wig is supposed to check with me every twenty-four hours. I lent him to you on that one condition. He hasn't called. I should have grounded him three years ago. I should have put him on permanent disability. But he'd die without the street. So I let him have the mayor's detail."

"Yeah. He and Mario Klein divided up the city between them."

"Rebecca's your mayor, Isaac, not mine."

"She appointed you, Sweets."

"You twisted her arm. Where's Wig?"

"At Mother Cabrini."

"You sneaked him in there with the cardinal's help, didn't you, Isaac?"

"Ah, Wiggy's scared you'll retire him."

"You have a short memory, Mr. Mayor. Wig hates your guts. And suddenly you're his champion."

"I'm nobody's champion," Isaac said.

They rode out of Brooklyn together.

"Sweets," Isaac said. "I don't think you'll have any more problems with the Knickerbocker Boys. They've run out of Geronimo Joneses."

"I hear you talked to Schyler Knott."

"You know about Schyler's involvement?"

"Isaac, you're not the only antiquarian in the world. Baseball fanatics have been calling in, leaving us tips. And I had dinner with Billy the Kid."

"Billy's touching all the bases, isn't he? Did he tell you about his niece's little boy? Oskar Leviathan."

"The Gov had to tell me about Oskar . . . once he told you."

They arrived at Mother Cabrini and went to Wig's room, nurses and nuns hovering around the white king and the black giant. But Wig wasn't there to receive them. He'd vanished from his bed. Isaac blundered through the hospital, but he couldn't find Wig.

"I don't blame you," Sweets said. "I blame myself. One more blackout and Wig might not recover."

But Isaac was dreaming of Anastasia and King Carol. He'd become addicted to *Pingpong Power.* All the young nurses looked like Nina Anghel.

Wig had escaped Sweets by half an hour. He'd put on his clothes and his two holsters, took his wallet from the night table where the nuns had left it, said good-bye to Jesus, and walked out of Mother Cabrini. He was fucking dizzy, and the daylight murdered his eyes, but he couldn't leave Harwood all alone to wrestle with his ropes. Wig stumbled down the hill to St. Nicholas Avenue, which was near enough to his own territory. A couple of strays from the Seventh Avenue Armory, who panhandled on St. Nicholas during the afternoon, discovered Wig. He fell into their arms.

"Wiggy, you ever gonna let us into the Purple Gang, huh?"

"Next year."

They got into a cab with Wig and escorted him to Convent Avenue, while he rocked between them, stars and moons in his eyes.

"Brother Franklin, Brother Ralph, take me to my door."

He was their chief, a police lieutenant and prince of the Purples, who looked after Harlem's homeless men. They brought him into his building, wouldn't accept money from Wig. He started to climb the stairs. He didn't panic now. He felt safe in his own lair. No one, not even Isaac or Sweets, knew his real address. He would invent different drops, mailboxes in other buildings, where his gun permits would arrive. He didn't have a mailbox here. He never chatted with his neighbors. He had none. He found his key and opened the door. Shit! He'd forgotten to bring Harwood some french fries. But he had a box of frozen Milky Ways in the fridge. He couldn't survive without Milky Ways. He'd hungered for them when he was a boy, but his mama couldn't even afford a refrigerator. A man's status was measured in the frozen Milky Ways he could devour. When the Purple Gang hid out, they couldn't worry about chitlins or hot corn bread. They lived on a diet of Milky Ways. And no supermarket in central Harlem could keep enough Milky Ways in stock. It hardly mattered that the Purples didn't exist. The legend was there.

"Harwood?"

The boy wasn't in his chair. The ropes had been cut. Who the fuck had entered Wig's fortress and grabbed the boy? A ghost? The FBI? Wig marched into the kitchen and opened his freezer. He had to have a hit of frozen nougat.

All his Milky Ways were gone.

19

Isaac dialed the FBI's Manhattan field office.

"Sidel here," he said. "I'd like to speak to Frederic LeComte."

"Sorry, sir. We have no Frederic LeComtes with us."

LeComte kept an office at St. Andrews Plaza, with all the other lads from Justice, but he wasn't vulnerable to a phone call. LeComte's secretary would only laugh at Isaac, while she recorded his conversation. He was a man between jobs. He could be trifled with for another few weeks. But LeComte was sensitive to his own image at the FBI.

"Please tell Frederic that I'm not crazy about pingpong on the Danube. I expect a piece of Nina Anghel."

"How do you spell the name, sir?"

"Like angel, but with an aitch."

He hung up the phone, whistled to himself, went to Rivington Street, and found Frederic in his tiny kitchen, eating a half-sour pickle from the king's icebox.

"Sidel, the Bureau is taboo, understand? Never call me at the Manhattan field office."

"LeComte, shouldn't your name be on the masthead of *Pingpong Power*?"

"What's your problem?"

"Margaret Tolstoy. You stole her out of my bed."

"Isaac, the lady has a mind of her own."

"But she doesn't have a passport. You gave her to Quentin Kahn and King Carol . . . nobody bothers to tell me that Margaret's out of the country. Is Nina Anghel one of your plants?"

"Isaac, I didn't invent Nina Anghel. She won the silver *and* the gold at the internationals in Barcelona. There's never been a phenomenon like her in women's table tennis. She can destroy most of the men."

"Then why does she need a nurse?"

"She's a kid, Isaac. Nineteen. From Bucharest."

"Why does she need a nurse?"

"Isaac, I didn't twist any arms. Margaret volunteered."

"For what?"

"To educate the kid. Teach her how to dress. Nina's a hillbilly. And now she's champion of the world."

"Who trained her?"

"Carol, of course . . . your coach."

"But I'm not a champion. I can hardly hold up my pants when I play. Why is Justice interested in Nina Anghel?"

"We're not. She's part of the sales package. We're interested in Carol."

"I thought you were protecting Quentin's schemes on account of the governor. You can't let Billy slide, or the Dems might pick another candidate. Isn't Oskar Leviathan sacred ground?"

"Yes, Oskar is. But we're not protecting Quentin and Carol worldwide."

"Quentin and Carol," Isaac murmured. "Like a comedy team with their own little hearse. But the fuckers made a mistake. They shouldn't have offed Rita Mae Robinson."

"And you shouldn't have gone to the Gov."

Isaac stared into LeComte's eyes. He could have strangled this commissar from Justice and delivered him to Plymouth Street. The king wouldn't have mourned LeComte.

"Are you telling me that Rita died because of my conversations with Billy the Kid?"

"I didn't say that. You complicate the picture and anything can happen."

"I saw Margaret and Carol holding hands."

"What?"

"In *Pingpong Power*. They were holding hands . . . it was a photograph."

"Isaac," LeComte said with a grin. "You can't blame me. I would have sworn that Margaret told you about her and Black Michael, the captain of Ceausescu's palace guard who catapulted himself into a king."

"I thought Carol was with the Securitate, and pingpong was his cover."

"He has many covers, Isaac."

"That doesn't mean he had to hold Margaret's hand."

"Margaret and Black Michael are like sister and brother."

"Sister and brother," Isaac said.

"Idiot, they were in the same orphanage. They grew up together . . . until Ferdinand Antonescu plucked her away, enticed her with ballet lessons, took her to Paris and Odessa . . . Michael Cuza is the only piece of family Margaret ever had. She's devoted to him. She'd kill for Michael."

"Maybe she already has," Isaac said. He could have learned to tolerate another lover. But not an orphan. "If Margaret is devoted to Michael, how will you trap him?"

"Any devotion has a price."

"And Margaret's price?"

"You," said LeComte. "This is her last gig. I'm taking her off the books. I can't have you sit at Gracie Mansion all alone. That would be indecent, Mr. Mayor. I'm giving Margaret to you."

"Frederic, I'm gonna steal Margaret. I did it before. I'll do it again."

"The girl has no nationality, Isaac. I can drop her in a boat and let her sail to nowhere. Who would take her in?"

"Gimme a month. I'll create a sanctuary for her. The FBI would look pretty stupid crashing into a mayor's house. You're on the rise, Frederic. You can't afford black marks.

Tell me about Michael. Why did he run away from Ceausescu's palace?"

"Isaac, come on. A former national champion. Who else could train Nina Anghel? He took a leave of absence."

"And ended up at Schiller's pingpong club, giving lessons to amateurs like me."

"That's no accident," said LeComte. "Have you had a look at Michael's other pupils? Oskar Leviathan. Jason Figgs. Papa Cassidy. Billy the Kid."

"I never saw the Gov at Schiller's."

"Isaac, the governor has his own table."

"And King Carol cuts a very wide swath. Where is he now?"

"Hard to say. Paris. Prague. Carcassonne. Nina's a fickle creature. She likes to give exhibitions without much notice."

"That's nice, but somebody has to have her agenda. Frederic, I could beat it out of you."

"Perhaps," said LeComte, removing another half-sour pickle from Isaac's fridge. "Delicious stuff." Two of LeComte's black commandos appeared on the king's fire escape. Another commando broke through the king's front door. "Shouldn't threaten me, Isaac. My boys are courageous."

"They were listening to every word."

"Well, I wouldn't walk into the lion's den without wearing a wire . . . you have a future, Isaac. Don't spoil it. I promised Margaret to you. Forget Black Michael and Nina Anghel."

"You planted Carol in Schiller's club."

"Not true. Carol had nowhere else to go. You've read *Ping-pong Power*. Schiller's is the last club in Manhattan. The man is a dinosaur. He could have sold out and made a fortune."

"He can't sell. Manfred Coen died at the club."

"It always comes down to Coen, doesn't it? Well, I'm not interested in ghosts."

Two black commandos climbed down the fire escape. LeComte left with the third commando.

"Ghosts," Isaac mumbled to himself. And he wasn't thinking of Coen.

20

Wig dreamt of his hospital room and that bronze Jesus on the wall. He liked all the nuns. But he couldn't sit there until the headaches blinded him completely or went away. He had to find Harwood all over again. Who could have kidnapped the boy and swiped Wig's last box of Milky Ways? Wig felt cheated, betrayed. It was his fortress, his own fucking crib. Some mother had *seized* Wig's address. He had to rest for an hour in the prisoner's chair, the same one that had held Harwood. But he must have dozed off, because it was dark when he woke. He heard himself whimper. Wig had a hole in his heart. He'd never considered how lonely he was for Rita Mae. He was Icarus, all right. Couldn't even drown in some unfamiliar sea. His wings had melted on the day he was born.

He had to find the boy.

He stole a car out in the street, started the engine with a strip of wire, and drove to the firehouse on Eleventh with a blur in both his eyes. The door wasn't even locked. Wig strolled inside, pulling the little .32 out of his ankle holster. He wasn't going to shoot up a firehouse with his Glock. The walls might have collapsed. He could hear a chirping noise in the background. The ambulance was gone. He bumped into a card table and two familiar shadows.

"Aw, Wiggy, you wouldn't hurt us. We playing chess, is all."

It was Brother Franklin and Brother Ralph, the two panhandlers from St. Nicholas Avenue who'd brought him home to his crib. He ran his fingers along the card table. He couldn't find one chess piece.

"Children, you play chess with invisible knights and kings?"

"Wiggy, we practicing the moves in our heads."

"Never heard of panhandlers in a firehouse. What the hell are you doing here?"

"Minding the ambulance for Arch."

"Ain't no ambulance I can see."

But he couldn't see much. Shadows. Buildings. Streets. He was as blind as Archibald Harris, without Archie's cataracts.

"Archibald asked us. Said we should come to the firehouse, so we come. We couldn't disagree. Didn't he start the Purple Gang?"

"Jesus," Wig said, "he's a blind baseball player left over from the nigger leagues."

"But wasn't he in Sing Sing?"

"Yeah, he had to knock off liquor stores to pay the rent."

But Wig began to worry. The myth of the Purple Gang only flourished *after* the war. Arch could have changed careers while he was still with the Brown Bombers, could have gone from catching baseballs to catching people. Wig couldn't believe it.

"Where's Brother William?"

"Holing up with a whore."

"Where?"

"That depends. He has a bunch of concubines."

"Yeah, redheads, blondies, and brunettes. Where?"

He pulled three or four addresses out of Brother Franklin and Brother Ralph. William kept his concubines in different cribs. But none of the cribs seemed to materialize. Wig struggled across Manhattan in pursuit of William. He couldn't uncover a single concubine. And then, cruising Harlem with the same blurry eyes, he spotted a fat man and a tall, skinny boy inside a playground at the foot of Morningside Park. He got out of the car, approached William and Harwood, who were huddled together, feeding on Milky Ways. The boy's nose was running. Brother William had a nasty cough.

Wig couldn't control his rage. He grabbed William, pounded him into the concrete while Harwood watched with the curious detachment of a crackhead.

"Wiggy," William pleaded. "I wouldn't have touched your candy unless we was starving."

"How'd you get into my crib? It's confidential."

"Aw, Rita was there once. She give me the address."

Wig couldn't remember making love to Rita on Convent Avenue. His past had begun to shrink. He was only one more Icarus waiting for a fire escape or a roof to fall down from.

"You drove her to Plymouth Street, didn't you, William? You were with Archie's ambulance corps."

"She was dead," William blubbered from the playground's concrete floor. "I couldn't do nothin' about that."

"Did you cry for her, William?"

"She was dead."

"Who found her?"

"I did. She was sittin' inside her booth at the Baba with a pig-sticker in her neck. Her hands were folded, Wiggy. She almost had a smile on her face. It was the spookiest thing. I didn't know what to do. I called Arch. He brung the ambulance. We wrapped her in a sheet."

"And you dumped her in Brooklyn. Why?"

"Arch was scared. We didn't have instructions. Quent wasn't there. Carol wasn't there. Only Eddie Royal. Brooklyn was Eddie's idea. He said we had to have at least half a borough between her and the Baba, or the cops would be on our tail. Plymouth Street belonged to the Maf, so it was a good place."

"And you reasoned with Eddie Royal like a fucking wise man in front of your own dead sister."

"Aw, Wig."

131

"Didn't even bother about who might have killed her."

"Could have been anybody, Wig."

"Like King Carol."

"Told you. Carol wasn't there. He was doing pingpong with Quent in one of them European capitals. Geneva or something."

"And what happened after you dropped off Rita?"

"I ran. Arch wanted me to stay with him, but I wouldn't. I knew I was next on the list."

"So you hid with one of your white whores."

"For half a day. She kicked me out. So I went to your crib. You never there."

"You broke into my place, you fat son of a bitch. You picked my lock and started living in the land of Milky Ways. Where were you when I brought Harwood and tied him to the chair?"

"In your closet," William said. "I woulda come out, Wig, I promise, but I was trembling and I pissed in my pants."

"And then?"

"I untied Harwood after you left. But I figured you'd come back to feed him. So I took all your candy and a pair of pants. I was desperate, Wig. And me and Harwood have been hiding ever since."

"In Morningside Park? I spotted you, William, and I'm the closest thing to a blind man."

"I used up all my money. So I called Arch. He's coming to collect us in his ambulance. We're gonna live with Arch for a while. Arch loved Rita. He cried like the devil when he saw Rita's ghost in the booth. He was with the Purples, Wig. I thought he was tough enough to protect her."

"How long have you been waiting for Arch?"

"Nine, ten hours. But it's all right. Arch has never failed us."

The ambulance arrived in half an hour, like some macabre angel of mercy, with its headlights on, Wilson Bright sitting up front in the cabin, all alone in his grotty uniform, wearing gloves behind the wheel. The back doors opened. Archibald

Harris peered out with his cataracts. He didn't seem disappointed when he saw Wig. "Hey, you desperadoes, get in."

Harwood climbed in first. Then Brother William and Wig. They sat across from Arch, who had his own narrow bench, the handle of his pigsticker poking out of his pants. And Wig didn't have to reinvent the act of murder or imagine the details of Rita's death. He was worse than Sidel. He'd let the romance of the nigger leagues blind him to Archibald Harris.

"Tell me all about it, Arch."

"What's there to tell?"

"How you started the Purple Gang. Was it 'forty-six or -seven?"

"Pish! I was playing with the Bombers in 'forty-seven."

"Old man, you had a dead career. You started stabbing people. You could go anyplace in Harlem. Who would have bothered a big celebrity like you?"

"Celebrity, son? I didn't have enough to eat."

"You invented your own team. Called it the Purple Gang. There was no gang. There was only you. Archibald Harris. You barnstormed in Harlem, and the legend began. I'd say you weren't even rich. The Maf must have been stingy with their new nigger prince. You had to supplement your income, knock off a few liquor stores. People forgot about the nigger leagues. You weren't so famous after Jackie Robinson and Roy Campanella and Willie Mays. You didn't even have to wear a mask. But one of the store owners happened to recognize a fucking worn-out phantom, or you would never have been caught."

Archibald laughed. "Brother William, I have my biographer sitting here. I went to jail when he was still dirtying his diapers."

"I never had diapers, Arch. My mama couldn't afford them."

"Then you must have had a wounded ass. Because you don't know shit about me or the Purple Gang. I aint a Purple. I never was. I wouldn't kill unless I had to."

"Breaks my heart to hear that. Because you killed rita Mae, old man."

Arch was cackling now. "Me? I'm blind."

"She wouldn't have let nobody near her neck like that unless she trusted him. And she trusted you. It was no stranger, it was no john. Did Eddie Royal give you a lot of nasty little dollars to off her? William was the chump who found the body. It was all planned. Quent was cleaning up his act, getting out of the business of buying children. And he had to separate himself from Rita . . . and Harwood . . . and Brother William. You were asked to kill all three. But William bolted on you and I found the boy before you could."

Archibald wasn't cackling any longer. The color of his eyes seemed to escape their cataracts. They looked profoundly purple and blue inside the ambulance. "Wiggy, I'm a casualty of war. I crippled myself in the nigger leagues."

"You killed Rita and you'll have to pay."

Wig was close enough to catch Archibald's moves. He reached into his ankle holster while the old man shoved him back against the ambulance wall with one hand, grabbed that pigsticker with the other, and tried to puncture Wig's throat. But Wig ducked under Archibald's arm and shot the old man in the mouth. There was a boom in the ambulance that sounded like a bowling ball. Archie's head slumped against his right shoulder. His mouth grew into an obscene red hole. Harwood and William had blood on their faces. They watched like children. The ambulance stopped. Wilson Bright peeked into the bowels of the ambulance. Wig poked his belly gun, his little .32, between Wilson's eyes.

"You be good now, Mr. Bright. And bring this ambulance home to rest."

Wig didn't have to bother about the gun. It wasn't registered. He'd toss it into the Harlem River soon as he was finished with Arch. The Harlem River had become a graveyard for Wig's guns.

There was a surprise waiting for Wig at the old firehouse. Brother Franklin and Brother Ralph had fled, but the firehouse had another homeless man. Geronimo Jones. He stood in his winter coat, like an orphan with sideburns, aiming his Glock at the ambulance.

"The Knickerbocker Boys," he said. "Lovely people. You're all under arrest."

"Brother Isaac," Wig said from his window. "You can't arrest an ambulance."

"Who's your latest victim, huh?"

"Archibald Harris."

"You whacked the best second baseman the Negro leagues ever had? That's criminal," Isaac said. "Wiggy, come down from that ambulance. I'll tear your heart out."

"Archibald killed Rita Mae."

"I don't believe it. He was my hero. He caught balls with his bare hand."

"And tattooed people with a pigsticker."

"I don't believe it."

Isaac climbed aboard the ambulance with his Glock. He saw Archibald Harris, lately of the Brown Bombers and the Baltimore Elites, slumped on a narrow bench with a big red wound where his mouth had once been.

"I could have sworn that Carol killed her," Isaac said.

"She didn't like Carol. But she would have done anything for the old man. That was her mistake. Trusting Archie Harris."

"Trust?" Isaac said, waving his Glock. "Get off this bus. All of you."

"Including him?" Wig asked, pointing to Archibald Harris.

"No. We'll deal with him later."

The Knickerbocker Boys climbed down from the ambulance, stood on parade in front of Isaac. Harwood's eyes began to drift. Wilson Bright bit his nails. William shuffled his feet. And Wig had to endure that metal ribbon in his head.

"Some gang," Isaac muttered, slapping Wilson Bright with his free hand. "Take advantage of homeless men. Your brother can't save you, Mr. Bright. Where did the corpses come from?"

"Mostly from Carol."

"Mostly," Isaac said. "That's an elegant word from a philosopher like you. Language is your special arena, isn't it, Wilson? You're the one who created the Boys' manifestos."

"Yes, Mr. Mayor. It was I."

"It was I," Isaac repeated. *"It was I.* Babble the king's English like a beautiful bird. But this bird steals poor men's pants and writes racist literature."

"I did what I was told."

Isaac slapped Wilson again. "Told by whom?"

"Carol . . . and Eddie Royal."

"Ah, the little magical jockey. Mr. Royal paid you in cash, didn't he? So much for each stiff."

"Yes. Three hundred dollars for pickup and delivery."

"And the abattoir was always the Ali Baba, wasn't it?"

"What's an abattoir?" William asked.

"A slaughterhouse," Isaac said. "Eddie Royal and Quent and Carol did all the work right under the FBI's nose. They had plenty of back doors, plenty of loading docks. Now I'll tell you who the corpses were, and you tell me if I'm right. Roumanian military men."

"Yes, Mr. Mayor. Military men."

"Members of Ceausescu's palace guard."

"I couldn't say. But they did have military titles. Lieutenant So-and-so."

"And who was the mortician? Who stripped them naked, let their beards grow, and dressed them in stinky clothes?"

"Me and Brother William and Brother Archibald."

"Three morticians," Isaac said. "Three blind mice . . . and you grabbed my name, didn't you, Mr. Bright? You decided to call each of them Geronimo Jones. That was your bit of genius."

"No," Wilson said. "I can't take credit for that. It was purely Quentin Kahn."

"purely Quentin Kahn."

"He took the initiative. We had the corpses. We dropped them in a dark hole or delivered them to a shelter. It was getting suspicious. So when we found out that you were boarding with us as Geronimo Jones, he got the idea. It came to him in a flash. He supplied the name of each Knickerbocker Boy. I did the notes."

"I was the gambit, I was the hat trick . . . and the fucking prototype."

"Yes, Mr. Mayor. You inspired the Knickerbocker Boys."

Isaac slapped him a third time. "Keep the credit, Mr. Bright. I don't want it. Did Margaret Tolstoy have anything to do with the corpses?"

"The woman with all the wigs? I wouldn't know. She was with Quent quite a lot."

"And Nina Anghel?"

"Never heard of her."

"Nina Anghel," Isaac said, raising his hand for yet another slap.

"I almost forgot. The lady champion. I only met her once. She has the biceps of a man."

"Did she enter any tournaments in America?"

"You'll have to ask Carol," Wilson said. "Pingpong isn't my game."

"And what is? Ghouling around in different graveyards?" The king was distraught. Welcome to the Knickerbocker Boys, he sang to himself.

"Boss," Brother William asked, "what we gonna do with Brother Archibald?"

"Deliver him somewhere. Like we always do. We're the Knickerbocker Boys."

But all he had in his head at the moment was Margaret's cropped gray hair. He wanted to sail the Danube with her, devour all of Europe. And here he was, stuck in an old firehouse with a dead man and a rotten gang of lunatics.

PART FIVE

PART FIVE

21

"Aunt Margaret, Aunt Margaret, can't you find us Mr. Baudelaire?"

She wasn't an aunt, or a mother, or much of a companion. She was touring the cemetery in Montparnasse with Nina Anghel, who was taller and sturdier than Margaret, with thick red hair that couldn't be braided or coiled into lengths of rope. Nina's hair was much too wild. Margaret had taken her to the best fashion shops on the rue de Grenelle, had bought her the sexiest stockings and shoes. She still looked slightly brutish, like some femme fatale with the heart and soul of a soccer player. But this was Nina's charm. Rawness and vulnerability. She wore red, red lipstick, rouge coquelicot from the house of Guerlain. She covered her freckles with liquid powder from Chanel. Teint Lumière. Her toenails were painted green.

Margaret was moved by this monster who couldn't bear to look at herself in the mirror, who was haunted by her own face. Nina Anghel terrorized all her opponents, female and male, but was like a gigantic brooding doll in silk underpants. She stumbled upon Baudelaire's grave and started to cry. Baudelaire was buried with his mother, Caroline, and his stepfather, General Jacques Aupick, ancient ambassador to Constantinople and Madrid. There were flowers and candles and trinkets on the grave. Nina couldn't stop bawling.

"I'm shocked," Margaret said. "A world champion crying like that. You'll lose your edge on the pingpong table. The biggest sissy will beat you."

"Son beau fils," Nina said, reading words off the tombstone. Doesn't it mean 'his beautiful son'?"

"Not at all. That's how the French say stepson. *Beau-fils.*"

"Then it's a language that tells lies. And I don't care to study it, Aunt Margaret."

"You'll be a greenhorn all your life."

"Girls from Bucharest are always greenhorns, Aunt Margaret. Ogres steal them from the schoolyards and introduce them to sex."

"Nina, how many ogres have you kissed?"

"None so far. But I'm an ugly duck, Aunt Margaret."

"With silk pants from La Perla."

"Pants can't make you a person. I have unruly hair. My face is like a road map, full with freckles. I'm nineteen and not one man has made love to me."

Thank the Lord, Margaret wanted to say. She was a concubine at ten and eleven, a bride at twelve, taking her honeymoon on the Black Sea, gobbling human flesh to keep alive. Margaret was the real ogre. But she hadn't eaten any orphans when she lived in Paris at the beginning of the war. Her protector, Uncle Ferdinand, was waiting to carve out his own little country in the Ukraine. The uniform he'd designed for himself was a little too green. It had gold lightning bolts. But Margaret didn't care. She lived right over the cemetery, on the boulevard Edgar Quinet. And the cimetière had become her own private Paris. Uncle Ferdinand took her to soirées, passed her off as a little dancing prodigy, but the only thing that gave her pleasure was stealing pieces of dark bitter chocolate that sat beside some German general's coffee cup. And she grew addicted to dark chocolate wrapped in gold foil. She'd been hungry for dark chocolate half her life. And Margaret was the one who was crying now. Because this cemetery, where she'd played years and years ago, sucking on her treasure of chocolate while most Parisians starved, was as much a home to her as her mansion on Little Angel Street. She didn't have a home in the United States, just a series of names and numbers in a very long address book.

"Don't cry, Aunt Margaret. Tell me about Baudelaire."

"Ah, he was a dandy who died of syphilis. He was paralyzed for a whole year. He forgot how to spell. He couldn't even pronounce his own name near the very end."

"That's a terrible thing for a poet."

"Or a pingpong player," Margaret said, without wiping her eyes. She could *feel* the trees, the alleys, the roads, the lanes, the tombs, the crypts of forty years ago. The crooked crosses. Stones sinking into the ground. The cimetière had its own boulevards and avenues and the Allée des Sergents de la Rochelle, which led to a stone tower that was shaped like a cannon shell, and where, she'd assumed as a child, a whole cadre of hunchbacks lived, marred by some magnificent disease. They ventured out at night, after the cimetière was shut, and tended the entire garden. Margaret could see their lanterns from her window. How she'd envied the hunchbacks of Montparnasse!

She entered another avenue with Nina Anghel and found the grave of Alexandre Alekhine, "Genie des Echecs de Russie et de France," who died in 1946. Another world champion, like Nina Anghel. But Alekhine had prowled the world of chess. There was an image of him sculpted into the stone, wearing a bow tie, and Margaret wondered if it was the same Alexandre she'd met at one of the soirées, the darling of the Gestapo, who also loved bitter chocolate and drank cup after cup of the blackest coffee Margaret had ever seen. This Alexandre's mouth was blue-black from all the coffee he consumed. He didn't have time to play chess. The war might end and he had to make his fortune selling the dark chocolate he'd swiped at the soirées.

Margaret went from Alekhine to the tomb of a fallen aviator, who'd been given the médaille du Mauroc and the couronne de Roumanie. Near the aviator was an unmarked grave with two figures jutting out of the stone: a pathetic skeleton leaning on his own scythe and a full-bodied woman holding a star above her head, the bad *and* the good angel of death. Which of them would Margaret have to choose?

"Auntie, where's Jean Seberg and Jean-Paul Sartre and Maria Montez?"

"Hold your horses," Margaret said. "I only grew up here. Without Maria Montez."

A man in dark glasses was waiting for them beside a statue at the heart of the cimetière, a winged creature clutching flowers, who was floating above the dead. Nina ran up to the man.

"Did you meditate this morning?" he asked, removing the glasses. He had blue eyes and tiny scars that couldn't have come from any dueling classes. He was practically born in an orphanage. But he had all the bearing of an aristocrat.

"Ask Margaret," Nina said. "I looked at a candle for an hour."

"And did you *move* into the candle?"

"Yes. I was making love."

His face started to wrinkle and the scars danced in the sun like tiny fish tails. That's how he revealed his displeasure, this complicated, merciless orphan who was methodically plundering treasure from a madman. Ceausescu.

"Nina, I could cut your allowance in half."

"I'm nineteen. I don't need an allowance."

"Idiota, I manage your life," said Michael Cuza, also known as Carol.

"I can sign my own checks."

"And give your dowry away to every beggar in the street."

"I don't have a dowry. I give exhibitions. People pay to watch."

"You're number one in the world," Michael said. "Who could ever beat you? Name me the woman or the man."

"I'm not a circus animal," Nina said. "I have feelings. I should fall in love."

"With whom?" Michael asked.

Nina sat down and contemplated that winged creature, looking for his genitals, which she couldn't find. She'd never been stroked by a man, never been kissed. She'd had an orgasm once, during a pingpong match. Her legs must have knocked in a magical way.

"She has the mind of an infant," Michael said to Margaret Tolstoy. "Some lout will knock her up, and her career will be over. I promise you, she'll give birth to a cow."

"Or a king," Margaret said. And Michael laughed. It cost her a lot to hear that rumbling music, invoked a past that was long before Angel Street, when she and Michael were guests of the State, charter members of the royal orphan asylum on Rahovei Road. He was always a princeling, her Michael, who played pingpong with his own jailors, protected Margaret from the groping hands of older boys and the jailors themselves. She was little Magda then, something of a beauty at eight and nine. She'd never known her mother or father. Michael was her only kin. She loved him like a gallant, loyal older brother. But the State seized Michael, sent him to military school, turned him into a cadet, and then Ferdinand Antonescu discovered her in a dancing class and plucked her out of the orphanage. He was a much sweeter jailor. And Margaret didn't seem to mind his caresses. Ferdinand was never rough with her. And he did bring her to Paris. She had her own rocking horse, a stash of dark chocolate, and a cemetery that she could conquer and explore.

Michael conducted business in the cimetière. He'd stand in the Allée Principale, where he could watch the exits and the cemetery guards in their dark blue kepis, and he'd meet with some antique dealer or silver merchant or agent of an auction house and present his "plunder book," his little catalogue that would vary from week to week, filled with items that his own henchmen had removed from the Palace of the Republic, right under the *diktator's* nose.

Ceausescu was too occupied with building yet another wing to the palace, with its six hundred clocks that were set from a console in the diktator's suite. He could create time according to his will, declare his own sunrise at two in the morning. The palace was swollen with artifacts, with money and jewels. Neither Ceausescu nor his wife could keep track. Their desire to accumulate was outside logic and the ordinary principles of human greed. The diktator had already squirreled away a billion dollars in foreign bank accounts; two billion, according to Michael. The diktator had been a reformer at the beginning of his reign. The little father of his people had condemned the Soviet invasion of Czechoslovakia. He organized clinics to control old age, battled illiteracy, protected the poor, the feebleminded, and the lame. But he quickly went from reformer to pharaoh. He tore up entire villages and turned them into industrial camps. And when Bucharest was ripped by an earthquake in 1977, the diktator designed his own mad city of haunted apartment houses on boulevards that dropped into an empty ditch . . . and a royal court, the Palace of the Republic, which he couldn't bear to complete. It sat in a huge lifeless park. Bucharest, Paris of the Balkans, was now a concrete garden and graveyard.

No one went there. It was a city that seemed to disappear from the map. And Michael was only stealing treasures from a country that was becoming a mirage.

His partners in crime were little princes of the palace guard, soldiers who imagined lives for themselves in that fairyland of America Michael had told them about. They would journey to Paris with the jewels. Michael would pay them a pittance and con them into getting onto a plane with a load of blue-eyed brats. Michael had promised them penthouse apartments and fat bank accounts. But they were talkative creatures and could have been turned around, used as witnesses against Michael. Besides, he didn't want to share his wealth. It seemed simpler and cleaner to kill them.

"He'll come after you," she said.

"Who? God? The Devil? Billy the Kid?"

"Your other pupil. Sidel."

"He's too busy chasing Geronimo Jones."

A buyer appeared with a pigskin briefcase. And Michael romanced him. He talked rapidly in French, introduced him to Nina Anghel, let him ogle Margaret, then took him on a tour of the cemetery, showed him the celebrity graves, while Margaret and Nina followed them at a distance.

Black Michael would earn a million francs this afternoon, selling off the diktator's jewels, which he carried in his pockets like some negligible merchandise. He wasn't even wearing a gun. He was Michael the trader, captain of Ceausescu's bodyguards and a colonel in the Securitate. The secret policeman. He'd always been reckless. He could fight ten wars at once, play chess and pingpong, but he'd never made love to Margaret. It would have been a sham, a performance, one more of Michael's masks. And he wouldn't perform with Margaret. He'd lie, he'd cheat, he'd steal, but he wouldn't perform. She was grateful for that. She'd have had to kiss him if he asked. That was her job. Kissing men for the Justice Department.

The briefcase bothered her. All that pigskin. It was a little too correct for carrying a million francs in the Cimetière du Montparnasse. And she wasn't startled when the buyer pulled a sleek Italian pistol out of the pigskin.

"Monsieur," he said, "the jewels, s'il vous plaît."

And Black Michael was shaking, not out of fright, but out of anger with himself. He should have recognized a robber, a gunman all dolled up as a merchant. The shaking stopped as violently as it began. Michael shrugged.

"Shoot me. I couldn't care less."

"Not you, monsieur. But the little champion. She's more valuable, eh?"

And that's when Margaret pounced. Nina Anghel had never seen a woman leap on a man like that. The robber lay on the ground. Margaret had kicked the gun out of his hand. Michael didn't ask any questions. He reached over and snapped the robber's neck.

"You fool," Margaret said. "This is *my* cemetery, Michael. We can't leave him here."

But Michael picked up the robber, held him close in his arms, and walked him out of the cimetière.

She was waiting for Isaac, could feel him inside her like a breathing child, her own special homunculus. But the homunculus must have gone to bed. The days passed. Isaac didn't appear. Michael went about his business, punishing people for that mishap in the cemetery. A band of mavericks, Hungarian emigrés, recycled policemen who had caught on to the tricks inside Ceausescu's palace, the constant, systematic looting. Michael dismantled the Hungarians, murdered their chiefs. Took him forty-eight hours. Meanwhile Nina Anghel had an exhibition at a pingpong palace on the rue Pascal, in the thirteenth arrondissement. It wasn't really a palace. It was a club that the city of Paris had built for its Metro workers, a bunker with a high metal fence and two floors of pingpong tables. The club had developed its own ecology, where instructors taught the children and grandchildren of these Metro workers, until you found three generations at the rue Pascal. And Manhattan had one prehistoric pingpong club that paid homage to a dead man, Coen. Pingpong itself had become a kind of fossil.

There were five hundred men, women, and children waiting for Nina Anghel. She moved among them, signed autographs, welcomed their touch. She went into the basement, where she changed into her pingpong clothes. People clapped when she emerged, her red hair just as unruly. Nina didn't have any women challengers, only men. She played the champion of Paris, a left-hander whom she wore down after several minutes. Her strokes were stronger than his. Her timing was perfect. They called her the redheaded lioness, la lionne rousse. She was docile, narcoleptic, almost numb when she wasn't behind a table. Her features were without charm or animation. But she turned lithe at the table. Her body did a ferocious ballet.

Quentin Kahn arrived in the middle of the match with all his cameras, like some perturbed photojournalist.

"Murder in the cemetery, huh? Margaret, you were supposed to watch."

"The guy had a gun. He was going to shoot Nina Anghel."

"All right. You disarm the mother. But did Michael have to break his neck? He gets rid of an entire network of Hungarians. That's wholesale slaughter. We could get kicked out of the country. I'm not a French national. And neither are you."

"You weren't so worried about wholesale slaughter at the Ali Baba."

"It wasn't wholesale," Quentin said. "And we could be particular. Michael's princelings showed up one at a time. We had our own chauffeurs and graveyards, and a sensational cover story."

"The Knickerbocker Boys."

"It still makes me laugh. King Isaac sleeping at a shelter."

"Don't misjudge his eccentricities. He'll shut you out of the real-estate market."

"Impossible. I have Billy the Kid on my side."

He stooped and took photographs of Nina at the table. Then Margaret whisked her back to their rooftop apartment on the boulevard Montparnasse. Black Michael had bought the entire building. It was a sandstone marvel that had been put up in 1907. Michael had become preoccupied with Paris real estate. He was sinking all his money into stone.

Michael sat in the kitchen eating a steak when Nina and Margaret and Quentin Kahn returned from the rue Pascal. Michael was naked.

"Cover yourself, for God's sake," said Quentin Kahn.

"Are you bashful, Quent? Worried about Margaret's honor?"

"It's the girl. Nina's never been with a man."

"I'm her coach. We've taken steambaths together. I've seen hers. She's seen mine."

"Michael, don't say that."

Margaret had to laugh at this Don Quixote of the yellow condoms who was so protective of Nina Anghel.

Nina went to take a bath. She didn't like to shower at ping-pong clubs. She preferred to sit and soak.

Black Michael continued eating his steak.

"I'm serious," said Quentin Kahn, circling the kitchen

table. "I won't have promiscuous murders like that. I'll pull out of the deal."

"And strand yourself, Quent? Without Nina? Without your little orphan army?"

"I'll sell the Ali Baba."

"You will not," said Black Michael. He'd been Quentin's guru once upon a time. Now they were partners with a bitterness between them. Quentin wanted to legitimize himself. Michael wanted to remain Michael.

"The ambulance runs are over, you hear? I'm getting out."

Black Michael abandoned his steak and walked out of the kitchen. Quentin began to sob very softly.

"Margaret, I can't handle it. I'm afraid of Michael. I can't handle it. He'll kill everybody. Me. You. Nina."

"Let him try," Margaret said. She was sick of all these millionaires. She didn't even have a bank account. She was Frederic LeComte's personal siren, seducing criminals for the Justice Department. She slept with Quentin Kahn, endured his little orgasms while she dreamt of Isaac, the ultimate gypsy, who couldn't find a home for himself. She was attracted to orphans. Isaac's dad had left him to become a painter in Paris. Joel Sidel. Margaret even had Joel's address on the rue Vieille-du-Temple. But she was reluctant to visit him, too shy. She would have felt like some daughter-in-law.

She went into her own room, locked the door, took off her wig. She was like an amnesiac who kept coming out of long sleeps to remember the worst details of her life. Starving in Odessa, on Little Angel Street. Uncle Ferdinand slept in a military tunic, with all his medals from the Gestapo and the German High Command. He'd run out of silver and gold and couldn't even hire a maid. All he could do was swipe orphans from the local asylum and eat them. Margaret ate them too. The Nazis had given her a nickname. Lady Macbeth.

They took the TGV train to Bordeaux. Black Michael, Margaret, Nina, and Quentin Kahn, the four musketeers. Michael was attacked on the train. He hadn't eliminated *all* the Hungarians. Two emigrés appeared in baggy coats, tried to kidnap Nina.

"Monsieur," they said. "We would like to see some cash."

"Gladly," Michael said, getting into the game.

He searched the pockets of his overcoat, plucked out dollars, francs, and deutschemarks, and while their eyes were on the money, he punctured their throats with the bodkin he'd also carried in his coat. It was Margaret who had to clean up the blood and help Michael escort the two dead Hungarians off the train at Bordeaux.

"Idiot," she told him. "Couldn't you let them keep the money . . . for a little while?"

"No."

He made a phone call. She walked *her* dead man outside the station. An ambulance was parked across the street. Quentin Kahn blinked at the ambulance and started to cry.

"This has to stop."

Nina Anghel seemed oblivious of everything. She sang to herself on the way to the exhibition, which was held at a sports palace in the suburb of La Bastide. Michael wouldn't let her give any interviews. He wasn't edgy. He wanted to distance himself from the dead Hungarians.

Nina destroyed Bordeaux's best player while sitting in a chair. Michael collected the exhibition fee. He hired a car and drove the musketeers to Toulouse. He picked an obscure hotel in the Arab quarter, where they hid for a day. Margaret watched the Arab men from her window. They would march in narrowing circles, retracing each of their own steps. There were no women in the street.

Nina played at a club on the rue de Languedoc.

Margaret still had the feeling that Isaac would come, that she'd look up and see his shadow across the pingpong table. But there was only Nina Anghel, growing tired of her desolation. No one could really challenge her, force her to work at the table.

The musketeers left Toulouse.

They drove to Carcassonne. Nina Anghel fell in love with

the ramparts, the old medieval walls. They had dark, delicious coffee inside the ramparts and little almond cakes called le petit carcassonnais, molded to look like a castle. Nina Anghel couldn't live without them. She'd hike the hilly streets with Margaret and a petit carcassonnais, while the two other musketeers plodded behind them, Quentin mopping his forehead with a handkerchief.

"Aunt Margaret, tell me a story . . . about Carcassonne."

She remembered the little tales Uncle Ferdinand had told her about an Arab princess who'd once lived inside the walls. Dame Carcas.

The Arabs had conquered the old Roman fort of Carcas in 725. Balaak, their king, was a merciful man. He didn't tear out the hearts of his prisoners and feed on them. He didn't hang any defeated warriors from the walls. He taught the new science of mathematics to the prisoners' sons. He married one of his own princesses, made her his Dame Carcas. She was as kind and as gentle as the king. She swore that no one would ever starve while she was there. But Charlemagne, king of all the Franks, grew jealous of Balaak. He arrived with his army at the bottom of the walls and demanded that Balaak surrender to the Franks. Balaak hurled hot oil down on their heads. Charlemagne ground his teeth. He moved his army out of range of Balaak's oil and sat for five years.

"That's preposterous," Nina said. "No king would ever sit for five years. He'd get holes in his pants."

"Shhh," Margaret said. "Who's telling the story?"

The Arabs began to starve during Charlemagne's seige. Their wells dried up. They ran out of drinking water. Balaak died, and so did most of his followers. At the end of five years only two creatures remained inside the ramparts: Dame Carcas and one tiny pig. Dame Carcas built dummy soldiers out of straw, placed them in strategic corners, and crouched from wall to wall, shooting arrows at Charlemagne. She let the pig swallow the last kernels of corn she had, and tossed it down to the Franks. The pig's belly split during the fall and most of the corn rained on Charlemagne, who continued grinding his teeth. If the Saracens had enough provisions left to stuff their pigs with corn, then Charlemagne had accomplished nothing with his siege. He rode away from the walls. Half mad from having lived among the dead so long, Dame Carcas stood on the ramparts and blew into one of Balaak's horns. But Charlemagne was a little deaf and failed to hear the horn. His own squire said, *"Sire, Carcas sonne."* Carcas is calling. But the king wouldn't return to the walls.

Nina didn't care about Dame Carcas. She wept for Charlemagne, the deaf king who was fooled by some silly kernels of corn. She went to the little house Michael had bought on the rue St. Jean. Black Michael was always buying houses. The house had its own printing press and little post office and a mountain of magazines. *Pingpong Power.* She couldn't even take a bath. She had to put on her skirt and rush out to the big château, where she was scheduled to play. It was only a castle inside a bigger castle called Carcassonne.

"Aunt Margaret," she asked, "what's my salary?"

"Shhh," Margaret said. "Michael is buying you a house."

"I'm not a baronness. I don't need a house."

A pingpong table had been set up in the castle's main hall. And Nina kept hearing in her own head, *Sire, Carcas sonne.* Her opponent wasn't even a legitimate champion, just a local boy who had entered a couple of tournaments.

"Aunt Margaret," she said, "I'll need a mask."

"What?"

"A bandage. A handkerchief. *Anything.*"

Nina grabbed Margaret's handkerchief and turned it into an eyeless mask.

"Christ," Margaret said, "you can't play that boy blindfolded. You'll never survive the match."

But Margaret hadn't counted on Nina Anghel's private sonar. Nina could position her bat according to the echo of the ball coming off the table. The boy stood like a straw soldier. He couldn't solve the mystery of Nina's mask. He'd offered to play Nina Anghel, not a blindfolded witch.

The boy left his bat on the table and ran away in the middle of the match. The crowd had its own cruel agenda. It started to laugh.

And then a man picked up the boy's bat. His shadow spilled onto the table. It belonged to Margaret's troubadour, Isaac Sidel.

"Miss Nina," he begged with his gypsy eyes. "I'd like to finish the match."

22

The king wasn't wearing sneakers. He hadn't intended to play Nina Anghel. But the boy's bitter duel had touched him. And so he volunteered himself. Isaac the jester. He'd stashed Harwood and Brother William in Gracie Mansion, where they wouldn't be hurt. He'd gone into the Ali Baba, prepared to beat Nina Anghel's schedule out of Eddie Royal. But the jockey had vanished. Isaac returned to his primary source: *Pingpong Power*. The city of Carcassonne was mentioned a little too often. It had to have some significance beyond the beauty of its walls. Isaac took the gamble. He flew to Barcelona, where his old enemies, the Guzmanns, had gone. He wondered how many Guzmanns were still alive. But he never even left the airport. He found a plane to Montpellier, then a bus to Carcassonne. The king could have rented a car. But he was nervous, had too much on his mind.

He crossed the Pont Vieux on foot, with its lanterns and crowns of metal lace, and climbed up to the medieval city. The king had to smile at his quick reward. There were posters advertising Nina Anghel. He'd preceded her by two days. He took a room at a tiny hotel on the place du Grand Puits, across from the castle where Nina would exhibit her strokes.

He had dinner on the rue du Comte Roger, sucked up a whole bottle of red wine. He couldn't afford a Pomerol, like Quentin Kahn. The king had a Cahors. He had a salad of

155

green and yellow beans, some salmon trout with steamed potatoes, and a pear tart. He devoured two baskets of bread, sat over a cup of espresso and a tiny brick of chocolate. It was like half a honeymoon, the king without his bride. He had no bride.

He wandered into the castle, hid among the spectators, and his heart beat like an ape when he saw *his* Anastasia, Margaret Tolstoy in a red wig, accompanied by Quentin Kahn and King Carol. With them was Nina Anghel, dressed to the nines. She'd come to play pingpong in a lovely little skirt. He was going to surprise them all after the match, knock out Black Michael's teeth. But his plans were ruined after Nina put on her blindfold and humiliated that boy, mocked him, belittled his adventure of dueling with a world champion.

His knees didn't shake once he held the bat in his hand.

"Who are you?" Nina asked under the blindfold.

"A friend of Black Michael's," he said.

And they started to duel with the bats. Isaac served the ball. Nina whipped it back at him, found a hole in his forehand. You have to love the ball, you have to love the ball, Isaac muttered to himself. This ball was yellow, like the condoms at the Ali Baba. Isaac wondered if the red lioness could read colors through her mask. What had ever happened to white pingpong balls?

The king served again. Nina ate him up. But he was one of Michael's wards, like Nina herself. He learned to love this yellow ball. He looked for Nina's weaknesses. He couldn't find one.

Nina served. Isaac cut under the ball, but she slapped it back into his face. She served again. Isaac pushed the ball over the net with a light kiss. She hesitated for a moment, could hardly hear the ball. She lunged a little too late. The ball struck her handle, and Isaac had his first point.

He broke Nina's game, hitting as softly as he could. Isaac's touch was outside her registers. Nina's sonar had failed.

The king caught Margaret's eye. There was a coldness in her face. She was angry at him for undermining Nina Anghel. He didn't care. He lobbed a slow, light bomb of a serve. Nina missed the ball, but Isaac was the good policeman. He could sniff some intrusion. A man in a blue hat had violated the perimeters of the game, had come a little too close. He was aiming a small silver gun at Nina's heart. Isaac tossed his bat. It knifed into the air and thwacked the man's forehead. The gun fell out of his hand. Isaac leapt over the table and tackled him. But the man in the blue hat was lifted out of Isaac's arms. Black Michael stood above Isaac, cradling the man in his own arms, while Margaret exhorted the spectators. "Calmez-vous, calmez-vous."

Then Isaac himself was lifted off the floor and hustled out of the castle with Quentin and Nina and Margaret and Black Michael, who was clutching Isaac and the man in the blue hat.

"Who is he?" Isaac growled.

"A Hungarian."

Isaac noticed something once they were away from the castle's walls. The Hungarian was dead. Michael had strangled him in all that confusion. A wind seemed to carry them down to the rue St. Jean. They entered Michael's house with the dead Hungarian, whom Michael sat in a chair. Quentin bolted the door and aimed the Hungarian's silver gun at Isaac. "We'll have to do him."

But Michael sprang at Quent, slapped him across the face. "Shut up!"

Quentin wiped the blood away from his mouth. Michael hadn't even bothered to take the gun out of Quentin's hand.

"We'll still have to do him. He can't come here like that. He knows too much. He's a pest."

"That's delicious," Michael said. "Spill out your life story. I'm sure Nina will love it."

"She has to grow up," said Quentin Kahn.

Margaret took Nina into another room.

"King Carol," Isaac said. "Is that the name you adopted for me, so we could talk king to king?"

"Yes, little father, it was tailor-made."

"I'll bet. And I'm the dupe of dupes."

"On the contrary. We had to be careful. We created the Knickerbocker Boys so you would keep out of our hair."

"You're a gambler," Isaac said. "Like me."

"But I have a certain advantage. I was trained by generals before I was twelve. I had German masters, then Russian masters . . ."

"Lemme guess. LeComte is running you. Your masters are American right now."

"Not really," Michael said. "Oh, I sell information. But Moscow doesn't trust Bucharest. So my secrets are very few."

"But you're a walking gold mine. A colonel in the Securitate. Justice lets you hump Ceausescu blind. And if you happen to kill some of Ceausescu's palace people along the way, no one's gonna cry. Not Ceausescu. Tell me, Michael, what is the Securitate's cut? Twenty percent? More?"

Michael smiled.

"You shouldn't have factored me into your fucking scheme," Isaac said, staring at the printing press and the stacks of *Pingpong Power*. "You don't print in New York or L.A. or Paris. You print here. But why Carcassonne? It's a tourist trap, a little wedding cake of a town."

"With perfect frosting," said Black Michael.

"Yeah," Isaac said. "Throw the hounds off your track. A company with world headquarters in Carcassonne."

"I thought you'd appreciate it."

"Michael," said Quentin Kahn, with blood in his mouth. "You're telling him too much. He's nosy."

"But I can't brainstorm with you, Quent. You're not a policeman. You've never even killed a man. You're good at moving money . . . and taking pictures of Nina. Go on, you have a pistol. Shoot Sidel between the eyes. I won't stop you. We'll bury him with the Hungarian. And you can caucus with Papa Cassidy and pick an emergency mayor. Shoot him!"

Quentin dropped the silver gun. His shoulders started to heave. He wiped his eyes with a bloody handkerchief.

"Get out of my sight. I can't bear to look at you, Quent. You have the soul of a chicken. I ought to rip your face off with my hands. I could, you know."

Quentin Kahn shuffled out of the room, his shoulders still heaving.

"He's brilliant with money, absolutely brilliant. But he'll bend on me, he'll break. He'll run into witness protection, and I'll get caught between the Mafia and the FBI."

Isaac pointed to the man in the blue hat. "Why did the Hungarian want to end Nina's career?"

"It wasn't personal. He belonged to a ridiculous cult of exiled cops. Cockroaches. They wanted to steal my product."

"You mean the palace jewels. That's some patrimony, Michael. The national treasure in your pocket. And most of your partners listed as John Doe and lying in a communal grave on Harts Island."

"Not John Doe, little father. Geronimo Jones."

"I could exhume the corpses, Michael, tie them to you and all the other Knickerbocker Boys."

"How, little father? Who's declared them missing? You have dead bodies that nobody wants. Where's the crime?"

"But didn't you know that once you decided on 'Geronimo Jones,' it would never leave my head? That I'd have to haunt you, Michael?"

"Ah, but we were getting out of the business. It was the endgame, little father. It bought us some time. And you can haunt me as much as you like . . . I'm proud of you."

"Why?" Isaac asked like an eager boy.

"You solved Nina's blindfold trick. You stifled her game, little father, swallowed the sound of the ball. You turned poor Nina into a mute."

"Remind me to give her a consolation kiss . . . Michael, you shouldn't have had Rita Mae Robinson killed."

"I was fond of Rita. But we had our orders. I'm not God, you know. We're part of a troika, Quent and me."

"And who's the third wheel?"

"I'd rather not discuss it."

"Then one of us is gonna die tonight . . . who is it, huh? Not Schyler. He has his own ideas about the nobility of bloodlines, but he wouldn't have ordered Rita's execution. Was it Papa Cassidy or Jason Figgs?"

"You're getting warm, little father."

"The other baron," Isaac muttered. "Judah Bellow."

"Correct. Judah had all the credentials. Most of our clients came from him."

"I talked to Judah. His daughter was a suicide. Natalie. And he was corresponding with a little Roumanian girl. She died of pneumonia. Did he blame Rita?"

"No. But Rita was our weak link."

"Her and Harwood and Brother William. They were the caretakers of Quentin's kids."

"We've stopped importing children."

"But I saw them," Isaac insisted.

"The last batch. And Rita might have compromised herself, snitched on us to protect her brother and the boy. Judah was being a good businessman."

"You're all fucking pharaohs. You bury and you build. Michael, I already warned you. One of us has to die."

The king jumped on Black Michael, who started to laugh. Isaac wrestled him to the ground. Michael kept laughing. He called out. *"Anastasia."*

It hurt the king to hear that name. *Anastasia.* It was the only thing he had left with Margaret Tolstoy, that totem word from the time when she was a princess at Isaac's junior high.

Margaret came into the room without her wig. Her cropped skull aroused him terribly. He'd have to go and seek a cure. Forty years, and the wound of her hadn't healed.

Isaac lost heart, but he didn't let go of Michael. Anastasia stooped over him. "Darling, if you kill him, you'll have to kill me. I'm sworn to protect Michael."

"You're not Nina's nurse," Isaac said. "You're Michael's babysitter, his bodyguard." He crawled away from Michael, got to his feet. "Margaret, did you help plan Rita's death?"

"No. But I wouldn't have stopped it."

"You're a Knickerbocker Boy," he said.

"And so are you."

PART SIX

PART SIX

23

The king returned to Manhattan.

He spent Christmas all alone. He had a hundred invitations for New Year's Eve. He turned them down. His own Party began to panic. Isaac hadn't leaked a word to the press about his administration, hadn't announced a single commissioner or deputy mayor. The pols began to predict that *their* king would flounder about in a rudderless ship.

But no one dared contradict him. He had the right to remain silent. A king didn't have a "voice" until his coronation. He wasn't idle. He walked down from the pingpong club to Emeric Gray's matchbox on East Fifty-sixth. This was the building that Papa, Jason, and Judah wanted to destroy. He could recognize Emeric in the pieces of limestone wedged into the corners of the building, like binders of a book, in the turreted brick tower that encased the water tank, in the blue awning above the revolving door, with a frosted deer sculpted into the glass. Emeric's markings soothed the king. He wasn't going to give up this building to the pharaohs.

He stood in a phone booth and got Jason Figgs' secretary on the line.

"What's your name, dear?"

"Cordelia."

"Please tell Jason that he can't have the matchbox."

"Matchbox, Mr. Mayor? I'm sorry. I—"

"Emeric Gray. He'll understand. If he touches that building, he won't get a dime from the City. No tax abatements. Good-bye, Cordelia."

He continued downtown, stopped on Orchard Street, searched in the clothing barrels, found a borsalino with a gorgeous feather, a pair of saddle shoes, a white shirt with someone's initials sewn into the pocket, *G.R.*, a pair of white socks with red piping, a double-breasted suit made of black wool, a winter coat with a mousy fur collar, a maroon necktie, and Isaac had his coronation clothes.

He went to his apartment on Rivington Street, but he had a strange feeling the second he opened the door. There was a poster in the kitchen, called "Pirate Ship." By Paul Klee. What the hell was it doing here? Had someone been living in his apartment while the king was in Carcassonne? He'd have to murder the landlord for lending out his keys. But it wasn't the landlord. It was Margaret who'd bought "Pirate Ship" at a little shop to decorate Isaac's barren walls when she moved in with him for a couple of weeks. She'd arrived without pajamas. Just her Glock and the clothes she was wearing. And her wig. The wig was part of her chameleon life as gangbuster and girlfriend to the Mob. She wouldn't take it into the king's bed. He fell in love all over again with this new Anastasia. The cropped hair made her look like Joan of Arc. Isaac had everything he wanted. Margaret and his own cappuccino machine, a gift from Jerry DiAngelis. Isaac would twist a knob and produce magical cups of coffee with steamed milk. But Margaret preferred her coffee black, with a bite of chocolate from a huge brick that she kept in her bag. The king tried Margaret's chocolate once. His eyes twitched from all the bitter cocoa. And when Margaret disappeared on him, Isaac stopped making cappuccinos . . . and "Pirate Ship" sank into his head.

Klee's ship had a smokestack, a paddle wheel, and two mainmasts. It had nine or ten flags. It had a navigator with yellow teeth and a captain with red eyes. The captain was a dreamer, lost in a maze of ladders, like Isaac Sidel.

He couldn't sit still. He rode uptown with a bottle of champagne. He had Wig's address in his pocket. He'd gotten it from Brother William, who was still in protective custody at Gracie Mansion. Isaac couldn't take the risk of losing him and Harwood to another one of Black Michael's wipe-out campaigns. William and the boy were running up a prodigious ice cream bill, which Isaac charged to his own administration. He didn't want to get Becky's cook into trouble.

Isaac hadn't seen Wig ever since they'd borrowed a coffin from one of Wig's undertaker friends and buried Archibald Harris in an upstate apple orchard that must have belonged to the Purple Gang. Isaac didn't ask any questions. But it pained him that Arch would have to lie in some anonymous grave without even *one* obit to portray his exploits in the Negro National League. Isaac had to wonder why Arch had never been inducted into the Hall of Fame. Cooperstown had started taking in celebrated ghosts from the Negro leagues, like Judy Johnson and Josh Gibson and Cool Papa Bell. Arch had been their equal.

Isaac got to Wig's place on Convent Avenue. The door was open. Wig sat in the dark. He didn't bother saying hello to Isaac. They'd shoveled dirt together, sang a little prayer to Arch in the apple orchard. That's how intimate they were.

"No disability pension, Brother Isaac. I'd rather starve."

"Wig, can you see what I'm holding in my hand?"

"A baseball bat."

"Jesus. It's a bottle of champagne."

"Well, I'm working at being a blind man. Takes a little time."

"Lemme bring you back to the hospital, Wig. You can convalesce."

"That's nasty shit. Nursing homes and Seeing Eye dogs. Okay, I get monster headaches. My sight comes and goes. But I aint no invalid."

Isaac put the champagne in Wig's freezer and had to dislodge boxes of frozen Milky Ways. Wig and Isaac had a feast. The nougat cracked in Isaac's mouth. It was much better than ice cream. They split a box of Milky Ways between them and started on champagne.

"To nineteen eighty-six," Wig said.

"I'd rather drink to auld lang syne . . . can you give me one good reason why Archibald Harris didn't get into the Hall of Fame?"

"Hall of Fame? That's for white trash."

"Josh Gibson is in the Hall."

"Window dressing," Wig said. "Arch was a convict. How could he get in? And even if they wanted Arch, he'd have to refuse. He couldn't promote his face. Arch was the Purple Gang."

"That's what everybody says about you. I guess Harlem has to have a Robin Hood."

"It aint got nothin' to do with Robin Hoods. Archibald hit on people for the Maf."

"I don't believe it."

"You're the blind man, Brother Isaac. And why are you defending that sucker? He made friends with Rita and then he finished her off . . . I hear you been to France. Did you catch King Carol?"

Isaac didn't have the courage to replay Carcassonne for Wig. He'd have to discuss his devotion to Margaret Tolstoy. He said nothing about Judah Bellow. He didn't want to send Wig on a dangerous chase.

They knocked off the bottle of champagne. Isaac opened another carton of Milky Ways. He began to stagger.

"Wiggy, will you join my 'ministration?"

"You looking for a doorman?"

"No, Wig. A bodyguard."

"You'll make history. The first mayor of New York with a blind bodyguard."

"Nobody will know except me and you."

"And Sweets."

"Sweets will have to live with it. It's an economy measure. We'll take you off his payroll and put you on mine."

"And what if I decide to off Eddie Royal?"

"I'll help you, Wiggy, but the little rider is gone."

"What about Joey? He could get jealous. He's your chauffeur, aint he?"

"He's my son-in-law," the king said. "I can't have him around all the time. People will accuse me of nepotism."

"Well, don't count on me driving, Mr. Mayor, unless you want to crash into a shitstorm on every block."

"Wiggy, can't you listen? Joe will drive us. When we need him."

"When do I start?" Wig asked between bites of nougat candy.

"Right away. You'll have to live with me around the clock."

"And what happens when you're making it with Margaret?"

"You'll close your eyes and be a good boy . . . but Margaret belongs to Black Michael."

"You talking about King Carol?"

"Carol doesn't exist. Carol's a joke, a tag Michael made just for me."

"We'll blow him out of the water."

What water? Isaac wanted to say. But he helped his bodyguard pack. Wig was as pathetic a homemaker as Isaac himself. Nothing made sense in this crib. Isaac had to search like a demon for Wiggy's socks and unlicensed guns. Wig needed a poster on the wall. Klee's "Pirate Ship."

Isaac packed whatever he could into one suitcase. More than one meant bad luck, according to Wig. He wouldn't let Isaac carry the suitcase down into the street.

"I do the carrying. I'm the bodyguard."

Isaac was relieved. Wig couldn't have survived much longer all alone. And neither could the king.

"We'll have champagne and Milky Ways on New Year's Eve," Isaac said and whistled for a gypsy cab.

A Cadillac halted in front of Isaac. A white limousine. Gypsy cabs must have been having their own renaissance. The door opened. A pesty man was holding a Glock on Isaac. It was the little rider, Eddie Royal.

"You been following me, Ed?"

"You bet. Come on. Climb aboard . . . but not him, not Wiggy."

"I don't go anywhere without my bodyguard."

The little rider started to laugh. "That's priceless. Your bodyguard is a hospital case. I'll count to three. And then I shoot."

Isaac looked into Eddie Royal's eyes.

"One," said the little rider.

Isaac smiled.

"Two."

Isaac shoved his belly against the Glock.

"Three."

Isaac clicked his teeth.

"Ah," said Eddie Royal, "be a sport, will ya?"

Isaac climbed into the Cadillac with Wig. It was like an enchanted cottage with a lot of jump seats. Eddie Royal sat near the floor. Behind him were Papa Cassidy and his wife, Delia St. John. She'd been a pornographer's model before she retired to Papa's bedroom. Most of Manhattan's political moguls had slept with Delia, who loved to dance in bottle clubs. She had long, joyous arms and legs. Her eyes seemed to reflect a permanent state of mischief. Not even papa knew Delia's age. She photographed like an eleven-year-old with pubic hair and breasts.

Delia had a grudge against Isaac, who'd closed down all her bottle clubs, but she cuddled against Wig and kissed him on the mouth.

"That's enough," Papa said.

"But Wiggy saved my life," Delia said. "You ought to be grateful, Papa."

"I am," Papa said. "We're all grateful to Wig."

Wig had escorted Delia to several of the bottle clubs when he was chief of Rebecca's detail and partners with Mario Klein. He'd kept all the clowns and unsuccessful suitors away from Delia. He'd also been one of Papa's bagmen.

Isaac turned to Papa and asked, "How's Jason and Judah?"

"Jason and Judah couldn't come. They're aristocrats. They don't like to dirty their hands. Isaac, you're not our mayor yet. You have five more days of freedom. If an accident should happen to you, it would only be a very minor catastrophe."

"Ah, I love the way you threaten people," Isaac said. Papa was his campaign treasurer. Isaac couldn't have raised a dollar on his own. He didn't know how.

"It's not a threat. You can't rule the City without us. You'll die. You have to give us *our* Emeric Gray."

"Not a chance," Isaac said. "I'm gonna landmark that matchbox."

"We've invested millions. We have Coca-Cola on a string . . ."

"What about Carcassonne?" Isaac purred at Papa Cassidy. "Will Delia dance while little Nina does her pingpong with a handkerchief over her eyes?"

"The man is crazy," Papa said.

"Papa, you shouldn't have gone into business with Black Michael. Too many fucking people had to end up in potter's field."

"Shut him up, will you, Mr. Royal?"

"It's my pleasure," said Eddie Royal with a huge grin. He wiggled about in the jump seat and waved the Glock in front of Isaac's eyes. But Wig slapped the Glock out of Eddie's hand, lifted him off the jump seat, and banged his head against the roof of the Cadillac. Eddie Royal began to twitch. His tongue clacked inside his mouth. Delia screamed. Papa Cassidy grabbed her hand and got out of the Cadillac. He stood in the middle of Convent Avenue with his bride. He didn't know what to do.

Eddie Royal's ears had gone deep purple. His nose was bleeding.

"Did you write Archibald a big fat check for doing Rita?" Wig asked Eddie Royal.

Isaac touched Wig's shoulder. "He isn't worth killing. He's only a messenger."

"Rita aint dying like that," Wig said. "Somebody's gotta pay."

"I agree."

Wig stuffed Eddie Royal between two jumps seats. Isaac knocked on the glass wall between him and the driver, who sat like stone.

"Rivington Street," Isaac said. "We're in a hurry."

And they rode downtown with Eddie Royal at their feet.

24

The State's chief judge, Jack Caution, swore him in on the steps of City Hall. Isaac took off his borsalino. He looked like Al Capone. He repeated his oath of office while a light snow began to fall. It wasn't much of a coronation. Isaac had arrived with Wig and Joe and Marilyn and Sweets and Cardinal Jim and Rebecca Karp, and his own baseball team, the Delancey Giants, kids he'd rescued from oblivion, delinquents who wore his colors and forgot how to steal. They stood in their winter jerseys—orange and black—Isaac's chorus and color guard.

The pols were also there, Democrats and Republicans, but Isaac avoided them. He was already sick of the mantle he would have to wear as mayor, that impossible cloak of power. He didn't have friends, only petitioners and penitents, people who were hungry for whatever Isaac had to give. His signature was better than gold. He could spawn entire industries with one scratch of his pen.

Reporters nudged his arm. He was supposed to have a press conference, talk about the Sidel administration and all the miracles it would accomplish. Isaac had a ghostwriter, Wilson Bright, that bandit guard at the Harlem shelter who'd created poisonous little notes for the Knickerbockers. He was the only scribbler the king could trust. He wasn't jockeying for position among Isaac's aides. Wilson was an amateur. He'd studied Descartes and was considered a dangerous man, because he was unpredictable and had never bothered to graduate from college. He'd been up two nights, preparing Isaac's maiden speech. It was pure poetry. Musical shock waves backed up with statistics about homeless women and the housing crisis. But Isaac didn't want to rock on the steps of City Hall like a renegade rabbi. He stuffed Wilson's speech into his coat pocket.

"The City's ungovernable," he told the reporters. "All I can do is stand up and take arrows in the head."

"Is that your job description for the mayor of New York?" asked a woman from *Newsweek.*

"Yes."

"Whose arrows are they?"

"Everybody's," Isaac said, winking at his Giants and racing down the steps. He'd gotten past his own advance men. He'd gotten past Wig. He'd only been mayor ten minutes and he was already out of communication with his staff. He was beyond the perimeter, a mayor lost in the storm of New York City. It wasn't supposed to happen. He had detectives and aides to track his every move. But he wasn't like any mayor there had ever been.

He went across the road to the Metropolitan Correctional Center, a federal prison near Police Plaza. That was the simple arc of Isaac's itinerary. He felt like a jailbird, sentenced to four years at Gracie Mansion and City Hall. But he couldn't just wander in. He had to wait for the warden.

"I'd like to get into the Heart of Darkness."

"I don't understand," the warden said. He was a cautious little man. Isaac couldn't remember his name.

"Heart of Darkness," Isaac said.

"You have no jurisdiction here. This is a federal facility. I could have you tossed into the gutter."

"But you won't. I'm on my honeymoon, warden. The Justice Department wouldn't want the mayor to be unhappy on his first day in office. Would you like to call Justice? Or should I do it for you?"

Isaac rode upstairs to the Heart of Darkness. It was a segregated cell block without windows where all the violent cases lived, mad bombers and murderers, traficantes who set people on fire, hacked off arms and legs. There were tiny slits in the walls, which gave off grim little rainbows of light. Isaac wandered from cell to cell. Prisoners whispered to him from their own private plots. He couldn't see their faces, only the corners of their eyes at the edge of each rainbow. They congratulated Isaac, wished him luck.

"I'll get you books, magazines," he said. *"Penthouse, Playboy, Moby Dick."*

"Fuck *Moby Dick.*"

Isaac fell out of the gloom of being mayor. "Who are you?" he asked.

"A shitbird, like yourself."

His heart began to thump. He peered into the cell. He still couldn't see a face.

"Who are you?"

"Herman Melville."

"Don't be cute. I could drag you out of there. I have the power."

"Didn't you get my letter?"

Someone had scribbled to him from this cell block. Isaac had the letter in his pocket.

Dear Mr. Mayor,

Hello from the Heart of Darkness. I'm inside the well at MCC. I have no contact with the world. They won't let me read. I can't survive without books. I don't miss the exercise yard. I don't miss the dining room. I don't miss the shower stalls. I don't miss conversations I never had. But I miss a book.

Yours,
The Reader

P.S. I preferred it when you were police commissioner. Now you'll have to kiss babies for the rest of your life.

"I know you," Isaac said. "I know that voice . . . you're one of mine."

"That sounds cozy, Commissioner. One of yours? Maybe we're kissin' cousins."

"We're a lot closer than that," Isaac said. And he drew a name out of his own dark well. "Terry Winch. You used to be my driver."

"Fuck you. I'm not Winch."

"You're Winch. You are. I lent you books."

"Yeah, your plugs are shot, old man. Try some vitamin E. I don't drive cars. I'm strictly baseball."

Isaac started to shiver. None of his Giants had ended up in the Heart of Darkness. He'd rehabilitated them with a base-ball bat and a small library of books. "Hey, Herman Melville, gimme a hint."

"Hint, you motherfucker. Who hit the home run that landed in the lion's mouth?"

Lion's mouth? Isaac muttered to himself. "Hector. Hector Ramirez."

Ramirez had pitched and played the outfield on the De-lancey Giants of ten, twelve years ago. He'd hit impossible home runs that bounced into the animal cages at the Central Park Zoo. He was Isaac's Babe Ruth, who broke every batting record in the Police Athletic League until he dropped out of sight when he was fourteen. Isaac searched and searched for the kid. But Hector Ramirez had become one more missing person in a town that loved to swallow up people, dead or alive.

"Hector, you could have been with the Yankees right now . . . millions in your pocket."

"Fuck you."

Isaac had to grab his own face to keep from crying. He'd been mourning Hector Ramirez while his mind detached itself from him.

"My little man," Hector said. "Isn't that what you called me?"

"Ah, it was harmless. I was proud of you, that's all."

"Hector Ramirez, superspic. My pappy was insane. He was fucking my little sister. I had to get out of the house . . . or one of us would have killed the other."

"You could have come to me," Isaac said.

"What? I watch you while you arrest my pappy? I would have been the hero of my block . . . I ran away with my sister, and what happened, huh?"

Isaac could make out the glint of Hector's eyes in that reluctant rainbow of light. "I'd rather not—"

"I slept with her. I beat her up. I became her pimp. I was a good little capitalist, wasn't I, Uncle Isaac?"

"I'm not your uncle. I never was."

"You were my teacher, my coach, my fucking tomahawk."

"You must be here under an alias, or I would have heard about it."

"I told you. I'm Herman Melville. I iced a narc, a snitch for the DEA. I cracked his skull with a Louisville Slugger, the same fucking bat you bought me for my twelfth birthday."

"Hector, I have some friends at Justice. I can . . ."

"No. I had enough favors. I'll do this on my own dime."

"Hector," Isaac said, "come close . . . I want to look at your face."

"What for? I never grew up. I'm a Delancey Giant."

Isaac rode downstairs to the warden. There was a terrible twitch in his eyes. "Melville," he said. "Heart of Darkness. He's here on a homicide. I want his cell filled with books. Not the usual crap. You find him some Dickens and Dostoyevsky . . . and bring him a lamp."

Isaac left the warden and strolled into a blizzard. The snow had fallen like cats and dogs while Isaac was upstairs with Herman Melville. Cats and dogs. A face emerged from the snow. It belonged to Larry Quinn, chief of Isaac's detail.

"Your Honor, we tried to beep you."

"I left my beeper at home."

"That's foolish, sir. We can't have you walking into a twilight zone. The city's connected to your heartbeat."

"Heartbeat," Isaac said. "I'm only the mayor."

And he disappeared into a wall of snow.

25

The pols were calling him Humpty-Dumpty.

They laughed into their fists. "All the king's horses, all the king's men," they said about Sidel. Humpty-Dumpty had run away from his own inauguration. Wouldn't even have a glass of wine with Judge Caution and Cardinal Jim. They were expecting complications. The pols would have to step in, rule the City from their clubhouses. But the chaos they had predicted wouldn't come. Humpty must have been working behind invisible walls. Suddenly there was a Sidel administration. The king had gone outside the Party for his chosen ones. He hired a new broom, Nicholas Bright, as his first deputy mayor. Nicholas fired half of Rebecca Karp's secretaries and other loyal souls.

The pols stopped talking of Humpty-Dumpty and made an appointment with *their* king. They crowded into his office, which still had photographs of Rebecca Karp with Barbra Streisand and Billy the Kid, with Mickey Mantle, Willie Mays, Arthur Ashe, Frank Sinatra, and hairy Isaac, her former Commish.

Her desk had never been cleared. Isaac sat behind it with his dark eyes. And the pols had to admit that the black wool he wore was becoming to a king. But whose initials were on his white shirt? *G.R.* Geronimo Rex?

"Your Honor, certain people have been punished, loyal followers, constituents who campaigned for you."

Isaac reached into a drawer and removed a slip of paper.

"Martha Hurricane, forty-six, member of the mayor's temporary typing pool. Vision impaired in both eyes. Can't distinguish between uppercase letters and lower ones . . . is she related to any of you, or all of you?"

"She's my wife," said one of the pols, a certain Tyrone Hurricane, who'd attached himself to the Bronx-Manhattan-Mozambique Independent Democratic Club. "Brother Isaac, who else will have her? She can't pass the civil service exams. Democrats ought to look after Democrats."

"You're right," the mayor said. "I'd rather move Mrs. Hurricane into personnel. She won't have to test her eyes or her typing finger . . . but all the other cuts will stand. Restrain yourselves, brothers and sisters, or I'll restrain you."

Isaac abandoned the pols, walked out of City Hall, and went over to sit in Jack Caution's chambers at State Supreme Court. Isaac smoked a cigar with the chief judge. Jack Caution was a man with silver hair. He'd reformed the State's judicial system, rooted out fraudulent judges. He was a year younger than Isaac. His father and grandfather had been minor magistrates. He was the most logical choice for governor if Billy the Kid went to the White House or retired. And Jack Caution would need a popular mayor at his side, a law and order man, the Pink Commish.

The chief judge's chambers filled with cigar smoke. A blue haze floated between Jack Caution and the king.

"Your Honor," Isaac said. "I'd like to shut down the Ali Baba. It's a filthy sink."

"Who's the landlord?"

"Quentin Kahn. He's a pornographer and a pimp. Brings children into the country, sells them off. His henchmen murder Roumanian mules. It's a slaughterhouse, Your Honor. Ali Baba is the home and headquarters of the Knickerbocker Boys."

"That's hearsay, Isaac. You don't have proof."

"I could present you with five or six corpses from potter's field."

"All Geronimo Joneses, eh? But you'd have to trace them back to the Ali Baba. And you can't. So leave it alone."

"Your Honor, I need a vacate order."

"Isaac, I can't undermine the courts as a personal favor to you."

"The voters will support us. I'm on my honeymoon."

"Isaac, I won't sign any order to vacate."

"Then I will. I'll forge your signature," the king said, removing a piece of paper from his pocket and depositing it on Jack Caution's desk.

"You're a scoundrel, Sidel."

"The worst."

"You could go to jail."

"Your Honor, I've already been to jail. It's no big deal." The king uncapped his fountain pen. "Sign!"

Jack Caution took the king's pen, stared at the document on his desk, signed it, and said, "Mr. Mayor, go to hell!"

The king could have gone to Barbarossa, who had a gold shield, but Marilyn the Wild would blame him, she'd conjure up the ghost of Blue Eyes, swear that Isaac was shoving Barbarossa into a battle zone, was dangling him, creating another Manfred Coen. He had to tap-dance very lightly around his daughter. Isaac was afraid of her wrath. And so he had to depend on Wig. They borrowed a pair of sledgehammers from the gardening crew at Gracie Mansion, put them in the trunk of the mayor's limousine, and Isaac got behind the wheel, drove himself and Wig down to the Ali Baba.

Isaac didn't want to scare the prostitutes and the johns. He carried the sledgehammers into the Ali Baba in a big shopping bag. Isaac showed his court order to one of Quentin's geeks, who served as house manager while Quentin was away. The geek was illiterate. His lips kept moving, but he couldn't decipher a word. He started to cry.

"Quent will kill me."

"He's finished, son. There's no more Ali Baba."

Isaac cleared out the customers and the working girls. He and Wig uncovered a curious kind of labyrinth. Half the Ali Baba had never been open to the johns. They found little apartments where the princelings from Ceausescu's palace must have stayed until Black Michael got rid of them with a bodkin. They found a room packed ceiling-high with yellow condoms. They found closets filled with correspondence, including a sheaf of letters from Billy the Kid's grandnephew, Oskar Leviathan, addressed to Quentin Kahn.

Dear Uncle Quentin,

I am so happy in America.

I am saying prayers to God every night.

Mama Rose says I will live in the White House one day with Uncle Billy. I love Mama Rose. I put wet towels on her head when she has the willies. I sing to her when she cries in her sleep.

I miss Aunt Rita. Uncle Billy says I shouldn't write to her. But she is not a bad person. She took me and Cousin Harwood to the movies. Cousin Harwood is not so nice. He steals coins from the candy machine.

If Mama Rose has to go to the hospital again, can I stay with Aunt Rita? . . .

Isaac stuffed the sheaf of letters inside his coat. He and Wig wandered into back rooms where Quentin's whores would hang out when they weren't behind the booths or sitting with johns upstairs in the hot tubs. These back rooms had forlorn cribs and playpens. The whores couldn't afford babysitters and had to entertain their own tots. There were jars of baby food on the shelves, there were rubber animals, and picture books that opened into panoramic jungle scenes. There was the faint perfume of piss and talcum powder.

"Wiggy, I hate this fucking place."

They took the sledgehammers out of the shopping bag and knocked down the walls. The playpens and the cribs sat in a sea of rubble.

They tore through the Ali Baba, waving their hammers like wild men. They destroyed Rita's booth.

I'll show you mine if you show me yours.

They ripped Quentin's own door off its hinges. They demolished his antique desk, a memento from an earlier robber baron. Quentin's safe had already been sacked by someone else. The steel door was unlocked. The shelves were barren except for a few scattered photographs of Margaret Tolstoy and Nina Anghel, both of them with red hair that looked like burning trees attached to their scalps.

They chained a padlock to the front door, then wrapped another chain around the padlock and locked that too. It could have been a religious ceremony. The king was exorcising a dybbuk, shutting down evil spirits in New York.

Reporters were waiting outside the Ali Baba. They swarmed around Isaac and Wig, who looked like angels with sledgehammers, standing in their own dust.

"Mr. Mayor, Mr. Mayor, will you close all the massage parlors and porno mills?"

"Me? I'm not a dictator. I'm just giving notice to Quentin Kahn."

"Didn't he contribute to your campaign?"

"That's his mistake," Isaac said. "Not mine."

"Mr. Mayor, are you signaling to us that this is going to be a hands-on administration?"

"I don't know how to signal," Isaac said.

Wig cleared a path for the king, who could escape reporters but not the PC.

"Get into my car," Sweets said, a dark fury on his face. They got into the back of Sweets' Dodge, but there was hardly any room for them. They were squeezed against the black giant.

"I could arrest both you motherfuckers."

"Sweets," Isaac said, "Wig and me are homeboys. But you're from the Hollows. You have the Revolution in your blood. Shouldn't call us motherfuckers."

"Albert Wiggens," Sweets said, "you should have a little more sense. Taking a sledgehammer to property that doesn't belong to you." He plucked out his commissioner's badge with its five gold points and placed it on the king's lap. "Mr. Mayor, I resign. I'm not going to spend my life chasing you down after each unlawful entry."

"Unlawful?" Isaac said. "I have Jack Caution's signature." He unfolded the order to vacate and handed it to Sweets, who put on his bifocals to examine the document and looked like an enormous, brooding genie let out of a bottle.

"Isaac, that chief judge is nuttier than you are. No warnings and not one arrest. You can't close Quentin Kahn. His lawyers will reopen the Ali Baba in twenty-four hours. And he'll probably sue the shit out of the City . . . Isaac, I let you have Wig, and you involve him in some dumb caper. The FBIs are watching the Ali Baba. They don't need Albert Wiggens."

"Sweets," Isaac said, "LeComte is running Quentin Kahn."

"Then he's Justice's headache . . . damn you, Albert Wiggens, why the hell are you with this man? You used to hate him."

"Still do," said Wig.

"Then collect your pension and disappear."

"It would be like committin' homicide, Sweets. The boss can't see straight. He thinks the world is white."

"Get out of here. Both of you."

Isaac returned the badge to Sweets and followed Wig out of the car.

26

The Ali Baba remained shut. *The Daily News* ran a feature on Isaac's war against prostitution mills. The mayor was photographed with Becky Karp. It was the first glimpse of Rebecca in months. She wore tinted glasses and wasn't sitting in her rocking chair. The pols quickly realized that the éminence grise of the Sidel administration was that corpse, Rebecca Karp. She'd risen from the dead. She sat behind closed doors with Sidel and helped him choose his cadre of commissioners, including Nicholas Bright. Nicholas had no political allies. He didn't vote Republican or Democrat. He didn't vote at all.

Nicholas attacked the Leviathan of New York City, chopped off whole departments, shuffled men and women around. But Isaac would start to dream whenever he had to examine the City's books. He wasn't like Nicholas. He couldn't fight the Leviathan, claw by claw. The king had too many details inside his skull. He couldn't stop thinking of that little Leviathan, *Oskar*. He would scan Oskar's letters in the middle of a meeting and permit his budget people to talk until their cheeks turned blue. There would be a shortfall in fiscal eighty-six unless Nicholas continued to chop and chop.

The Sidel administration began to find its very own shape. There was Becky Karp in the background. There was

Nicholas and his brother Wilson, the ghostwriter who was sort of Isaac's secretary. There was his bodyguard, Albert Wiggens, and two mysterious aides, a fat man called William and a boy with a runny nose. They would brew coffee, fix rebellious machines, arrange for homeless men and women to tour the mansion.

Gracie was growing into a little Versailles. Isaac encouraged his chef to prepare a battery of lunches and dinners for the homeless. The king himself ate at these lunches. And his "democratic dinners" were soon a daily ritual. The cardinal would stand in line with the homeless and suck on a cigarette. He preferred Isaac's table to the Four Seasons. He could wolf his lasagna and guzzle two glasses of wine.

Billy the Kid came down from Albany to be photographed with all these beggars. He sat near Isaac with a paper plate and a plastic knife and fork.

"Been waiting for you, Billy, waiting to give you this." Isaac jumped up, pecked Billy between the eyes, and sat down again. "I always kiss a man before I fuck him over. I like to bring my enemies very close."

Billy's hand was shaking. Isaac had to cut the lasagna for him, feed the governor like a boy.

"You had Rita killed, didn't you, Billy? You gave the order. You panicked. You had fucking presidential fever."

"You're berserk. I could have you institutionalized, Sidel."

"I'd welcome it, Billy. I'll take the bed next to your niece. Rose Leviathan-Smith."

"Shut your mouth."

"Judah was the cutout, the safety value. He was your own little mailman. He talks to Quentin Kahn, and Rita is dead. How could she have harmed you? Oskar was crazy about her. What did he write? *I miss Aunt Rita.* She was more like a mama than Rose could ever be. You son of a bitch."

"Not so loud, Sidel."

"Come on. No one's listening. People love to eat."

"While you conduct a kangaroo court."

"I'm fond of kangaroos," Isaac said. "My favorite animals.

Did you ever see them fight? They can punch with their hands and feet."

"Sidel, let's go upstairs to your study."

"No. I insist. I do all my dirty deals in the dining room."

"I'm your master, Sidel. I sit on the Financial Control Board. I can throw your City into continual darkness."

"Try," Isaac said.

Billy the Kid coughed into his napkin, stood up, and stepped out onto the mayor's porch. Isaac finished his lasagna, had some coffee and cake, then joined Billy outside. The Gov had turned off all the lights. Isaac sat with him on the porch steps, watching a tiny whirlpool in the waters of Hell Gate. The governor's lips were moving.

"Can't hear you, Billy. The wind is ripping too hard."

"I said *blackmail*."

"Now there's a twist to the caper, your very own whirlpool, but I'll strangle you, Billy, before I get sucked in."

"Oskar was lending them his pocket money, and then it became more than a loan. Rita brought them around, that fool brother of hers and the boy."

"William and Harwood."

"Exactly. Rose was in and out of the hospital. I would borrow Rita from Quentin, ask her to babysit whenever Rose was gone. There was nothing crooked about it. I paid her, of course."

"You didn't need Rita. Oskar Leviathan could have stayed with you."

"That was impossible."

"Yeah. You're a regular nomad. You shuffle from your mansion in Albany to your town house in New York. You have an army of chauffeurs and maids. And a wife, Billy. What about your wife? You couldn't afford to advertise Oskar Leviathan, the lost boy who was slightly illegal. So you invited Rita into Rose's house. Some rendezvous. Did you sleep with her, Billy?"

"Once or twice."

"Cost Rita her life. And don't start your blackmail stories.

William and Harwood were always looking for cash. They would have robbed Rose's faucets if they could. They rifled Oskar's piggy bank, bullied him a little, and you tossed them out of the house. William, Harwood, *and* Rita. And then you got scared. The Democrats' dark horse. You were dreaming Pennsylvania Avenue, the Rose Garden, the Lincoln Bedroom, one more mansion in your curriculum vitae. The White House, the bloody White House."

"Could have been worse," said Billy the Kid. "Don't you play pure at heart. You've bedded down with the Mafia. Your mistress is LeComte's pet rattlesnake. And the angels you collect have a mediocre survival record."

"Manfred Coen."

"I'll break you, Sidel, if you start to meddle. This talk never took place. I had nothing to do with Rita. She was Oskar's governess for a while. That's all you'll get out of me."

Billy the Kid marched back inside, grabbed his coat, shook hands with some of the homeless men, and left the mayor's house.

Isaac crossed his legs in the cold and started to meditate. But he couldn't reach the white glow of alpha. Coen could find alpha in a pingpong ball. Isaac couldn't. But he could hear the slap of the porch door, feel a shadow sit down next to him in some kind of negative alpha, a soft dark glow. It was Becky Karp in her rocking chair.

"Isaac, you'll have to give the Gov what he wants."

"He had a friend of mine killed. Rita Mae Robinson."

"It makes no difference. You're not a cop anymore. You owe your allegiance to him."

"He's a psychotic prick."

"True. But that psychotic prick is the titular head of your Party. You can't escape it, Isaac."

"Then I'll escape him and the Party."

"My poor silly man," said Rebecca, rocking above Isaac, who was still on the steps. "You'll turn your life into a rough little game of the hounds and the hare. You can hide in your mansion, Isaac, but the hounds will get you. It will be a very slow kill. They'll corner you, raise their hind legs to pee, cry at the moon, and tear your limbs. It could last for months. You won't even feel yourself bleeding until it's too late."

Isaac searched the dark of the porch for Rebecca's eyes. He discovered two warm white spots. "Becky, will you be with the hounds or the hare?"

"The hare, Isaac. But I can't help you. The hounds will eat me alive."

27

The hounds arrived before the end of the meal, looking like real-estate barons. Judah, Jason, Papa Cassidy, and Quentin Kahn.

"Gentlemen," Isaac said to the first three barons. "I won't talk to you in front of that piece of shit."

"Quentin is with us now," said Papa.

"He's moved out of pornography," said Jason Figgs.

"But he'll be sad without his yellow condoms."

"Isaac," said Judah Bellow. "You closed the Ali Baba. He didn't fight you, and he could have. But we must insist. You took something that belongs to him. A batch of personal letters. They're his private property. Letters from a certain Oskar Leviathan."

"That's lovely, Judah. A certain Oskar Leviathan who happens to be the grandnephew of Billy the Kid."

"You don't have any proof," said Jason Figgs.

"Yeah, Jason. Boys can disappear just like Geronimo Jones . . . fuck all of you," Isaac said. "I mean it. You can be the hounds, but you won't catch shit."

"He's hallucinating," said Quentin Kahn. "Sidel likes to talk in his sleep."

"I'm going into alpha. That's the only weapon I have against you guys."

"The letters, please," said Judah. "We can get our own injunction. You have stolen property, Mr. Mayor."

"Ah, Judah," Isaac said. "You were with the gods. Worked under Emeric Gray. And now you're Billy the Kid's mailman and messenger boy . . . you're trespassing, gentlemen. You'll have to leave."

"That's preposterous," said Papa Cassidy. "We're all taxpayers. This house belongs to us."

"You're wrong. It's open to the public by invitation only. I could give you a guided tour, Papa. But you might not get through it."

The barons put on their winter hats. "We'll see you in court, Sidel," said Jason Figgs.

"I don't think so. Oskar would have to take the stand, talk about Bucharest and all the different mothers and fathers and uncles he's had. Good night, gentlemen."

The king walked upstairs to his bedroom. He had a combination lock on his door that couldn't be opened with any key in the world. It was designed to thwart assassins who crept into the house. The door itself could withstand explosions and earthquakes. But none of the armor soothed the king. His bedroom had all the coziness of a tank.

He caught a glimpse of himself on the ten o'clock news. His hair had gone white in a week. He was hurtling through time at a faster clip than other men. His coronation was destroying the king.

He got into his pajamas and started reading *The Great Gatsby*. He couldn't quite recover from the shame of being a college dropout. He knew Gatsby by heart, had studied it like a Talmudist. But he still felt deprived, longed for some college instructor to reveal the book to him, illuminate Scott Fitzgerald's lines. Gatsby seemed closer to Isaac than his own skin, the guy who rose out of nothingness, a bootlegger with a couple of months at Oxford behind him.

Wig knocked on the king's door at two o'clock in the morning. "You got a guest."

Isaac put on his robe and came downstairs. Judah Bellow

sat in the living room all alone. Isaac gave him a glass of schnapps. Judah's fingers were frozen. Isaac crouched in front of the fireplace, built a pyramid of paper and logs, so that Judah could warm his hands in the fire.

"I didn't care about the others," Isaac said. "They're Billy's. But you shouldn't have done his bidding, you shouldn't have sentenced Rita to death."

"There was no other way. Billy was beside himself."

"You could have delivered your message and then told her to run."

"Fat chance," Judah said.

"Your own daughter killed herself. Quentin finds you a pen pal, Natalia, and Rita is the letterbox. But Natalia dies of pneumonia, and things got confused in your head. You blamed Rita, right?"

"Wrong. I pleaded with Billy. I stated my case. I was awful fond of her, Isaac. Nothing sexual. She never stripped for me inside her booth. But the Gov was adamant. Said he couldn't be safe with Rita around. Her brother was blackmailing him."

"And you believed Billy the Kid? . . . I met Black Michael in Carcassonne. He told me about the troika."

Judah quit rubbing his hands in front of the fire and licked his schnapps like a cat. "What troika?"

"You, Michael, and Quentin Kahn."

"Michael's a murderer with a very quick imagination. There was no troika."

"But why would he imagine himself into a partnership with you? To tease me, Judah? Throw me off the track?"

"To beguile you. He fancies himself a sorcerer. Isaac, he's my coach too. Did he ever hypnotize you across a pingpong table? Did he ever make your whole body rigid, turn you to stone for half an hour?"

"No. He was stingy with his powers. But there was a troika. Quentin was a thug with a college education. And Michael was an outcast. Without you they could never get near Billy the Kid. You arranged all the marriages. You got Quentin into the Christy Mathewson Club, introduced him to Schyler Knott. You're Knickerbocker number one."

"Nonsense," said Judah Bellow. "I don't even understand baseball. I never did."

"Was it money problems, Judah? Ali Baba was the perfect cash cow. No receipts. No records. Nothing. And you welcomed Quent into your own little club of barons. You took his filthy lucre. And you conspired with Black Michael, you profited from Ceausescu's jewels . . . I didn't close the Ali Baba. I just delivered the final kiss. I'm a public servant. I don't have the mentality of a pharaoh. I was fumbling in the dark. You figured I'd go to Jack Caution. You anticipated it. Eddie Royal ransacked the Baba, picked it clean. But he forgot about Oskar Leviathan's letters. He didn't even know that Oskar could write."

"Isaac, sooner or later you'll have to give the letters back."

"Nah, Judah. I treasure them. I read Oskar's letters all the time."

"They're dangerous for you."

"What isn't? I put my nose into everything. That's my nature . . . ah, you should receive a memorandum from the mayor's office. I typed it myself. I'm tossing you and Jason and Papa off the Landmarks Commission."

"We're your main builders, Isaac. You won't have much of a commission."

Judah finished his schnapps and went out into the night. It was a quarter to three. Isaac cursed himself. The trivia of his job, the sheer weight of it, was sinking him into forgetfulness. The Sidel administration was incomplete. The king had neglected his most important commissioner.

He couldn't find his bodyguard. He dressed, got past the gatekeeper, and drove down to the Christys. Nothing had changed in the last month. The club was still boarded up. Isaac took out his pocket flashlight and let himself in through the cellar door.

Schyler was sitting in the same royal chair. His beard was

a little longer. He had cartons of Chinese food at his feet. Ah, he might have been a lot healthier on a diet of Milky Ways.

Isaac shone the light in Schyler's face. Schyler blinked.

"Jesus," Isaac said, "why the hell are you here? You're not a fugitive. No one's even looking for the Knickerbocker Boys. No one gives a damn."

"But I do. I'm not reopening the Christys. There's nothing out there for me."

"So you sit here like Rip Van Winkle. You give up the fucking fight. You're a twelfth-generation New Yorker."

"Thirteenth," Schyler said.

"You're related to Peter Stuyvesant, for Christ's sake."

"Peter Minuit."

"The biggest landgrabber in history. He robbed the Indians blind."

"He was just a speculator. Like your friends, Jason Figgs and Judah Bellow."

"They're not my friends, and I threw them off Landmarks, together with Papa Cassidy . . . Schyler, you've been a ghost long enough. I need you with the living. I won't have a Landmarks Commission without you. The pharaohs will steal my pants."

"Isaac, I'll landmark every window, every wall. The pharaohs will have to build in hell."

"That's fine with me."

Isaac returned to the mansion. It was almost five in the morning. He couldn't sleep. He had a frozen Milky Way out of the fridge. His bodyguard arrived a few minutes after him. They both munched on Milky Ways.

"Brother Isaac, are you gonna ask me where I been?"

"I don't have the courage."

"Yes you do."

"Then I'd say you've been settling accounts with at least one of the Knickerbocker Boys. Quentin Kahn."

"He was getting it off with some bitch at his suite in the Pierre. I snuck past security. I picked Quent's lock, stood outside the boudoir. I let him have his love grunts. He came out of the bedroom whistling to himself. I grabbed ol' Quent and pushed him into the toilet. 'Rita,' I said. One word. He pissed on his own leg. I offed him. Nearly pulled his neck out of its socket. He perished with his eyes open. You gonna call the police, or should I do it?"

"Ah, let's wait," Isaac said, sleepy all of a sudden. He climbed upstairs to his bedroom, but he couldn't recall the combination. It was Albert Wiggens who had to monkey with the king's lock.

28

Smut Lord Tycoon Found Dead at the Pierre.

Quentin's picture was on the front page of the *Times*. "Police suspect foul play." He was thirty-nine years old. He'd attended Swarthmore, Williams, and Wesleyan. He was worth close to a hundred million dollars. His real name wasn't Quentin Kahn. He was born Louis Lister near the Bronx Zoo. His dad peddled shoelaces and died in a madhouse. His mom had deserted him when he was five. He'd been an entrepreneur at eleven, controlling a small monopoly of newspaper routes. He'd never finished high school. But he changed his name, invented new parents for himself and a high school diploma, and got into Swarthmore, paying his own tuition. But the college soon discovered lapses in the education of *their* Louis Lister/Quentin Kahn. And Quent forged his way into Williams, then Wesleyan, then returned to Manhattan island, where he opened a massage parlor at nineteen.

The Bronx's own Jay Gatsby. Isaac preferred Louis Lister to Quentin Kahn. He was going to make a pilgrimage to Bronx Park, seek out the apartment house where Louis was born. Could it have been an Emeric Gray? Probably not. Emeric had never wandered that deep into the Bronx.

No one from the NYPD arrived to arrest Wig. The D.A. didn't even ask to question Isaac. Papa Cassidy called, seemed very humble. "I won't complain about getting bumped off Landmarks, Mr. Mayor. I serve at your pleasure. And I'm proud of that."

It was all blather. Papa was backing off. And Isaac began to wonder if the whole damn world was blind. Wasn't anybody gonna arrest Wig? Isaac studied his own detail. Larry Quinn, who was constantly fighting with Wig, now purred in his presence. The maids brought Wig's breakfast up to him on a silver tray. The tour guides saluted him. The pols who visited Isaac couldn't take their eyes off Albert Wiggens.

Isaac slapped his own head. "I'm a fool," he muttered. The town knew that Wig had waxed Quentin Kahn. People were frightened of the Purple Gang. Wig could walk into the Pierre and kill any pharaoh. The Purple Gang was now in residence at Gracie Mansion.

Isaac went down to City Hall with Wig. The reporters, photographers, secretaries, and guards all buzzed behind Isaac's back. "The Purples are coming, the Purples are coming."

Isaac canceled his appointments. But there was an unexpected guest waiting in the corridors. Rose Leviathan-Smith. He had Wig escort her into his office. She'd aged, just like the king. Her iron-colored hair was turning brittle. The tic in her cheek was more pronounced.

"Sit down, Mrs. Smith. Can I get you something? Coffee? Tea? Orange juice? A Milky Way?"

"I think I'll stand, thank you," she said. Her eyes had stopped focusing. She'd glance at the mayor, but her mind could have been on another planet. "You have ruined my life, sir."

Isaac wasn't sure what he had done, but he had the urge to apologize. That death at the Pierre couldn't have ricocheted off Rose.

"I'm sorry, Mrs. Smith."

"You compromised Oskar, stole his letters, I believe."

"It's part of an investigation. I wouldn't hurt the boy."

"But you already did. You understood the terms of his adoption. We didn't hide the irregularities from you. Oskar isn't really mine. The governor had to protect himself. He took Oskar away from me."

"Ah, I'll return the letters, Rose."

"It's too late."

She was holding a pistol in her hand. It could have been a toy, or one of those derringers that gamblers were always using in cowboy films. Isaac wouldn't flinch. But Wig leapt in front of the king, knocked him to the ground, offered his own body as a target to Rose Leviathan-Smith.

"Ah, Wiggy. She's distressed. The woman won't shoot."

There was a soft clap, like the cry of a hummingbird. Isaac thought the sound had come from Rose herself until his ear started to sting. Rose dropped her gun onto the mayor's carpet.

Isaac and Wig both climbed to their feet.

"Rose, I promise you. I'll get your boy back."

He picked up Rose's gun in a handkerchief and locked it inside his desk. He had Wig accompany her home to Yonkers in a police car. He called Billy the Kid, but he couldn't get through. The Gov had removed himself from the mayor of New York.

Isaac looked up. There was a vulture at his door. LeComte.

"Your ear is bleeding."

"I scratched myself."

But LeComte borrowed a first-aid kit from one of Isaac's secretaries and dressed the injured ear.

"That'll do," LeComte said. "But you'll have to see a doctor. Wouldn't want you to die of blood poisoning."

"It's a masterpiece," Isaac said, looking at his ear in the mirror. "Frederic, you told Sweets not to arrest Wig."

"Let's say I discouraged him. He doesn't have much of a case. You'll swear that Wig was at the mansion all night."

"I can't. I was out, visiting with Schyler Knott."

"But Sweets doesn't know that. And I didn't volunteer the information."

"Frederic, shouldn't we go outside and sit in the park? My

office has to be bugged. How many intelligence divisions are monitoring me?"

"Five or six, including Justice. But my sweepers neutralized all the other bugs. I look after you, Isaac. I consider you my own child."

"I'm twenty years older than you are."

"You're still my child."

"Yeah, that's how it is in the secret services."

"Justice doesn't have a secret service. It's not included in our mandate. We have undercover agents. But that's another story."

"I'll bet. Talk to me about Black Michael. And no legends this time. You could have solved the case of the Knickerbocker Boys in a week. Your wizards are the best in the world."

"You must be mellowing. That's the first compliment we ever got out of you."

"Lemme finish. They could have scratched under the fingernails and found whole histories for each Geronimo Jones."

"But we knew their histories beforehand."

"Yeah," Isaac said. "Yokels from Roumania. Farm boys who were trained by the Securitate and moved into Ceausescu's palace. And all they could dream of was America."

"Mr. Mayor, that's a tough dream to beat."

"Then why didn't you stop the carnage? What was so important about having them killed?"

"They were sacrificial lambs. We couldn't interfere. We might have lost Michael."

"So you had an informant inside the Securitate. Big deal. Your own captain or a colonel. Frederick, wake up. It's honeymoon time. The KGB honchos can't survive without their Cadillacs. They're moving into General Motors and IBM."

"You're the one who's archaic. Forget about spies. Michael's a mercenary. He does odd jobs for us. He's a kamikaze who always comes out alive. Works for Air Force Intelligence, the DEA, whoever needs him. If there's a Turkish arms smuggling ring we want to stop, we send in Black

Michael. A traficante in Panama who's particularly obnoxious. Michael takes him out. Doesn't even ask for dollars."

"Why should he? You let him collect his plunder however he can. I'd call him a pirate. And his lucky medal is Margaret Tolstoy."

"But Margaret might not be so lucky for him, Mr. Mayor."

"They're a brother and sister act. Playmates from the Bucharest orphan asylum."

"Margaret's the only one he can trust."

"She's his bodyguard," said Isaac.

The crown prince and cultural commissar of Justice started to laugh. He looked like a clever marionette wrapped in blue. "Michael doesn't need a bodyguard. She's his babysitter . . . and his executioner."

"I don't get it."

"Michael's a temperamental bastard. A murder artist. He might go over the edge. And if he becomes an embarrassment to us, well, Margaret has orders to terminate . . ."

"Orders to terminate," Isaac said. "Congratulations, Frederic. You don't miss a fucking trick. And what happens if it's Margaret who becomes an embarrassment? Is there a double bind? Does Black Michael get to terminate her?"

"That's not in the current curriculum."

"Then what is? Your commandos have a base inside the Ali Baba, and when I go through the premises with a sledgehammer, that base is already gone."

"Oh, we knew you were coming, Isaac. We closed shop, that's all."

"But why were you there in the first place? To protect Black Michael? Help him off the Roumanians, huh?"

"We had to control him. He was running wild. And we never cared much for Quentin Kahn. He was a bad egg. We were glad when you got rid of him."

"I didn't get rid of him," Isaac said.

"Really? Shades of the Purple Gang."

"Frederic, don't confuse me with your stinking myths."

"Aren't we bashful this morning. If you'd rather not take

credit, that's all right. But Albert Wiggens is also an artist, blind as he is."

"He's my bodyguard," said the king.

"I understand. Your bodyguard."

"I thought you were building a case against Quentin Kahn's children's market."

"We were, Isaac. We stopped the flow, didn't we?"

"What happens to Oskar Leviathan?"

"Oskar? He's off the screen at the moment. In transit somewhere. Don't worry. We'll find him. But you shouldn't have provoked Billy the Kid . . . Isaac, I'll have to relieve you of Oskar's letters. We can't have them floating around. They might surface one day and damage Billy."

"Cross my heart," Isaac said. "I'd never smear the Gov. Return Oskar Leviathan to Rose Smith, and you can have the letters. But I'll need a favor."

"We're always good at granting a mayor's wish list."

"I'd like you to spring Herman Melville."

The cultural commissar stared at Isaac. "Will you repeat that?"

"Hector Ramirez. Calls himself Herman Melville. He's in the hole at MCC. Brained a narc with a baseball bat."

"Then how can I help him, Isaac?"

"He was one of my Delancey Giants. Best natural hitter I ever had. Get him into witness protection. I don't care. Work a miracle."

"Isaac, I have a limited repertoire when it comes to convicted felons."

"You're the Justice Department. You can do whatever you want . . . where's Margaret?"

"I'll talk to this Hector Ramirez, but I can't promise."

"Where's Margaret?"

"Who knows? Somewhere east or west of Carcassonne."

"Good-bye, Frederic. Thanks for the tip."

He left City Hall and returned to the mansion, sat in his living room like a blind man. He didn't even open his eyes when Larry Quinn said, "Your Honor, there's a woman at the gate.

I've seen her once. At your daughter's wedding. She's gorgeous and she's funny-looking. You'd swear she was bald. Says she's Anastasia."

"Show her in."

29

Isaac wanted to be Michael the murder artist and dispatch this woman with her helmet of short gray hair. She'd come to Gracie without her wig. He had to hold himself back from hitting her. Love had turned him into a blind man . . . and a pig. It was all a great big bloody game. He'd have to woo Margaret with a hatchet in his hand. But she didn't have the look of a temptress in her eye.

"Margaret," he said, "did you bring your chocolate brick? I think I'll have a bite."

She reached into her handbag, broke off a bit of chocolate, and fed it to Isaac. He was much less giddy with that jolt of bitter cocoa.

"Isaac," she said, "it's like Little Angel Street . . . the mansion, I mean. I could shut my eyes and swear I was in Odessa."

"Odessa, Margaret? Make yourself at home."

"We had our own little park . . . and a porch. Our gatekeeper was Albanian. He deserted us when Uncle Ferdinand ran out of money."

"But you've been here before. Why the sudden revelation?"

"That's the beauty of it, Isaac. I looked at your mansion and it triggered something. I fell down a hole."

"Yeah," Isaac said. "Like Alice in Wonderland. But Alice didn't wear a Glock."

"You're so suspicious, darling. I'll never tire of you."

"LeComte sent you. You're his little siren."

Margaret reached into her handbag again, pulled out a plastic envelope, and tossed it at the king. Isaac plucked the envelope out of the air and started to tremble. It was filled with baseball cards. Isaac could see the luminous colors inside that plastic pouch. He was holding a fortune in his hands. A rare DiMaggio. The best Willie Mays. Shoeless Joe Jackson from Fatima cigarettes. Lou Gehrig from Goudy gum. And then Isaac's fucking heart stood still. Mingled with this dream team was another team: forgotten men out of the dinosaur leagues. But these cards had a crispness and a telegraphic bite. "Tobias Little, Batter. Louisville." "Monte Ward, Pitcher. Providence." "Jay Penny, Champion Base Ball Catcher." Isaac's very own Knickerbocker Boys. They all wore the old nineteenth-century style of cap with a flattened top and a hard bill. They looked like fraternity brothers who belonged to some forbidden dueling club. But none of them had scars on his face.

Isaac was in a frozen realm. He could neither accept the cards nor relinquish them.

"Anastasia," he growled. "I was just with LeComte. He could have given me the cards himself."

"They're not LeComte's cards," she said. "They're a present from Black Michael. He took them off a drug dealer in the Hamptons," she said.

"Michael's in America?"

"As of yesterday," she said.

"And he finished the dealer for LeComte . . . or some of LeComte's agencies. The cards were spoils of war, part of the treasure he collected for himself. Does he know how valuable they are? Why is he so generous?"

"He wants to make peace, so he won't have to kill you."

"Yeah," Isaac said. "Black Michael's never harmed a pupil of his . . . Anastasia, what do the cards mean? That if I interfere with him again, he'll have to kill me. The cards are a kite, something to remind me how careful Michael is, how well he can choose. In that case, I can't accept his gift. Because I will interfere with Michael until one of us dies."

"Darling, didn't I tell you? You'll have to kill me first."

Isaac dropped the plastic pouch onto his living room table and stared into Anastasia's almond eyes. "Maybe I will."

She reached into her bag a third time. Isaac was expecting her Glock. But she moved much too swiftly for him. He blinked once and she was wearing that orange wig from Carcassonne.

He didn't even realize that he'd made a fist. And Isaac, who'd never been rough with a woman, hit her in the face. Margaret didn't buckle. She absorbed the blow. It was Isaac who felt weak in the legs. He was like a king with one leprous fist.

"Anastasia . . ."

She fell without warning onto the king's couch. He reached over and rocked her in his arms, kissed Anastasia's eyes. She opened them for Isaac.

"Darling, I never even noticed. Your ear's all white."

" 'S nothing," Isaac said. "A little tattoo from Oskar Leviathan's mom. Anastasia, I . . ."

"Shhh," she said. "You're a wife beater. I'll have to get used to it."

"Couldn't you stay here?" he said. "On Little Angel Street?"

"I have to get back to Michael."

"Ah, the immortal one. The new Captain America. Tackles terrorists, yakuza, arms dealers, traficantes for Uncle Sam. LeComte told me about it. Michael has complete immunity. Are you his accomplice?"

"Michael works alone."

"How's Nina Anghel?"

"She can't quite recover from that blindfold match with you. And you're not even a champion."

"But she shouldn't play pingpong in a mask. Margaret,

does Michael have a code name . . . when he's on his suicide missions for Uncle Sam?"

"Black Star Galactica."

"Lovely. Black Star Galactica. That's grand. He is like a galaxy of black stars. Full of bitter explosions. Billions of light-years away. I can't read Michael. I can't read you. It's like an endless world of mirrors. Margaret, I'm floating in negative space, and I'll never get out."

"Darling," she said, "I better go."

The king couldn't seize her wrists. He was still petrified. She stood up and wobbled out of the room.

"Darling, better lock your doors while Michael is in town."

"Ah, my bedroom is fortified . . . you are his accomplice, aren't you? One of his black stars."

But Anastasia was gone. The king looked down and saw the plastic pouch on his table. A galaxy of baseball players.

30

Isaac was sitting in the dark when Wig returned from Yonkers. That Tolstoy woman had been in the house. She always left a path of perfume. It was like sniffing wildflowers in a gigantic jar. Wig couldn't get away from that smell. It could hypnotize a gang of monkeys . . . or a man. And it was deadlier in the dark.

Wig went to the main switch and put on all the lights in the house. The mansion bloomed like its own wildflower.

"You're wasting electricity," Isaac groaned from his couch.

"And you're wasting yourself."

"That's none of your business, Mr. Wiggens."

"You are my business, Massa Isaac. I'm your bodyguard."

"Is Rose all right?" the king asked, coming out of his gloom.

"I fixed her a cup of tea, put her to bed."

"Wiggy, Michael's around. And we can't lay a finger on him. He's like a diplomat . . . or a pirate king."

"Fuck him. I eat pirates for lunch."

"But Uncle Sam is on his side."

"Then I'll have to do Uncle and his pirate."

Wig went upstairs to his room. He had to hug the banisters, or he might have plunged into the stairwell. He'd burnt his hand on Mrs. Smith's stove, because he couldn't see the wisps of fire. He'd cracked two of her cups making coffee. He'd spilled sugar on his shoe. The blindness would come with its own crippling speed, catch Wig unawares. He was a bodyguard who couldn't even guard his own body. He would fumble and fall.

Enough niggers had died! Archie had offed Rita, so Wig offed Arch. He wasn't proud of shooting Archie in the mouth. But he'd gone into Whitey's mecca, the Hotel Pierre, and got Rita's main assassin, ol' Quentin Kahn. And now he had to find that Roumanian mother, Black Michael. Like black was mean, or black was bad.

Wiggy must have nodded off in his street clothes. Tulip, the nigger girl, woke him with a cup of coffee, a croissant, and a pot of marmalade. She'd have crawled under the covers with him if he'd asked. But she wasn't *his* fox, only a maid in the king's house. He didn't know what to do about Harwood. William couldn't raise the boy. William was a buffoon.

He was smothering that croissant in marmalade when he happened to look up. He could make out a fat man in the morning sun. With all the wisdom of his good eye. But he didn't have a good eye. He had to guess at Brother William from his thick outline.

"If you're bringing me bad news, Will, you'll regret it. Here, have some of my croissant."

"Can't eat that Frenchy cake. It crumbles in my mouth . . . Harwood got a phone call this mornin'. Real early. And he just walked out."

"You didn't think to follow him?"

"I was busy with somethin' else."

"Like climbing on one of the maids."

"No, Wig. I was paintin' the porch roof, winterizing it."

"In January? Winter will be gone by the time you're through . . . where was Harwood going?"

"He didn't say. But Harwood wouldn't move unless it was rainin' money somewhere."

"He aint supposed to leave this mansion."

"I couldn't prevent him, Wiggy."

Wig dreamed of the territory in front of him and managed to cuff William on the ear. "Like you couldn't prevent your sister from dying, huh? . . . Who am I, Will?"

"The Purple Gang."

"And what's the Purples' strongest point?"

"Killin' people."

"Now surprise me, William. Did Harwood say anything before he left?"

"He mentioned a pingpong ball."

Wig measured the air like a stalking bird and plucked William's throat. "Who plays pingpong, huh?"

"Isaac."

"Who else?"

"Michael Cuza . . . King Carol."

"And you let Harwood fall into Carol's hands?" Wig could barely see a big fat blubbering face.

"I forgot all about Carol."

"Go on. Get out."

He didn't run to Isaac. Wig had his own war to play out. He put on his ankle holster and his Glock, got a cab at the gate, started downtown to the Ali Baba. It was only a hunch. Black Michael could have lured Harwood inside that haunted house. And then Wig muttered to himself, *It's me he wants.*

The king's bodyguard rode uptown to Convent Avenue. There was no one inside his crib, but he could feel a certain presence, as if the Devil had come to town and parked his ass close to Albert Wiggens. He checked the fridge. He still had his stash of Milky Ways. It was freezing in his crib. And if he hadn't been such a blind man, he would have realized a little sooner that the window was open. Now he could recognize Black Michael's technique. That open window was an invitation for Wig to climb up to the roof. His whole damn future depended on some fire escape.

He stepped outside the window, stood on that metal landing, which had already begun to rock. There were white curtains around him, billowing sheets stretched across endless clotheslines in the back yard. They looked like the haphazard sails of a pirate ship.

Wig climbed that lunatic ladder and arrived at the roof. Black Michael stood with a cigarette in his mouth. He had Harwood in front of him, with the point of a pigsticker scratching Harwood's throat. Michael was only a couple of feet away.

"Ah, you're early," Michael said. "Congratulations. I wasn't expecting you for another hour."

"Let the boy go," Wig said. He didn't reach for his Glock. He could have rolled onto the tarred floor, got out his belly gun, but Harwood might not have survived that scramble. The boy was crying, and Wig wanted to clap his hands over his ears, because the sound was ripping at his heart. He was the only papa Harwood would ever have.

"Let him go."

"Couldn't," Michael said. "You'd kill me. You're a notorious outlaw."

"Harwood never hurt you."

"But you did. You walked into a fancy hotel and made Quent give up his ghost. Personally, I'm rather glad. But he was my partner, Wig. And what will people think of me? That I couldn't even protect my own partner? It's bad for business."

"I'm here, aint I, Michael? You can have me."

"That's much too simple. Bang bang. Wig is dead. Michael shoots the Purple Gang. I need a bit more adventure. What if Harwood and I climb onto the ledge and you have to capture us? It would be like a game of tag."

"You can fuck yourself, Mr. Black Michael."

"Mustn't curse, Wig. I hold all the cards. There's no more Harwood if my elbow should slip."

Wig beckoned Black Michael with his hands. "Come to me, bro'. Do me with your dagger. I aint shy."

But Michael shoved Harwood onto the lip of the roof, kept him from falling, then climbed up, balancing himself like an acrobat with the blade of his hand.

Motherfucking maniac, Wig mumbled to himself. He had sun spots in his eyes. And that reflection off the white sheets sickened him. He had to face an eternity of clotheslines.

"Waiting for you, Wig."

He growled deep inside his throat. He wasn't going to let a Roumanian child stealer mock him in front of the boy.

"Harwood," he said. "Hold on. I'm coming up to meet ya."

He stepped onto that narrow lip. He didn't look down. But the sun and the pull of rope between the buildings made him dizzy.

He looked into the fierce blue of Michael's eyes and all the dizziness went away. He was dueling with the Devil. But it was peculiar, because it seemed to Wig that Michael was holding him, keeping him on that ledge, with the power of his eyeballs. Black Michael had him on a string, and Wig was doing his own dumb dance.

"Michael," he said, "you're mine."

"Yes," Michael said in a tender voice, a voice Wig might have used with Rita when he was courting her. Michael had some powerful shit, like voodoo, and Wig was flooded with a crazy kind of peace. The steel band had gone right out of his head.

He reached toward Harwood and fell.

He didn't moan about his miserable life. He was Icarus, the guy who was destined to fall from roofs. His ears swelled with blood. He heard a great whooshing sound, and he wondered if God was a baritone or if that Devil on the roof was playing one more trick. He'd bump, bump into clotheslines, and the white sheets would cling to him like so many parachutes. But nothing could break his fall or oblige him to black out. He was as lucid as a church bell. Detective Lieutenant Albert Wiggens, Disabled. On special assignment to the Honorable Isaac Sidel. The mayor's own marshal. Black Icarus. Couldn't live or die.

PART SEVEN

31

It was Barbarossa who knocked on the king's door. No one else dared summon him out of bed. Isaac traveled to Harlem Hospital in his bathrobe, with Barbarossa behind the wheel. Wig had been lying six or seven hours in his own back yard, bundled up in clotheslines. It was Harwood who finally claimed him, called the police, after hiding on the roof. He was waiting at the hospital for Isaac and Barbarossa, with red marks on his throat, his mouth a bitter blue, his hazel eyes without luster, his fingers frozen. Isaac gave him gloves to wear, and lent him Barbarossa's overcoat, said one word—"Michael"—and the boy began to cry.

"Mr. Isaac, that man say, 'Little brother, don't move.' I couldn't help Wiggy. I couldn't save him."

"Joey," Isaac whispered, "the kid's in a trance. Will you get a doc for him? I have to look for *Lieutenant Wiggens*."

Isaac had never called him that. Lieutenant Wiggens. He found Wig in the emergency ward, inside some derelict closet, with Sweets and the hospital chaplain hovering around him. Sweets was holding Wiggy's hand.

"Don't you die on me, you hear? You're our last commando, Wig."

Sweets glanced up at Isaac with a fury on his face. He whispered something to the chaplain, then motioned to Isaac

with one of his huge paws. They convened on the far side of
the closet, Sweets towering above the closet's canvas walls.

"I gave him to you," Sweets said. "It was supposed to be
his glory hour. Wig shouldn't have been out on any roof."

"Black Michael conned the boy, kidnapped—"

"Black Michael's your coach."

"He's also coaching Billy the Kid and Judah Bellow."

"Not anymore. I banned him from New York City."

"He's FBI," Isaac said. "A one-man task force. LeComte
sends him on suicide missions."

"He should have kept away from Wig."

"Banish him," Isaac said. "You're the PC."

"I am not. I'm a floater. You never swore me in."

"That's ridiculous," Isaac said. "Everybody knows you're
my Commish. Who cares about a ceremony?"

"I care."

Sweets turned his back on the mayor, shoved between the
canvas walls, and went to Wig, while Isaac stood at the edge
of nowhere, the pariah king.

Wig had his own wheelchair within a week. A deputy inspector arrived at the hospital, got Wig into his dress uniform,
and drove him down to the Blue Room with all his medals
and a pair of white gloves. All the pols and Manhattan moguls
kept pumping his right and left hand.

Wig stopped shaking hands after a while. He didn't want to
soil his gloves. He sat next to the Commish, Carlton Montgomery III, Carlton's wife, and Carlton's three little girls,
while Isaac stood under the City's seal and swore Carlton in
as his police commissioner. The wife was called Florence,
and she'd come out of the same aristocracy as Sweets.

She brought Wig a glass of punch and an almond cake. She
had high cheekbones like Rita Mae. Wig was almost in love
with her, but he wouldn't have messed around with Sweets'
wife.

"I'm serving notice," Sweets said, clutching the microphone with his paw. "I won't tolerate hidden venues in my

town. The law doesn't recognize magicians and invisible men. There's only one paradox in New York City, and that paradox is your police commissioner. I don't like to sit on fences. I'll give a good slap whenever I have to. I've learned that from Isaac Sidel."

The pols cheered and raised their glasses of punch. Sweets was sending LeComte a kite. There would be no more Knickerbocker Boys in Manhattan, no more Carols. LeComte should have been at Sweets' little party, but he wasn't in the Blue Room. Neither was Billy the Kid. All the other nabobs had come to celebrate Sweets. Martin Malik lurked in the corner, biting into a macaroon.

Becky Karp, who'd risen out of her rocking chair to have some punch in the Blue Room, gripped Malik's elbow and danced him toward Sidel.

"We're hiring Malik," she said, "stealing him away from Sweets."

"We are?" Isaac said.

"Yes. We need a broom. I'll figure out his title and his salary."

"But Malik hates me," Isaac said. "Don't you, Malik?"

"It doesn't matter," chirped Rebecca Karp. "He can knock off our enemies while he hates you." And she danced Malik back to his corner.

Isaac had a sudden urge to commune with someone out of his own past. Not Joey or Marilyn or his brother Leo. It had to be baseball. He could have gone up to Washington Heights and visited with Harry Lieberman, but the Bomber had no affection for Isaac and wouldn't talk baseball with him. Herman Melville, he'd go to Herman Melville.

He left City Hall. It was snowing, like the last time he'd been to the MCC. The warden gave Isaac a wispy little smile. He went up to the Heart of Darkness, passed all the tiny bullets of light in the walls, but Herman Melville wasn't inside that segregated cell block. Isaac went back down to the warden.

"Where's Hector Ramirez?"

"Your Honor, I haven't a clue. Federal marshals stole him right out of his cell with Dostoyevsky and all his other books. They had some kind of writ that smelled of the Justice Department."

LeComte had gotten Herman Melville out of the Heart of Darkness as a favor to Isaac. Or was it a favor?

Isaac took a cab up to Little Angel Street. He sat in Rebecca's rocking chair. Wig might never walk again. The king was responsible for his own bodyguard. If he hadn't gone near Rita, imposed himself upon the Ali Baba, she might still be alive. Black Michael was the king's own poisoned rabbi. Michael had taught him to meditate and to love the ball, had sent him a fortune in baseball cards as some memento mori, had almost murdered Wig, and then disappeared into a crack between Carcassonne and Bucharest. The king couldn't find him. He had a few spies, remnants of his former secret police, the Ivanhoes, who'd checked with their associates in France. Nina Anghel had dropped out of the pingpong circuit. The red lioness didn't have one exhibition scheduled anywhere.

Isaac sat on the porch with his plastic pouch. He began shuffling the baseball cards. Tobias Little. Monte Ward. Jay Penny had a baseball green in the background and a magnificent blue and orange sky. The king searched this sky for some clues.

The telephone rang.

"Your Honor," said one of his secretaries. "There's a maniac on the line. Mr. Herman Melville."

"Put him through."

Isaac could hear a click and then a hoarse whisper. "It's your little man . . . meet me at our clubhouse in half an hour."

"Clubhouse?"

"Yeah. You figure it out."

Isaac would often have breakfast or lunch at Ratner's with his Delancey Giants. He drove down to Delancey, parked the car, and entered Ratner's with such a scowl the waiters left him alone. One little boy asked him to sign his name on a napkin. "Jay Penny, Champion Base Ball Catcher," he wrote, and the little boy returned to his table.

The waiters brought him barley soup and seeded rolls, a bottle of celery tonic, three cups of coffee, and a prune Danish. He couldn't stop eating. He'd come out of his coma a year ago and had been famished ever since. He had to eat for the dead man who was still inside him and for the tapeworm that had vanished from his intestines when Isaac was shot under the Williamsburg Bridge.

A tall man in a black leather jacket appeared at Isaac's table. Two other men, also in leather jackets, were waiting for him at Ratner's front door. These men were babysitters. And Hector Ramirez, who couldn't have been more than twenty-six, had that gray complexion of a guy who'd been living without sunlight. He ordered a celery tonic.

"Don't you dare pity me," Hector said. "And if you sniffle once, I'll strangle you inside your favorite restaurant."

"You're in witness protection," Isaac said.

"Thanks to you. I was happy. I had my books. I didn't ask for this cowboy stuff."

"I told LeComte to pull you."

"And now he has me doing capers. But you kept your word. The warden let me have Dostoyevsky. I read *The Brothers Karamazov* sixteen times. I am what I am because of you."

"That's unfair. I got you a uniform, and gave you a small allowance, so you wouldn't have to work after school."

"Don't forget the Louisville Slugger."

"All right," Isaac said. "You crowned a narc with it, but was that my fault?"

"What does Ivan Karamazov say? Eternity is a bathhouse full of spiders. Well, I sent the narc over there with your baseball bat . . . coach, you're paler than I am, and you didn't spend three years in the Heart of Darkness."

"I'm looking for a guy," Isaac said. "It troubles me. I can't sleep."

"What's his name?"

"Michael Cuza. Some people call him King Carol."

"Black Michael? The FBI's own fucking ninja."

"He was my pingpong coach."

"On rainy days," said Hector Ramirez. "Don't move. Have another celery tonic. I'll be back in a couple of hours with all you need to know about Black Michael."

"You can't," Isaac said. "LeComte has you under a screen . . ."

"I was born under a screen, but I taught myself how to walk and talk."

Hector Ramirez marched out of Ratner's with his two babysitters. And the king started to cry. He didn't even get the chance to talk baseball with his greatest prodigy. The king and Cardinal Jim could have gotten Hector into the big leagues if the boy hadn't disappeared from the Delancey Giants and left Isaac with a bunch of orphans who dropped into last place. Isaac's only championship had come with Hector Ramirez. The cardinal's team took over the Police Athletic League and the Delancey Giants had a quick fall from paradise.

Isaac didn't have to watch the clock in the window. He nibbled on a poppyseed cake and knew that Hector wouldn't return to Ratner's. He was on his fifth celery tonic when the FBI burst into the restaurant in the form of Frederic LeComte and the same two babysitters in leather jackets.

"I spring him for you, Isaac, and this is how you repay me? You're never to see Hector Ramirez again. If you approach him, if you exchange one word, the kid goes back into solitary and sits for the rest of his life."

"Come on, LeComte, you gave him a ticket to ride because I happened to discover him in your little house of detention. You couldn't afford the bad publicity. Here I am, the virgin mayor, with one of his ex-Giants tucked away in the dark. A Puerto Rican kid who's passionate about Herman Melville. The media would have had a love affair with Hector Ramirez."

"I still freed the kid."

"And got your mileage out of him. How many capers has

he done for the FBI? He knew all about Black Michael. Was he out in the Hamptons with Michael and Margaret Tolstoy? Did you use him as Michael's lookout man?"

"You're talking silly," LeComte said.

Isaac tossed his plastic pouch onto the table. "Silly, huh? Margaret says this is from Michael. Spoils of war. He knocks off a drug ring for Uncle Sam and comes up with an incredible batch of baseball cards. A terrific find. But Michael isn't that much of a magician. He doesn't know dick about baseball, and neither does Margaret. It's an FBI package. The cards are from you."

"No," LeComte said. "They're from Michael. I merely appraised the value for him."

"Merely appraised," Isaac said. "I want Black Michael. Where is he?"

"Michael's been erased from our books. He doesn't exist."

"He existed long enough to have Wig thrown off a roof."

"You'll have to find a new pingpong coach."

"Yeah," Isaac said. "Michael made a real booboo. Sweets doesn't like it when the FBI lets a mad dog fuck over his head. Sweets is fond of Wig. And now you're on his shit list."

"Mr. Mayor, you'll have to heal that rift. He'll lose a giant portion of his budget if he dismantles our joint task force."

"Sweets won't dismantle anything. He'll just narrow you a little and cut your heart out. He had a good teacher. Isaac Sidel."

"But there's one more ingredient," LeComte said.

"Margaret Tolstoy. She's in limbo with Black Michael. You sent her there, didn't you, LeComte? And if I'm not your boy, Margaret stays where she is . . . here, finish my celery tonic, you miserable cocksucker."

Isaac picked up his plastic pouch and vanished from Ratner's restaurant.

32

Little Angel Street.

The mansion held no meaning for Isaac without Margaret Tolstoy. He had his own rocking chair installed on the porch. He would either rock alone, or with Becky Karp, then walk down to the fireboat station at the edge of Carl Schurz Park and ride one of the launches with his fire patrol. He felt calm on the water, as if he could shed that rough political skin he had to wear as mayor of New York. He would cross the channel into the whirlpools of Hell Gate, cruise up the Harlem River, while people waved to him from the broken docks, his thick sideburns suspiciously clear under the metal brim of his fireman's hat.

But Isaac couldn't live out on that launch. A seafaring mayor was still locked to the land. It was lucky for him that he had Martin Malik. Malik ran the City while Isaac rode on the river or rocked in his chair. But the king had a sudden longing for pingpong. He went to Schiller's on foot, passed the kibbitzers' gallery, and paused at Manfred Coen's table. He missed Coen more than he cared to remember. Isaac was always finding and losing angels. He sat near the wall and started to meditate. But an angel crept out of the wall. And the king shivered like he'd never shivered before.

"Coen?" he said. "Blue Eyes?"

The angel wouldn't answer him. And then Isaac understood its source. One more phantom visiting Schiller's pockmarked walls. The lights were constantly playing tricks. But this phantom wouldn't go away. It had a black leather coat. Herman Melville had come to haunt him at Manfred's pingpong table.

"Coach, I can't stay."

"Ah, Hector," Isaac said. "LeComte's preparing a little crucifixion. He'll kill you if he catches you around me."

"I promised you Black Michael's address, didn't I?"

"That's the problem. He doesn't have an address."

"Yeah, the sucker has his own château. It's near a town with a lot of towers."

"Carcassonne," Isaac said.

"That's it. Carky. Michael has his own lake and a black forest. It's called the château of the forest. You can't miss it. Isaac, I have my spies. Just like you and LeComte. We're a band of brothers and sisters, all the FBI's undercover rats."

"Did you and the rats ever work with Michael?"

"Michael works alone."

"That's the record I keep hearing. *Michael works alone.*"

"He was trained by a monk. They were in a dungeon somewhere. The monk taught him how to catch colors in the dark and breathe without breathing. Michael can make his own heart stop."

"A miracle man," Isaac said.

"He cured my rheumatism. You remember. I had a rheumatic thumb. Michael rubbed his hands together until they were hot as hell. He put them around my bad thumb, transferred all the heat from him to me, and I was cured. Michael cooked my thumb."

"How?" Isaac asked. "When? I thought you never worked with Michael."

"Ah, I met him once. Coach, you'd better bring some heavy shit. Because you can't beat Michael. And even if you could, the guy has clearance all the way up to God. He can shoot the governor, and it wouldn't be considered a crime."

"Then I'll have to take my chances," Isaac said.

"I almost forgot. Michael raises animals. He has a deer farm."

"Don't you mean a deer park?"

"No. Definitely a farm."

And Hector Ramirez ran out of Schiller's in his black leather coat.

The king couldn't jump on a plane like a private citizen and satisfy his wanderlust. He belonged to the City of New York. His signature, his touch, his voice were needed in case of an emergency. He could ride on a fireboat, vegetate in a rocking chair, as long as he could be reached. It was forbidden for a mayor to disappear.

He sat with Rebecca Karp on his own porch, which felt like a dead planet to him. "Becky, I have to go to Carcassonne and kill a man."

"Be my guest."

"But I can't pretend I'm on a trade mission."

"Isaac," she said. "You're dying. I can see it on your face. We'll get you a plane ticket. No fuss. Kill whoever you have to kill, but call in every six hours, understand? Malik will cover for you. And if they arrest you on your flight home, we'll have a team of lawyers at the arrival lounge . . . it's that Tolstoy woman, isn't it? Anastasia."

"No. It's Little Angel Street."

Isaac climbed upstairs to his fortress and started to pack. He was at JFK in four hours. With Rebecca Karp. She carried his ticket, his passport, and a small bundle of traveler's checks. The king was flying business class. He gave no interviews at the airport. But it was obvious to everyone that Isaac was leaving the country. He kissed Rebecca, realized that this rough ex–beauty queen was his only ally.

"Come back to us," she said.

Isaac arrived in Carcassonne the next afternoon. He had a marvelous coffee at a café near the ramparts. He could hear a siren calling him under the call of the wind. *Isaac. Isaac.* Was it Sophie Sidel, his poor mother, the junk queen who'd been trampled to death? Was she warning her older son away from violence? "Mama," he said, "sometimes you have to kill." He was like a madman talking to the wind.

Michael's house on the rue St. Jean was locked. Isaac peeked through a tiny crack in the shutters. There wasn't a soul inside. The king got into his rented car, drove down the rue du Grand Puits, crossed the Aude River on the Pont de l'Avenir, and rode into the Montagne Noire, the black mountain where Michael had his retreat. It was cluttered with gold mines and game preserves and lugubrious places, like the Waterfall of the Bad Death. It was Carol's country, all right. Le Château du Forêt was in the Forest of the Dead Crab. Isaac could have torched the place with a couple of matches. But it wasn't a real château. It was more like a hunting lodge in disrepair. There were huge gaps in the stone porch. The chimneys had started to crumble. The roof looked like the beginning of a landslide. There was a fence near the lodge that enclosed a long barren field. But the field wasn't so barren. Tiny spotted deer emerged from all the emptiness. They moved in packs of five or ten with a startling swiftness. First they stood frozen, staring at Isaac, and then they leapt like human lozenges. This was the deer farm that Hector Ramirez had been talking about. Isaac had never noticed such perfect creatures in all his life. Midget brown deer with red spots. The males had bumpy little horns. They slid across the field with their own silent music.

The king was hypnotized. He couldn't bear to take his eyes off them. He would have murdered his own father for the privilege of remaining where he was. It was the only society he would ever need. But someone called him from the house.

"Mr. Sidel."

It was Oskar Leviathan, wearing the dark clothes of a hunter. His eyes were pure blue in Michael's forest. Isaac entered the house. It had a fireplace, a few pieces of furniture, a fridge, and a pingpong table. The redheaded lioness, Nina Anghel, sat on a very bare sofa, without lipstick or nail polish. She seemed indifferent to Isaac. Black Michael was with the lioness. He wasn't wearing any shoes. Good, the king thought. He'll trip and break his ass.

"Been expecting you, little father. Did you bring a gun?"

"I wouldn't point a gun at my own master," Isaac said.

"That's wise. Because I could sit here and catch all your bullets in my hand."

"Just like the late Archibald Harris," Isaac said. "When he was in the nigger leagues. He would catch baseball bullets with either hand . . . did Billy the Kid pay you to hide Oskar Leviathan, huh?"

"He's a cautious man, like any presidential candidate. He couldn't afford to have Oskar in his dossier, not after you started trampling around. You broke his niece's heart."

"I'd like Rose to have the boy, no matter what happens to you or me."

"Nothing will happen to you, little father. You're blessed. But you really ought to think like a politician. You could blackmail Billy if Rose gets Oskar back."

"That's not my style."

"Your style might change. And Billy can't risk that."

"Then bury me in potter's field. I'm the original Geronimo Jones."

"Harm my best pupil? Wouldn't dream of it."

"You'll have to dream of something else, because I'm taking the boy to Rose."

"Ask Oskar if he'll go with you. He likes it here."

"I live with Nina now," said Oskar Leviathan. "And Black Michael."

"What about Rose and Uncle Billy?" Isaac asked.

"Rose was America," the boy said.

"But you loved Willie Mays."

"True," the boy said. "But I will recover."

The king gnashed his fists together. "Michael, I'm sorry, but I have to kill you."

Black Michael started to laugh. "But I have protectors. Nina and Oskar and my *daims*, my spotted dear. They're much better than watchdogs. They sniffed you from miles away. When they're agitated, little father, their feet start to whistle on the ground."

"You should have kept away from Wig. He's my man. And you tricked him into falling off a roof."

"He's alive, isn't he, little father? He landed in a lot of clotheslines. And it's his own special fate to fall off roofs."

"You put him in a wheelchair."

"Perfect. He'll have to avoid all roofs . . . but why should we argue? We'll settle this at my pingpong table. If you score one point against me, I'll close my eyes and induce my own death."

"Like a monk, huh?"

"Ah, you've been chatting with your baseball orphan, Hector Ramirez. He told you about the monk I met while I was still a policeman."

"The monk was your cellmate."

"And the best teacher I ever had. We exercised together in a room that was the size of a dumbwaiter. I had no fear of dying after I was with this monk. I longed for it. I kissed the belly of the beast. I'm just like you, little father."

"What happened to the monk?"

"Had to turn him in. It's a pity, but I'd been sent to prison to spy on him . . . it's time for pingpong. All you have to do is make one point."

"Do I get Oskar Leviathan?"

"Of course. And the lioness can fend for herself. But you won't break up my family, little father. Not you or LeComte or Ceausescu's palace princes. I'm waiting for you. Pick up your bat."

Isaac faced Black Michael across the net. "I'm not like you. I'm not a fucking death machine."

"Score on me, little father. One point, and you're rid of me forever."

Isaac picked up the Butterfly that was on the table, crouched, and delivered his very best cut serve. Michael slammed the ball back into Isaac's face.

225

Oskar and Nina Anghel watched this game that wasn't a game. Isaac couldn't even see the spin on Michael's serves. He lunged, he groped like a ridiculous bear. But he'd outlast this lousy king of the dead. Michael's eyes began to flutter. It was almost as if his spirit had left the table.

"Where are you, Michael?"

"With my spotted deer . . . if you could see the colors I see, hear the sounds, you would fall on your knees and die with delight. You're a blind man, Isaac, and you'll always be."

"Good. But I'm going to fuck you out of a point."

His mouth was dry. And he began seeing double. It felt like he'd been hitting the ball for hours. One of his eyes closed. He almost screamed, because Black Michael looked more and more like Manfred Coen. The king should never have agreed to this match. He could no longer lift his arm.

"Where's Margaret Tolstoy?" he asked before the Butterfly fell out of his hand and he crashed into the net, the table collapsing under him like a coffin.

33

The same Hungarians were chasing her, exiled police chiefs who wanted Michael's money. But she couldn't glock them in the street. This was Montparnasse and the boulevard Edgar Quinet, not the badlands of New York. The gendarmes weren't on such intimate terms with anarchy, and the crime squad wouldn't appreciate a gun-toting mama from Odessa with a Parisian past. She had to close all of Michael's companies, collect as much as she could from his bank accounts, and not cause any suspicion. The bank managers knew her as Michael's married sister, Madame Tolstoya. The best defense, according to Black Michael, was to embroider the truth with only the least little lie. Michael and Margaret were as close to brother and sister as any pair of orphans could ever be. Michael trusted her with all his accounts.

She was carrying a fortune in francs and doing fine, dodging all those Hungarians, when she saw a picture of Isaac in the *International Herald Tribune.* Her darling had two headlines devoted to him.

MAYOR OF NEW YORK MISSING
SIDEL BELIEVED TO BE IN FRANCE

Was that cuckoobird in Carcassonne? She called Michael in the Montagne Noire. But Michael must have been busy with his spotted deer. He wouldn't pick up the telephone. How could she find the cuckoohead *and* continue collecting money? She arrived on the boulevard Arago and climbed six flights to Nicolae Mars' chambre de bonne. Nicolae was a Roumanian novelist. There were a hundred of them in Paris at the moment, and it seemed to her that Michael was supporting every one. Most of them lived in maids' rooms, like Nicolae Mars. A few of them had French publishers. Nicolae was the doyen of these emigré novelists. He was fifty-five years old. He wore thick glasses and had a slight paunch. He'd once been a member of the Securitate. But he'd fallen out of favor with Ceausescu and the secret police. He looked like a beardless Santa Claus.

French had always been Roumania's second language. Bucharest was the Balkan paradise, *un petit Paris,* until Ceausescu began ripping up the streets and building his nightmare boulevards. The State publishing houses had already silenced Nicolae Mars and declared him a dead man. Still, he might have stayed. But he was a hypochondriac, and it was this that saved him. He worried about what might happen if he ever fell ill. The hospitals in Bucharest had run out of medicine. The operating rooms were open at random hours. There were incurable shortages of electricity. Nicolae was convinced he would die on an operating table in the middle of a blackout. He ran to Paris without a kopeck. It was Black Michael who set him up in the attic. Michael had romantic notions about literature. He loved the smell of books. Margaret was a little less attached to the written word. Novels held no future for her. Besides, she found Nicolae unreadable in Roumanian and French. He couldn't keep away from love stories. But the passion he described in his books seemed dull and predictable to Margaret. Nicolae's men were always leaping on dark-eyed girls and announcing their devotion in pathetic little poems.

She'd brought a stack of "Molières" to Nicolae, five-hundred-franc notes. It was the last bundle she would ever bring. Nicolae couldn't believe it.

"Michael's going out of business. He's been caught between several agencies. He'll retire in the Montagne Noire."

"Margaret, without Michael how shall I live?"

"You have a French publisher."

"Who never pays royalties," said the novelist. "How shall I live?"

"Ah," she said, "I'll help you. I'll become a patron of the arts."

Nicolae measured her with his owlish eyes. "Would you marry me, my dear Margaret?"

"I'm a widow," she said. "I couldn't ever marry again."

"But I have been warming up to you."

"It's the money, Nicolae. All the Molières."

"No," he said. "I'm not a gold digger. I have a weakness for women with red hair."

Margaret took off her wig, revealed her sudden baldness to Nicolae Mars. "You imagined me one way, Nicolae. Now you have the other."

But her baldness seemed to inflame Nicolae. His nostrils flared. "Darling, lie down with me."

"Nicolae, Nicolae, who has the time?"

He pounced on her like one of the characters in his books. She was startled by Nicolae's strength. He wasn't such a Santa Claus! But he grew paralyzed when he saw the Glock in her hand. She danced around him and put her wig back on. Her "bridal bag," a simple velvet sack, was still open. He was staring at the fortune of francs inside. He could almost move the money with his eyes. She closed the bridal bag and left him there in the attic. He'd never even thanked Michael. What could you expect from a novelist?

She got into a taxi near the green lion of Denfert-Rochereau. The lion had always amused her. It marked the limit of her walks as a child in Nazi Paris. The German soldiers would visit the Eiffel Tower or the Sacré-Coeur, loll around Montmartre with all the little aging artists, but Margaret had her lion.

She crossed the river and rode into the Marais. If she couldn't find her dumb darling, she'd visit with his dad. Joel Sidel, the portrait painter. She got out of the cab with her sack, wandered around on the rue Vieille-du-Temple, went through an opening in the wall, discovered a dark court with magical blue earth, like a cemetery where golems might sleep. Some curious instinct rubbed at Margaret and led her up a stairway to Joel's door. He was supposed to have a Vietnamese companion, a mistress-wife. But she wasn't inside the flat. The walls were pale green, like her lion. Joel was lying in bed with a goatee that had gone yellow. He looked like a starving man. Margaret would have fed him noodles or something, but the cupboards were bare. There couldn't have been a lady in this house.

"Who are you?" he asked.

"Your son's fiancée," she said, assuming she'd have to lie a little to this old man or he might suspect she'd come to rob him of all his valuables: the pale green walls, trinkets of dust.

"Leo's getting married again?"

"Not Leo," she said. "Your other son."

His face grew resentful under the goatee. "Ah, the mayor. Him with his black heart. Can't forgive his father for coming to Paris. Only he can have a new life."

"Mr. Sidel, you'll have to get dressed."

"Call me Joel. You're almost in the family, even if you are a stranger. Where are we going?"

"To my place." She didn't have a place. It was the last of Michael's apartments, on the boulevard Montparnasse. She hadn't sold the building yet. She didn't want to make the *trésor public* suspicious. The tax people might come after Michael. The building was in Nina's name.

She helped the old man dress.

"Joel, what happened to your wife?"

"Mauricette? She died on me last month. I wanted to bury her in Montparnasse, but we didn't have the money. You know, a grave near Jean-Paul Sartre. It means something to me. My son the mayor doesn't understand. I'm a mediocre painter. I don't have the gift. But I've been happier doing portraits than living like a bedbug in Manhattan. Kill me, Isaac's fiancée, but I can't stop loving Paris."

"I'm Margaret," she said. "Margaret Tolstoy."

"Tolstoy. It's nice to be named after a genius."

Margaret got him down the stairs, past the golems' court with the blue earth, and onto the rue Vieille-du-Temple, while she clutched her velvet sack with Michael's millions. Her mouth started to shape a scream. She was looking into the eyes of a bandit with a blue face. Joel had distracted her. She'd forgotten all about the Hungarians. But this Hungarian had a familiar grin. It belonged to the missing mayor. Isaac Sidel.

"No excuses," she said. "Abandoning your father like that. Joel was starving to death."

"I was waiting out here. I didn't have the courage . . . and then I saw you go in."

"You were in Carcassonne, weren't you? And Michael was foolish enough to let you out of his forest alive."

"I'm confused," the old man said. "Is it my son the mayor? He looks like the wolfman. His cheeks are all blue."

"He is the wolfman. He hasn't shaved in a week."

Margaret maneuvered father and son into a taxi. They rode out of the Marais, along the same route where Leutnant Lodl of the Service Juif had once driven her. Lodl was in love with her, a little girl of twelve called Magda Antonescu. The Marais had been full of women and children with Jewish stars on their chests. Magda hadn't been able to find any men in the streets. Lodl had a Jewish mistress. There was going to be a roundup, a *grande rafle,* and Lodl, who had helped plan it, was also hiding Jewish children, sending them into monasteries, delivering them to friends he could trust. Lodl was like a handsome Frankenstein. The escape routes he designed for the children were almost as efficient as his plans for the *rafle.* The leutnant had a love of detail.

"Lodl," she'd asked, "can I keep a Jewish boy or girl under my bed?"

"Quiet, you little mouse."

He'd stroke her calf, but he wouldn't kiss her on the mouth. She was a child, after all, though Uncle Ferdinand would marry her in six months. And when Magda returned to the Marais in July, after the *grande rafle,* she couldn't discover any children. The Marais was swept with ghosts, like a bitter cemetery . . .

She began to cry in Michael's kitchen on the boulevard Montparnasse. Margaret hadn't expected house guests. She'd organized her own *rafle,* rounding up Michael's money. But she couldn't get Lodl out of her mind. She had onions and potatoes and turnips and leeks. She had a can of tuna fish, a loaf of rye bread, a bottle of wine, some blue cheese. She hadn't made a sit-down meal in months. Margaret was always eating on the run. But she prepared a salad, served the two Sidels in the dining room, which opened onto Paris like a magnificent flower garden.

"Delicious," said the old man, his goatee hovering over the salad bowl. He didn't even look at the view, this Gauguin whose eyes had gone inward. And he wouldn't look at Isaac.

"All right," Joel said. "I abandoned you. Are you happy now?"

"Mom died like a dog," Isaac said.

"But I didn't step on her bones. And you were nineteen years old, twenty, when I left. Where's the crime?"

"Papa," Isaac said, "you could have painted in New York."

"No. It was Paris or nothing."

"Where are your canvases?" Isaac growled. "You painted portraits in a tourist hotel like a refugee from Montmartre."

"That was my privilege," Joel said.

"I ought to rip out every hair on your face."

"Isaac," Margaret said. "You shouldn't talk to Joel like that. Remember. I'm wearing my Glock."

"Let him talk," Joel said. "He was always a wild animal."

"Yeah, Papa. I'm the wolfman."

There was a knock on the door. Margaret rose from the table with her gun. "Who is it?"

"Nicolae Mars. I'm in trouble. Let me in."

His simple plea unsettled her. Margaret opened the door. Nicolae crashed into her arms, propelling Margaret toward her blind side, where she could only see the wall, while six Hungarians entered the apartment with Italian pistols. Margaret shoved away from Nicolae and could have shot one or two of the Hungarians, but those other murderers would have gotten to Joel. She didn't want that old man from the Marais to die in Michael's house.

"Margaret dear," Nicolae said, cleaning his eyeglasses with a foul rag, "you really ought to give me your gun."

"Nicolae, if I die you die. Remember that. You shouldn't have gone to the Hungarians."

"Had to, dear. Michael retires, just like that. Never even consults us. I'm his ward."

"You're close to sixty," Margaret had to remind him.

The novelist exploded with indignation. "I'm fifty-five . . . Margaret, you have two visitors. One of them is famous. I recognized Sidel. The mysterious mayor of Manhattan. We might have to kidnap him."

"You'll kidnap shit."

Her dumb darling had come out of the dining room. He'd wrecked Margaret's equilibrium. She'd never get the drop on those Hungarians."

"Maître, the money, the money," said the chief of the Hungarians, a shriveled ex-policeman who wore an eye patch.

"Margaret," Nicolae said, "see for yourself. They're impatient boys. Michael's already butchered their compatriots. Their guns might go off. It could create a frightful accident . . . I'll relieve you of the money bag and then we'll disappear."

"You'll relieve her of shit."

"Isaac," Margaret whispered, "go back to your father. This is my fight."

"Nah," Isaac said. "Margaret, I'll take the little fish. I'll crack his head."

"Who's a fish?" Nicolae asked, indignant again.

The ex-policemen aimed their pistols at Isaac's eyes.

The door opened. Oskar Leviathan strolled into the apartment with Nina Anghel. The Hungarians smiled. Michael's precious *enfants* walking into their little trap. But Isaac understood the battle plan. It was a new variation on the Trojan horse. Michael's horse was metaphysical. He'd sneaked his warriors inside the murderers' den. He was on another suicide mission. But it was Nicolae's suicide, not Michael's.

The murderer with the eye patch dropped to the carpet with a bodkin under his ear. An arm reached around the door with the suppleness of a snake and snapped the neck of another murderer. Then Michael's face appeared, like an unholy mask, his eyes practically hollow, and he let out a scream that almost shattered Isaac's eardrums. It was a kamikaze call. The king couldn't move. His arms and legs were frozen. He was like some spectator in a tiny field of toy soldiers. Michael moved from soldier to soldier, snapping their necks.

Isaac heard a strange meow. It was Nicolae crying.

"Maître," Michael said. "I loved your words so much." He strangled Nicolae in front of Nina Anghel and Oskar Leviathan. The novelist died with the same meow.

Joel Sidel wandered out of the dining room, saw the dead bodies, and scolded his son. "Isaac, I can't keep up with all your tricks." Then he returned to the dining room, shut his eyes, and fell asleep in his chair.

34

The king was welcomed home with incredible panache. There was a parade of boats in the harbor, with fireworks that exploded Isaac's phantom image across the sky. A few Orthodox rabbis complained. No town should worship idols, they said. The Committee to Re-elect Isaac Sidel, which financed the fireworks, issued an apology, and the rabbis withdrew their complaint. Isaac couldn't understand all the fucking sound and fury. He'd run to Carcassonne to kill a man, had failed, had been out of touch with New York for a week, and came back a hero.

It was LeComte who had woven a legend around the king, prepared little leaks for the press and then a full dossier. The mayor of New York had gone undercover and followed a gang of murderers across France, the very gang that had been killing homeless men. The leader of the gang was Michael Cuza, aka King Carol, a notorious Roumanian cutthroat, smuggler, and jewel thief, operating out of pingpong parlors.

LeComte went to Harts Island off the coast of the Bronx, visited potter's field. All the Geronimo Joneses were pulled out of their communal graves and discovered to be former members of Nicolae Ceausescu's palace guard who'd swiped treasures from the great dictator. Michael had lured them to Manhattan and murdered every one, dumping their bodies at different homeless shelters, while he hid behind the mask of a pingpong coach.

Enter isaac Sidel. Police chief and mayor-elect and Justice's first Alexander Hamilton Fellow. "He's a natural nightfighter and an awesome, original detective," LeComte was quoted in *New York* magazine. "Sherlock Holmes on the new frontier. It shouldn't be much of a surprise that Sidel tracked Michael Cuza to a pingpong parlor, offered to train with him and become his pupil, so he could uncover Michael's modus operandi."

And according to the article, this New Age Sherlock Holmes had gotten between Black Michael and his gang, and it was the gang that killed Michael in his Montparnasse lair. But the photograph of Michael Cuza's corpse in *New York* magazine looked suspiciously like that cherub, Nicolae Mars.

The king burnt the article in his fireplace. He took to wearing his gun at Gracie Mansion. He would stop strangers in the hall, like a highwayman. He went after Martin Malik. "Who started the Committee to Re-elect Isaac Sidel?"

"I did," Malik said, standing his ground.

"I haven't been in office a month, and there's already a committee to re-elect?"

"It's standard practice, Mr. Mayor. If you don't start early, you're dead after a year."

"Fine. Who's the chairman?"

"We have two chairpersons. Papa Cassidy and Rebecca Karp."

Isaac groaned. "Papa once took a contract out on my life. Did you know that, Malik?"

"You can't survive without a committee to re-elect."

"And you can't have fireworks. How much did it cost to put my face up in the sky?"

"Ninety thousand dollars."

"Malik, imagine how many homeless men and women I could feed with ninety thousand dollars."

"But the committee can't feed them. It would be a misuse of funds."

And the king ran from Malik, who was the real mayor. Isaac was only marking time on Little Angel Street. His dad had moved into the mansion with him. He did portraits of the mayor's employees. He wore his beret and climbed up and down the stairs with an easel and leaky tubes of paint. Joel had made his own Paris inside the mansion's walls. He never went out. He was over eighty and seemed content to immortalize the Sidel administration.

But the king wouldn't sit for his own portrait. He couldn't decide whether to kiss his father or kill him. He'd seen Joel twice in thirty-five years, and now they were practically roommates. Isaac wore slippers, like his dad, and stuck to Little Angel Street.

The doorbell rang around midnight. The king had been dozing near the fire. He got up, wondering if any of the Hungarians survived the slaughter in Montparnasse and had come to kidnap him. Isaac opened the door and found a black man with scars on his face . . . and two wire crutches.

"Wiggy, what happened to your wheelchair?"

"I smashed it. Told the hospital I couldn't leave you all alone. Asked the doctors to outfit me the best they could."

"Ah," Isaac said, "it's fucking good to see you."

And the king had his bodyguard again.

He was asked to give a speech. Schyler Knott had reopened the Christy Mathewson Club and wanted Isaac at the inaugural dinner. The king couldn't refuse. He came with Wig. They looked like a couple of killers in black tie. Schyler Knott, that purist of white baseball, had started a drive to induct Archibald Harris into the Hall of Fame.

Isaac had a very odd dinner companion. The melamed, Izzy Wasser. Why would the Maf's biggest brain come to the Mathewson Club? But Izzy was a baseball freak. And Isaac was an idiot. The melamed was here to celebrate Archie Harris for another reason. It had nothing to do with the nigger leagues.

"Iz, you hired him."

"Isaac," the melamed said, "do you have to speak riddles?"

"Archie Harris. You hired him."

"Not so loud. I wasn't with the Family in 'forty-six. You were a schoolboy and I was a struggling melamed and second-story man. And that's when Archie flourished. In 'forty-six . . . but I hired him later. He did a lotta piece work for us until your bodyguard shot out his tonsils."

"Wig had a reason," Isaac said.

"Sure he had a reason, but he ended Archie's career."

"Then it wasn't a myth. About the Purple Gang."

"Isaac," the melamed whispered, "we held Harlem in place with one man. Archibald Harris. He terrorized all the colored numbers men. I loved Arch. We talked baseball for hours."

A lectern was brought to Isaac's table and hooked to a microphone. The king stared out at his audience and started to cry. He couldn't control himself. Wig stood up on one wire crutch and put his arm around the king.

"Should we cancel, bro'?"

"Wiggy, I'm all right."

They formed a curious pietà, Albert Wiggens and Isaac Sidel. The bodyguard and his crippled king. Wiggy sat down again.

"Met a princess at this club. *Anastasia*. She was born in Bucharest, the little sister of Carol, the boy king. Carol was a real sweetheart. He robbed people and played pingpong in the royal palace. Anastasia and Carol were quite a team. When royalty went out of fashion, they joined the secret police and traveled all over the world. The princess appeared at my junior high school in nineteen forty-three. And appeared again forty years later at the Christys. Still a secret agent. But she and Carol now free-lance for the FBI. They also raise midget deer on a mountain north of Carcassonne when they're not whacking people for the FBI's own little darling, Frederic LeComte. And thinking about the princess made me cry. But I shouldn't be so personal. Schyler invited me here to talk about Archibald Harris and black baseball . . ."

Isaac laughed when he saw the limo waiting for him outside the Christy Mathewson Club. He put Wig into his own limousine. "Wiggy, I have to do a solo."

"I'm your bodyguard."

"Yeah, but I'll be safe. It's only the FBI."

He sent Wig home to Little Angel Street and climbed into LeComte's limo. The cultural commissar was in a rage. He held a gun on Isaac, a nickel-plated target .22 that he must have grabbed off the firing range at the FBI Academy. "That was some fairy tale, Your Honor. Can I quote you? . . . *when they're not whacking people for the FBI's little darling, Frederic LeComte.*"

"You bugged the Christys."

"Of course I did. How else could I keep up with you? You're a firecracker. Isaac, you're not to mention Anastasia or King Carol, not ever again."

"Frederic, my fairy tales are as good as yours. You shouldn't be giving interviews to New York magazine. You're the FBI."

"But I had to untangle the mess you made. It wasn't easy. Michael Cuza is dead, Isaac. Is that understood?"

"Dead until you need him. And what happens to Oskar Leviathan and Nina Anghel?"

"They're part of the fallout, part of the flak. But they won't suffer very much on the Montagne Noire."

"With Margaret Tolstoy."

"She's Michael's now," said LeComte. "I promised her to him. That's part of the deal. You can live without Margaret Tolstoy."

Isaac grabbed the target .22 out of LeComte's hand and dug it against his throat.

"Frederic, I'm not afraid to shoot. You believe me?"

"Yes."

What could the king do? LeComte was like a mean fairy godmother who kept him and Margaret alive. Isaac was almost a son of the FBI.

"I'll get lonely without you, Frederic, swear to God."

Isaac returned the .22, got out of the limo, and hitched a ride to Gracie Mansion in a police car. He didn't bother to undress. He slept on the sofa.

The king made himself a glass of orange juice in the morning. He had a guest. Schyler Knott. The king was still in black tie.

"Your Honor," Schyler said, "I'm giving the barons their matchbox."

"What do you mean?"

"The Emeric Gray on East Fifty-sixth. I'm not going to landmark it."

"Why didn't you say something at the Christys last night?"

"I didn't want to disappoint you. And I never mix baseball and landmarks . . . Your Honor, Jason and his partners have agreed to set aside two million dollars for the homeless."

"It's a bloody bribe."

"I don't agree."

"But none of Emeric's buildings can ever be replaced. You're the one who said it, Schyler. Every fucking stone is our second skin."

"You brought me out of the basement, Isaac. I'm a politician now."

Isaac marched upstairs. He found Wig in Harwood's bedroom. The truant officers had come to Little Angel Street, but they couldn't get Harwood to go back to school. Harwood had the imprint of a mayor's mansion behind him. He lived with Isaac Sidel. But he couldn't recall the letters of the alphabet. And the brutal policeman, Albert Wiggens, was teaching him how to read again.

"The white man goes to humdrum heaven and humdrum hell, but the nigger goes to the poor man's paradise."

Wig stood up on his wire crutches when he noticed Isaac at the door. And it hurt Isaac to watch Wiggy walk, twisting his torso as he stabbed the ground.

"Wiggy, I'd like to borrow the Purple Gang."

"How's that, bro'?"

"To finish off Papa Cassidy and Judah Bellow and Jason Figgs."

"You'll leave yourself an orphan."

But the Purple Gang couldn't move on crutches. And Wig had Rita's boy to raise. Why should he follow Isaac's whims?

The king returned to his bedroom. Someone would always be there to manipulate him. He couldn't preserve a lousy matchbox. The whole planet would diminish with one less Emeric Gray. He had to have a portrait of that matchbox for his own meager eternity. He captured Joel Sidel with his easel and his cans of turpentine and drove him down to Fifty-sixth Street, where he set the easel up across from Emeric Gray.

"Paint," Isaac told him. "Paint."

"What?" Joel said, angling his beret over one eye.

"The building, Papa. It's a masterpiece."

"I don't paint buildings."

Joel collapsed his easel and returned to the car.

The king was forlorn. He drove his father back to Little Angel Street. Joel took off his chapeau and dangled it like a courtier. Suddenly the old man seemed radiant. Isaac couldn't understand all that bliss until he turned around and discovered a bald lady in his dining room.

"How are you, Madame Tolstoy?" Joel asked, kissing Margaret's hand.

"I was fine," she said, "until I saw your son's face."

"Isaac's always like that. Gloomy."

The king's gloom was his own business. He didn't like the scenario. LeComte would lend out Anastasia and then recall her to the Montagne Noire . . . or deposit her with another brigand.

"You can invite Madame Tolstoy to dinner, dad. I'll warn the cook."

Margaret tossed a little blue booklet at Isaac, who recognized the eagle on the cover, with its olive branch in one talon and arrows in the other. He opened the booklet, saw a photo of Margaret without her wig. It was almost magical. LeComte had outfitted Margaret with an American passport. Nothing was phony, and everything was phony, with Frederic LeComte.

"Margaret," Isaac asked, like a begging boy, "how long can you stay?"

"Somewhere between forever and half an hour . . . don't ask me questions, Isaac."

The king heard a thump. Joel stood behind his easel. "A portrait," he said.

"Papa, not now."

"I insist. You and the lady."

"Isaac," Margaret said, clutching the king's arm. "Listen to your father. For once in your life."

Joel Sidel was already lost in a world of colors. He didn't see Isaac or Margaret Tolstoy. He saw swirling plateaus, the shifting planes of a cheek.

"Papa," Isaac said.

The king had a revelation. He was his father's son, not Frederic's fucking agent. LeComte couldn't control him with a little blue booklet. Isaac had his bald bride, and he'd escape with her into some fifth or sixth dimension.

"Margaret," he whispered, "I love you."

What could she do about her dumb darling? The Devil's microphones were all over the place. Margaret herself had planted one or two the last time she was at the mansion.

"Shhh," she said.

"Margaret, I love you."

She fondled his chin in front of Joel. "Isaac, the walls have ears."

"I know."

And she kissed her dumb darling on the mouth. Why should it worry her where the Devil lived? She was on Little Angel Street with Isaac Sidel.

616